THE LOST GARDEN

MODERN CHINESE LITERATURE FROM TAIWAN

LI李昂ANG

TRANSLATED BY

THE

SYLVIA LI-CHUN LIN

LOST

WITH HOWARD GOLDBLATT

GARDEN

A Novel

COLUMBIA UNIVERSITY PRESS   NEW YORK

Columbia University Press wishes to express its appreciation for assistance given by the Chiang Ching-kuo Foundation for International Scholarly Exchange and Council for Cultural Affairs in the preparation of the translation and in the publication of this series.

The translators acknowledge with gratitude a publication subvention from the National Taiwan Museum of Literature.

COLUMBIA UNIVERSITY PRESS
Publishers Since 1893
New York   Chichester, West Sussex

cup.columbia.edu

Library of Congress Cataloging-in-Publication Data

Li, Ang, 1952-
[Mi yuan. English]
The lost garden : a novel / Li Ang ; translated by Sylvia Li-chun Lin with Howard Goldblatt.
pages   cm. — (Modern Chinese literature from Taiwan)
ISBN 978-0-231-17554-8 (cloth : alk. paper) — ISBN 978-0-231-17555-5 (pbk.) —
ISBN 978-0-231-54032-2 (electronic)
I. Lin, Sylvia Li-chun, translator. II. Goldblatt, Howard, 1939- translator. III. Title.
PL2877.A58M513   2015
895.13'52—dc23
2015017756

Columbia University Press books are printed on permanent and durable acid-free paper.
This book is printed on paper with recycled content.
Printed in the United States of America

C 10 9 8 7 6 5 4 3 2 1
P 10 9 8 7 6 5 4 3 2 1

COVER AND BOOK DESIGN: VIN DANG
COVER PHOTOGRAPH: ANTONIS MINAS
COVER MODEL: ALEXIA GALATI

WHAT SEPARATES US FROM CHINA

WHAT SEPARATES US FROM CHINA is more than spatial, temporal, even cultural distance; it is more like a gulf between hearts.

My ancestors once lived in China, which they called Tangshan, a place with a highly developed culture, where people wore silk and satin and used fine china.

When I was a child, my father taught me in Taiwanese to recite Chinese poetry. When Taiwan was under Japanese rule, he called himself a Han; for a while he even admired Chairman Mao, whom he considered to be the savior of the laboring masses. But we were given a drastically different view of China from those who arrived in Taiwan in 1949. The tangled emotional ties, grievances, and resentment have never ceased to exist, even now.

In the oppressive climate of White Terror during Taiwan's four-decade-long martial law era, we diligently worked at piecing together the history of Taiwan of the sixteenth and seventeenth centuries, when the island was frequented by competing merchants from Japan, China, the Netherlands, and Spain, all of which treated Taiwan mainly as a site for trading silk and silver.

This is a promised land that has enabled me to construct a story of the Zhu family, whose ancestors were pirates, and whose curse was passed down through the generations, until its eventual realization.

I have spent years with friends in Taiwan's opposition camp. Comparatively speaking, Taiwan has been luckier than most countries, for it became democratic without a bloody revolution, an accomplishment worthy of making all Chinese proud. Democracy and freedom have made it possible to write about taboo subjects, which is critical for writers like me. But the key is to write a good novel, a work that can withstand the passage of time.

Things change with time, but the issue of national identity explored in this novel exists not only in the past, but in the present, and in the future as well. It is an eternal polemic, since it originates from the gulf between hearts.

Whatever separates us from China, and other related issues, has always been the heart, the gulf between hearts.

LI ANG

IN THE EARLY DAYS OF 2015

TRANSLATOR'S NOTE

PUBLISHED IN 1990, three years after the lifting of martial law in Taiwan, *The Lost Garden* was the first full-length novel to re-create in fictional form the White Terror Era, reference to which was a political taboo for more than four decades. Showcasing Li Ang's talent to convey poignant insights through well-crafted details and innovative narrative techniques, the novel also marks a turning point in her writing career, expanding her scope from a predominantly feminist approach to increasingly multifaceted portrayals of contemporary Taiwan. The novel has attracted considerable scholarly attention in Taiwan and elsewhere since its publication. A French translation has been in print since 2003; now an English version is finally available for a broader audience.

The garden (*yuan*), with its multitiered metaphoric and symbolic role, has been the central focus of scholars who have analyzed and written about the novel. "*Mi*," the first word in the Chinese title, has been variously interpreted as "strange," "mystifying," "labyrinthine," and more. After consulting with the author, I have chosen "lost" to signify the loss of the garden to its rightful owners during Yinghong's father's time. The sense of "loss" is further conveyed in the second strand of the narrative, in which decadent and lavish banquets are a manifestation of an island lost in materialism. In addition, "lost" hints at how individuals became lost in the garden, thereby encompassing the mystifying sense of a labyrinth suggested by scholars. During the translation process, I have striven to adhere as closely as possible to the tone, the sentence structure, and the images of the original text. *The Lost Garden* is narrated in a semiformal language and quasiclassical style, which I have attempted to duplicate in my rendition. Words in languages other than Chinese are in italics throughout the novel.

The translation and publication have been made possible in part by a translation fellowship from the National Endowment for the Arts and a translation grant from the National Museum of Taiwan Literature. I am grateful for the encouragement of Jennifer Crewe, director of Columbia University Press, which has published a large corpus of fiction from Taiwan. I thank the two anonymous readers for their meticulous checking of the translation. Rather than supply footnotes, as they recommended, I have provided explanations and clarifications in the text where appropriate. The term *waishengren*, literally, those from outside the province (of Taiwan), commonly refers to residents who emigrated from China to Taiwan at the end of the civil war in 1949. I recommend Joseph Allen's *Taipei: City of Displacements* to those interested in learning more about Taiwan's capital city, and *A New Account of Tales of the World*, translated by Richard Mather, for further reading of the text Yinghong's father consulted.

Howard Goldblatt read many versions of this translation and offered considerable editorial suggestions, which merits listing him on the cover. I thank my old friend, Li Ang, a supremely gracious writer and a delightful author to work with, for her timely assistance in responding to queries and for assisting in the application for a publication grant from the National Museum of Taiwan Literature.

SYLVIA LI-CHUN LIN

BOULDER, COLORADO

THE LOST GARDEN

PROLOGUE

IN THE DOG DAYS OF SUMMER, sweltering heat permeates every corner of the Taipei Basin, pressing down on this coastal city with stifling heat and sultry air.

The basin is like a magnet for oppressive heat that smothers the city in clammy dampness, like colorless, odorless foam rubber that fills up and encases the high rises and dense residential districts, as well as the meandering streets, with no prospect of ever leaving. All seems submerged in molasses.

When night falls, the sun loses its power, if only temporarily. An occasional breeze from the surrounding hills might set the stagnant heat in motion, but it feels more like a pot of boiling water that has just been removed from the stove top—water roils on the surface while the steamy heat is buried deep down, stubbornly unmoving.

The heat is interminable. Given the island's subtropical location, it experiences only moderate differences in temperature from day to night. Heat that takes over the city in the day refuses to back down at night, hovering like a fire-spitting beast regardless of time of day. Over the long summer months, it stays put, persistent and relentless.

2

Zhongshan District, near the Tamsui River, was dotted with small American-style bars. Lacking neon signs, most were lit up only by streetlights, recognizable late at night by simple English letters burned or carved into ebony wooden plaques.

One of the bars, *Red Wood*, stood out, for its cursive letters were highlighted by suggestive pink light from the pink-and-green neon sign of the barbershop next door.

It was nearly midnight on a Friday, the beginning of the weekend for foreign-enterprise employees. The bar was half full, with mostly men who, with their loosened ties, were obviously entry-level white-collar workers.

The corner was outfitted with a modified, short Taiwanese-style bar, with stools now occupied by Caucasian customers who were smoking in silence. Unaccustomed to stools, the local Taiwanese preferred to sit with friends at tables.

With the air-conditioner going full blast, cigarette smoke hung in the air before slowly dissipating. Ear-pounding music sounded anxious and rushed, making it difficult to tell whether the muffled voice of the singer came from a man or a woman, who was screaming as though his or her mouth was full, but with little energy. The customers had to shout, even when sitting across from each other, so most simply sat there, not knowing what else to do. Those who couldn't stand the boredom looked around the room with glazed eyes.

Suddenly the door opened and in swarmed a half-dozen people led by a short, frail man in his twenties dressed in a black tank top and jeans. A paper sign a full meter in length hung from his neck down to below his knees. Two bright, eye-catching words had been scribbled in red on the white paper:

Help Charlie

Below the English words was a Chinese phrase written from left to right: *Cha-li bing le.* Charlie is sick.

Someone snapped off the stereo, creating an abrupt silence that prompted those facing inside to pause in their survey of the bar and turn to look toward the entrance. The young man with the sign walked in slowly, followed by a tall, even younger-looking man, who was also wearing a tank top that showed off his rippling chest, shoulders, and arm muscles. Despite his brawny appearance, he seemed shy and timid; coins clattered in the tall tin can he was shaking.

"Charlie's sick and we're collecting money for him," he said in badly accented Mandarin, glossing over the four tones in a sort of affected monotone, like a foreigner trying to converse in the Beijing dialect. Phony sounding, he was obviously putting on an act.

The bartender, an ordinary-looking woman in her late twenties or early thirties, wore light makeup for the sake of her job, but it was clear she did not rely on looks to succeed in her line of work. No, her competence and experience came through as soon as she opened her mouth to greet the newcomer.

"You're Xiao Shen from the *Lighting House,* aren't you?" She paused. "Isn't Charlie your manager?"

"Right. He's in the hospital . . ."

"Ai! Isn't he the one who got *AIDS*?" a waitress with a serving tray blurted out before Xiao Shen finished.

A momentary silence descended on the bar before animated discussion among the patrons erupted, while Xiao Shen, struggling to be heard over the din, stammered an explanation in English: *"Charlie is sick. We wanna help him."*

One of the three men at a table near the entrance, who had unbuttoned his shirt and loosened his blue-and-red tie, reached into his pocket and took out his wallet. His face red from drinking, he picked out a hundred-NT bill with fair, delicate hands that had also turned red from the alcohol.

"*To* Taiwan's first *AIDS* case," he mumbled.

Shen came up with the can, which noiselessly swallowed the bill.

"Thank you. *Thanks.* Thank you very much." The other newcomers joined him in thanking the man.

Money flew as noisy drunk patrons began making donations, the occasional laughter adding a cheerful note to the atmosphere. It felt more like the end of a party, when the money is collected or when raffle tickets are drawn. Everyone seemed to be having a great time; gone was the earlier boredom, gloom, and ennui. When someone tossed a handful of coins into the can, the metallic clang and the noise from the bar created a festive air.

The din continued until Shen had made the rounds and was walking to the door, when someone at a table said in a loud voice:

"*AIDS* is a condemnation from above, God's punishment. It's contagious. You should congratulate yourself he wasn't arrested and thrown in jail. How dare you come here to collect money?" The speaker was a young white-collar worker. Though his tone was calm and detached, his face was a deathly white, either from alcohol or, possibly, his natural complexion.

A look of loathing flashed in Shen's eyes, but then disappeared as his expression turned anxious and fearful.

"This is Taiwan's first *AIDS* case," he beseeched deferentially, forgoing his earlier toneless foreign-sounding Mandarin. Now it had a Taiwanese accent. "We worked with *Charlie*. Don't you think we're afraid of catching it? *Tell you true*, we're scared to death, but we have to help him. Saving his life is the same as saving our own. Besides, *just think*, Taiwan's first *AIDS* case has historical significance. We have to take this opportunity to find a way out for Taiwan's *gays*."

"I'll give you some money."

A Caucasian at the bar cut him off in standard Mandarin as he took out a five-NT coin. Everyone turned to observe him on his bar stool, hand raised high over his head. He showed off the coin like a magician before letting it drop in the can, where it banged crisply against the side before falling silently to the bottom.

"*Thanks.*" Shen thanked the man in the same obsequious, anxious tone. "Thanks a lot." Looking around and seeing that no more donations were forthcoming, he waved at the bartender and left with his friends. She didn't look up, merely acknowledging his gesture with a faint smile.

The pleasant, cheerful voice of a young woman was heard before the door shut and the rock music started up again:

"They could be partners, the same type, *you know*. How scary. *It's terrible. The world's upside down.*"

None of the newcomers turned to look at her.

A rush of stifling summer-night heat enveloped them in sticky warm air the moment they walked out of *Red Wood*. Their sweat glands, dried and sealed by the air-conditioning, went into overdrive, and they were quickly drenched in sweat, which, with the combined effects of body heat and the sweltering night, turned hot and wrapped itself tightly around them.

"*Damn it*. Fuck. Shit!" Shen wiped the sweat from his forehead with his hand. "That foreigner was a real shit. Five NT! That's ten cents, a *dime*. That's no way to treat people. Damn him!"

No one said anything as they crossed the street and entered a narrow lane flanked by flashing neon signs that formed a colorful stream.

"He gave us money," the short guy carrying the sign said cautiously. "That showed his good intentions."

Shen rapped him on the head with his knuckles.

"You ought to be ashamed of yourself, forgetting who you are in the presence of a foreigner."

When they reached the end of the lane, they turned onto a major thoroughfare, where cars surged in waves. A wall of flashing TV screens blocked their view.

"Wow!" they cried out in unison. "That's amazing."

They were facing six rows of six twenty-eight-inch TV sets filling the storefront of an electronics shop. It was almost midnight and the TVs were showing the late-night news. A pavilion and a terrace by a pond of water with long, curvy, swaying willow trees that sent tiny ripples across the surface appeared on all thirty-six screens. The multiple display of identical exquisite terraces gave the impression of a continuous, endless row of pavilions, water, and willows, creating a sense of unmatched prosperity, as though, for thousands of years and over hundreds of generations, the willow tips never stopped touching the water and the terrace and pavilion would go on forever. After a while, the rippling water and terrace began to change from screen to screen, becoming dreamlike phantasms, thirty-six separate views running contiguously and endlessly. One pond followed another; each pavilion merged into the next. For a brief moment, the thirty-six screens appeared to morph into an enormous garden crisscrossed with endless terraces, pavilions, and towers.

The voice-over narration was by a female newscaster in a clearly enunciated, professional, and yet emotionless voice:

> Ms. Zhu Yinghong, descendant of Taiwan's famed gentry family from Lucheng, followed an original design in completing the renovation of Lotus Garden, built by her ancestors two hundred years ago. It was once a private residence, but Ms. Zhu recently established the Lotus Garden Foundation and opened the garden to the public. Now more people will have a chance to visit one of Taiwan's rare natural beauties. A ceremony held earlier today was attended by both government officials and members of Lucheng's gentry.

The camera shifted and the buildings disappeared, replaced by a shot of a crowd, before moving to a medium shot of a woman. For a moment, the thirty-six screens were filled with the face of a woman in her late thirties.

On that face was a pair of large, beautiful eyes, more sunken than those on most Asian faces, giving the face a clearly defined outline, though the nose bridge was not particularly high. Her thick lower lip contrasted with a much thinner upper lip, lending an unquestioned sensuality to her face. For some reason, she looked anxious, perhaps because the slightly gaunt face displayed an agitation more commonly seen on older women. She was wearing a simply cut, lacy white dress with a V-neck; the sleeves, made of tightly woven, soft lace, barely covered her shoulders. A long white scarf of the same material was wrapped over her head; curls of black hair peeked out from one end of a scarf that dangled across her chest. Strands of hair quivered under an early summer morning breeze, as dazzling sunlight shone down on her scarf and dress from treetops; the V-neck opening was highlighted by a diamond clearly weighing more than ten carats.

The professional voice-over now turned affectionate, with a hint of a smile: "Zhu Yinghong was able to renovate Lotus Garden with the help of her husband, Lin Xigeng, a real estate tycoon. It is rumored that he promised the renovation as a wedding gift to his beloved wife."

The camera moved from a sweep of the government officials and local gentry to a close-up of a man in his forties. The face, which must have been very handsome in the man's younger days, had filled out, but that added a measure of self-assurance and confidence that bordered on haughtiness. His tightly pressed lips were thin but nicely outlined; the glasses resting on his high nose lessened the severe look and added a genteel air. With sunlight reflecting off the lenses, it was hard to see the expression in his eyes, only that they seemed dark and harsh. A unique sense of confidence betrayed an untamed expansiveness, particularly when he turned his head to look around, chin held high.

The voice-over resumed its flat narration:

Lotus Garden, built prior to 1850, is more than ten acres in size, and, owing to the hills around it, has the feel of a mountain forest. Some of the terraces, pavilions, and vegetation are arranged in clusters, others set off by themselves. Undulating structures of varying heights are a sheer delight. Lotus Garden is centered on a large pond filled with lotus flowers and flanked by rocky heights from which a waterfall cascades. Surrounded by a number of paths, winding verandas, high towers, and terraces, the garden is a perfect place for a visitor to lose himself as he becomes one with nature, his mind soaring freely.

The camera paused on an octagonal doorway, where an unusual rock formation and a stand of short bamboo were framed by a red-brick door through which the camera entered, taking the viewer to a long meandering loggia that seemed to twist and turn without end. Before long the camera panned over the lotus flowers and tilted upward to display a tower. A quick turn around the tower led the viewer to a terrace, a pavilion, and the waterfall.

As the camera moved faster and faster, it traveled through dense trees and flowers, past swallow eaves and green-glazed tiles, over red bricks and white walls, all repeated on each of the thirty-six screens. The group had been focusing on one screen, but it was hard not to look at the entire wall of screens for fear of missing something. As the viewers' gazes shifted, the thirty-six screens seemed to move, creating a surreal tapestry, so they all quickly looked back to the first screen, but by then everything had changed; it was hard to shake a feeling that they had missed something when their eyes moved from screen to screen. The endlessly shifting gazes increased the illusion that everything was undergoing continuous change.

"Wow! It's like a labyrinth," Shen said as he rubbed his eyes.

"Hurry. We have more bars to visit."

At that urging, the short young man with the cardboard sign turned around; framed by garden scenery on thirty-six TV screens, the blood-red writing on the sign looked shockingly gaudy. The red paint looked like intertitles on the TV screens:

Help Charlie

And the Chinese text beneath it:

Cha-li bing le.

It was nearly midnight, but the summer night was still plagued by the high temperature and humid air that wrapped itself around the thoroughfare, with its endless flow of traffic, car horns, and engine noise. Neon lights along the street turned into a river of colored light shining down on sidewalk stalls suffused with the din of clamoring people. On this bustling, noisy, chaotic, and yet colorful street in the city of Taipei, the large wall of TV screens continued to display a breeze blowing over flowing water and swaying willows. Terraces, towers, and pavilions, with their soaring eaves and green tiles, seemed to replicate themselves as they turned into a fantastic illusion of an endless sequence of images.

PART I

ONE

"I WAS BORN IN THE LAST YEAR OF THE FIRST SINO-JAPANESE WAR..."

Zhu Yinghong's teacher had chosen the word "I" as the theme for the first assignment in her third-grade writing class. Nine-year-old Yinghong picked up her pencil, sharpened to a fine point, and wrote the opening sentence in her notebook without hesitation: I was born in the last year of the First Sino-Japanese War.

What next? She wrote something on her cheap notebook, erased it, wrote something else, and erased that, until the thin paper was creased and torn by her pencil point and eraser, and the board she was writing on had slipped off her desk more than once, and still no second sentence. Finally, she picked up her copy of *Sample Essays*, turned to the "I" section, and finished her first essay in accordance with the sample given in the book. Naturally, that included all the third-grade practice sentences like "I have a Papa and a Mama. We are a very happy family. I also have two elder brothers. We live in the middle of a large garden." When she couldn't write a Chinese character, she used the standard phonetic system.

Her teacher, known by her Japanese name, Keiko, was a small woman with stumpy calves that, visible beneath her skirt, were devoid even of the normal curve of ankles. Yinghong had heard from someone, probably the maid Mudan, who had come along with Mother when she was married, that those were called "turnip legs," the shape a result of all that kneeling on tatami mats. Only a few years had passed since the Japanese had been repatriated, and the adults were now saying that "turnip legs" were ugly.

Her mother often sat on her legs too, but they didn't look like turnip legs to her. And every time her mother tried to get her to sit that way, she refused unrelentingly, harboring a secret dread; not only did adults call those turnip legs ugly, but the very thought of them terrified her somehow. There was a time that whenever the maid muttered "You don't look right whether you're sitting or standing," Yinghong petulantly refused to do what she was told, and all Mudan had to say was "You'll wind up with turnip legs" for her to turn obedient.

Turnip legs were, of course, white. Mudan loved to say that "Keiko's skin was as white as a Japanese woman and as puffy as a pastry," and Yinghong would never forget her teacher's white, round face and her fair, soft, gentle, red-tinged hands.

Turnip legs and the color white, these distinct characteristics of her teacher, formed enduring impressions of Zhu Yinghong's childhood. Even many years later, they had not gone away.

And that afternoon, as Keiko stood at the rostrum, calling out the names of the students and handing back notebooks with their essays, Yinghong walked up and, as always, kept her eyes fixed on her teacher's hands so as not to look at her legs; her notebook was clutched in one of those soft, white hands. Suddenly, she heard her teacher abandon herself to loud laughter.

"Zhu Yinghong, so you were born at the end of the First Sino-Japanese War!"

She was laughing so hard she could barely get the words out. Everyone in the class, infected by their teacher's laughter, started laughing.

"If you were born in the last year of the First Sino-Japanese War, do you know how old you are now?"

Zhu Yinghong shook her head. Tears glistened in her large eyes.

"Go home and ask your papa, and next time watch what you write."

Keiko forced herself to stop laughing so she could pass out the rest of the notebooks. A red tinge suddenly showed on her fair face, after briefly returning to normal; deep blushes spread out evenly on her snowy white cheeks.

The teacher's face turned red easily, usually when boys in the class disobeyed her or when girls were arguing. Yinghong, a third-grader, was well aware that in the two years Keiko had been her teacher, this was the only time she had laughed out loud, and she had no idea in the world why her teacher blushed afterward.

By the time Yinghong finally understood that her teacher had blushed owing to embarrassment over a momentary loss of self-control, Keiko had by then chosen marriage over her teaching career and become a mother of five.

That was what he said when he met her for the first time:

"You look like you were born . . .born in the last century, the end of the last century."

"Eighteen-ninety-something."

"That's about right."

He nodded, and she was still smiling. Then, without thinking, she blurted out:

"Sort of like I was born in the last year of the First Sino-Japanese War . . ."

Even if Keiko hadn't told her to, Zhu Yinghong would have gone home and asked her father. The way her teacher had, uncharacteristically, laughed so hard that afternoon, and then blushed afterward, had humiliated and frightened Yinghong more than at any other time in her life. Always the class leader, the girl with the best grades, she had simply written an essay in which she'd said she was born in the last year of the First Sino-Japanese War, and her teacher and all the students in the class had laughed, followed by the teacher blushing. What had she done? She had to know.

During those years, her father had suffered from poor health. When school was out, she knew that he had probably just gotten up from his afternoon nap and was still at Flowing Pillow Pavilion. Not wanting to wait till she reached Upper House to put down her school bag, she ran, passing under the archway where the words "Lotus Garden" were written in cursive script. At Yinghong Pavilion, she could still read the parallel lines on the red pillars in the late-afternoon sunlight:

At a quiet little garden startled wild geese fly off on the wind
In the fields of green leaves winged guests enjoy stirring up shadowy red

Every time she came to Yinghong Pavilion, she reached out and touched the last two words—*ying hong*, shadowy red. It was where she'd gotten her name, from this garden and this little pavilion, and even the illiterate Mudan knew that her name and this pavilion were linked.

But on that third-grade afternoon, she was in such a hurry to find her father she ran and skipped all the way to Flowing Pillow Pavilion without stopping to touch "Yinghong" on the pillar for the first time ever.

She pounded on the door with the back of her hand, yet only managed dull, barely audible thuds. Her father had told her she was always to knock before entering his room. It was a heavy, sturdy door, and her little fingers could hardly produce a sound, but he would not permit her to slap the door with her palm, so the only way to make any noise at all was with her knuckles and a shout:

"Is Otosan in?"

"Come in, Ayako."

Recently, Father had taken to calling her by her Japanese name, Ayako, and had told other members of the family to do the same. Mother, whose fluent Japanese was well known in Lucheng, called out in a lovely soft voice that made her name pleasing to the ear. Mudan was the only one who could never master the language, and usually called out: "Aiya! Kou!" especially when she was out in the yard calling her to come in: "Aiya! Kou!" "Aiya! Kou!" If Yinghong did not want to come when called, she'd have to plug her ears with her hands. Fortunately, Mudan usually forgot even how to "Aiya! Kou!" and simply called out "Ah-hong."

For as long as she could remember, everyone had called Yinghong "Ah-hong." Her playmates were Meizi and Wuxiong, for her father had originally banned Japanese names. She had no idea her name was Ayako. But when her schoolmates began using their Chinese names, he took to using Japanese; that went for every member of the family.

"Otosan, I need to talk to you . . ."

Yinghong pushed on the door, but it didn't move; it was bolted on the inside. She felt a momentary sense of panic. For some reason, in recent years Father had gotten into the habit of locking doors in the house, and once he did that, there was no way to open them. And he wouldn't open the door until he was sure who it was.

She was about as tall as most third-graders in public schools, which meant that when she tried the door, she would push at the exact spot of the long wooden bolt on the other side. That presented a formidable obstacle. Had she been taller, say the height of a young woman, she'd have been pushing above the bolt, which would have caused the old door to creak and move a bit.

For years she had been frightened by the prospect of a bolted door, and on the afternoon in question, she tearfully waited for her father to open the Flowing Pillow Pavilion door.

He saw the tears at once and pulled her inside. Between sobs, Yinghong told him about her "born in the last year of the First Sino-Japanese War" essay.

Instead of laughing, as she'd expected, he surprised her by asking sympathetically:

"How do you know about the First Sino-Japanese War?"

"Mudan told me about it. When she tells me stories, she says 'During the First Sino-Japanese War,' or 'Back then, back then it was like this and like that.' I was born a long time ago, so why can't I say I was born during the First Sino-Japanese War?"

"Hold on." Signs of a gentle smile creased Father's face. "A moment ago, you said the last year of the First Sino-Japanese War, that you were born during the First Sino-Japanese War. But do you know what 'last year' means?"

Knowing how her father doted on her, Yinghong said confidently:

"The last year? That means I was born last, later than Mudan and later than Otosan."

Father had a good laugh over that, a rarity in recent years. He got up out of his carved sandalwood bed, and walked up to put his arms around her, having to bend over to do so, since he was so much taller. She recoiled briefly when his beard touched her face, but then quickly leaned back toward him. Father took her over to a bedside table, where he picked up a thick Japanese book and, without even opening it, began:

"The Sino-Japanese War broke out in 1894. This is now 1952. So tell me, if you were born in the last year of the First Sino-Japanese War, how old are you?"

She had already memorized her multiplication tables, so simple addition and subtraction were no problem.

"Fifty-eight," she said and began to laugh, her eyes still filled with tears.

He obviously didn't know when the First Sino-Japanese War had taken place, so when he heard her say she was born in the last year of the First Sino-Japanese War, he said, without thinking, "Indeed!"

She didn't correct him. Rather, she asked:

"Why do you say I was born in the last century?"

"Because there aren't many girls like you these days." He thought for a moment, then added: "You're too smart and, I'm sure, very competent."

After he'd gotten to know her better, she asked him the same question, and he'd said:

"I wasn't wrong. You're as competent as you are precisely because you were born into that family. You have the mannerisms of the matriarch of a large clan."

After they'd been married many years, she asked him again:

"Do you still feel that I was born in the last century, the end of the last century, during the First Sino-Japanese War?"

This time he merely looked somberly out the window without answering.

. . . You can say you were born at the end of the First Sino-Japanese War if you want to. The war broke out in August 1894. In September, the Manchu court lost a battle in the Yellow Sea. On the twelfth of February in the following year, 1895, the Japanese defeated the Northern Fleet and Ding Ruchang committed suicide. On the seventeenth of April, the Treaty of Shimonoseki was signed, ceding Taiwan and the Penghu Islands and the Liaodong Peninsula to Japan for thirty years. On May twenty-fifth, Taiwan declared itself the "Democratic Republic of Taiwan," with Tang Jingsong as its first president. Tang fled the island on the sixth of June. In October, the Battle of Guangzhou was lost, and Sun Yat-sen fled to Japan. During that same month, Japan crushed all opposition in Taiwan . . .

The letter was written in Father's simple and concise Japanese, and touched upon his rereading of modern history in his old age. The more he thought about these major events, the more he felt that, at some level, his daughter hadn't necessarily been wrong when she said she was "born in the last year of the First Sino-Japanese War."

Yinghong finished her father's letter from home with tears clouding her vision. Snow fell heavily outside her New York window, the worst snowstorm the city had seen in half a century, according to meteorologists. As dusk settled in, large, dry snowflakes kept falling, and as the snowfall continued, it increased to the point where it was a wall of shifting white, a haze that blurred heaven and earth.

In her mind, that afternoon in Flowing Pillow Pavilion was a clearer and more concrete image than anything else she had seen in her third year at school. More than a decade had passed, and now, as she stood there watching snow fall on New York, the passage of years merged with her memories, creating a picture more detailed than those memories, until they were no longer merely impressions of things seen by a third-grade girl.

Father had his back to the light. His living quarters faced south, looking out on a large lotus pond. In late October in central Taiwan, the sun set slightly to the south, which meant that Lotus Garden, built at the foot of a hill, blocked the sunlight shining westward, casting shadows on one side of the garden. Early autumn scorching heat, what the locals call the autumn tiger, was not to be taken lightly, and the garden was brightly lit; Flowing Pillow Pavilion, too, was, for the most part, washed in sunlight.

Father was in his room, in which a warm, yellow glow from the sunlight slanted in through windows shaped like two fans with overlapping sections. He sat on a Chinese-style armchair with his back to the window. He was only in his forties, and, though he was gaunt and pale from a long illness, he was still an undeniably handsome man. Deep-set eyes so typical of the Zhu family were lusterless. A high nose bridge and full lips were set off against an angular face with high cheekbones that seemed even more prominent because of his bony features.

She had always thought her father was tall and slender.

When she was in high school, a lesson in her Chinese literature textbook dealt with *A New Account of Tales of the World*. One day her father, struck by a sudden whim, took out an ancient-looking book lying flat on a carved sandalwood bookcase; it was a woodblock edition of *Wondrous Tales of the*

World printed on bamboo paper. The bound cover looked well worn and the thread in the covers was coming loose, all signs of frequent use.

"It should be in the language section," Father mumbled to himself.

He opened the book to reveal comments and annotations in vermillion ink that filled the yellowed pages, like red flower petals lodged between the lines. Flipping back and forth, he made the flowers flutter among the inky black characters.

"No, so then it must be . . ."

Quickly he turned to "Wit 25" and pushed the book over to Yinghong, who began to read word-by-word lines that had been punctuated with vermillion ink.

"Sun Zijing, when he was young, had wanted to become a hermit, so he said to Wang Wuzi that one should use a rock as a pillow and flowing water to rinse one's mouth. But it came out incorrectly as 'using a rock to rinse the mouth and sleeping on flowing water.' Wang objected by saying that water could not be used as a pillow and that a rock cannot rinse one's mouth. Sun retorted that one could use flowing water as a pillow in order to wash one's ears and a rock to rinse one's mouth in order to sharpen the teeth."

Yinghong let out a soft cry. As a little girl, she had once sat on her father's lap and listened to him explain the origin of "Flowing Pillow Pavilion": using flowing water as a pillow. How can that be done? she recalled her father asking. Back then she'd hated it when Mudan dragged her up to a red wooden bucket and made her squat down to wash her hair, so she answered without thinking:

"Sleeping on flowing water means you never have to wash your hair."

He roared with laughter. Unlike other people she'd seen laugh by cracking open their mouths and making tiny sounds, teeth still hidden behind stretched lips, her father would open his mouth wide to show his white teeth, and release loud, clear laughter, a sign of true delight.

His laughter stopped her from discovering the true meaning of "using flowing water as a pillow" until that afternoon, when she held the ancient edition of *Wondrous Tales of the World* in her hands. With a cry of surprise, she said:

"So it meant to use flowing water to rinse your mouth and pillow your head on a rock, but he made a mistake and reversed the two."

In high school, Yinghong was slightly over five feet tall, which placed her seat in the middle of the classroom. But a slender figure made her seem much taller. Standing by the bookcase with the thread-bound copy of the *Wondrous Tales of the World*, she was only half a head shorter than her father.

So he was not particularly tall after all, and could only be considered a man of medium height among people of his generation. But he favored Japanese-style dress, a locally made cotton gown in a grayish blue. When he walked down the uneven verandah of Flowing Pillow Pavilion, he had to hike up the hem of his robe with one hand. Wind around the low hill in the open space would then be able to travel freely inside his robe, puffing it up enough that his normally gaunt body looked pleasingly trim and slender.

It was not until high school that she had a true understanding of her father's height, for before then she'd always had to look up at him; it was also about the same time when, through the allusion to "Flowing Pillow Pavilion," that she began to have a vague understanding of her father's admiration for Sun Zijing's "Pillowing flowing water to wash one's ears and rinsing with rocks to sharpen one's teeth." But at the time she was still unable to glimpse the profound meaning below the surface.

Was it because of the name, then, that her father had always been partial to the pavilion among the many pavilions, terraces, and towers in Lotus Garden? She recalled that, according to a legend passed down by generations, the pavilion got its name because there happened to be a rivulet flowing by the small pavilion terrace when the garden was completed.

Flowing Pillow Pavilion was on the west end of the garden, at the tip of a pond with irregular sides. A smaller pond of little more than a couple hundred square feet had been created by piling rocks near the pavilion; long wooden planks had been placed atop four stone pillars made of Jiaping white stone from Tangshan set in the pond, thus creating a small terrace that soared above the water. Flanking three sides of the terrace were hardwood bench seats, where one could sit and reach out to touch water lilies in the summer, when they bloomed profusely amid the graceful leaves. In mid summer, the lotus leaves might even reach across the bench seats, their lush, green figures spreading out to the middle of the pavilion.

By the time October came to an end, the lotus flowers had long since turned into seedpods and the leaves were mostly dried up. Father would sit by the fan-shaped windows in the pavilion, keeping himself mostly in shadow. Perhaps because of the darkness around him, his face remained blurred in her memory. What she remembered most vividly was actually a dying lotus branch framed by the fan-shaped window. The lone stem was bathed in the light of the yellow setting sun, looking brilliant and glorious, as if gilded. But in no time, the autumn sun set, and she could no longer make out what she had written in her notebook: "I was born in the last year of the First Sino-Japanese War...."

I had always thought that the Sino-Japanese War was simultaneously the beginning and the end for the Taiwanese, for from that moment on, the fate of the Taiwanese was destined to be decided by others. My arrest and imprisonment, as well as the extermination of the Taiwanese elite, were simply another unavoidable continuation of the tragic fate of the Taiwanese. Except that, fortunately or unfortunately for me, I was released when they believed I was too ill to live much longer, which allowed me to drag on in my feeble existence to be an eyewitness as I awaited a Taiwanese future that could be even more tragic and deplorable.

Which is why I'm convinced that on this land there can be no true paradise, no justice, no hope. In order for you, my beloved children, to start over in a new, unsoiled place, I sent your two older brothers to study abroad when they were young. I arranged for them to live in Japan and the United States of America with the express hope that they would have a clean, fresh start, without the entanglements and hindrances of the past. Only you, Ayako, my favorite little girl, were kept by my side because of my love for you. I was really worried that if you were to leave home at too young an age, a fragile girl like you would not know how to deal with the vast outside world. I therefore sought to console myself that you, Ayako, were, after all, a girl, for whom the most significant matter in life was to find a good husband. And that was why I indulged myself with this selfish desire and kept you by my side till you graduated from high school.

But now that I have turned sixty, I cannot help but wonder every once in a while if I had any right to make these arrangements for all of you. As they have been away from a very young age, your brothers have basically forgotten about this land, their bloodline, and their familial continuity. They did indeed enjoy a new beginning, just as I had hoped. But if this new beginning turned out to be the ultimate break, then it will be I who severed the three-hundred-year continuance of the Zhu family in Taiwan. I may have given the Zhu clan two sons, two outstanding sons who hold doctoral degrees, but spiritually I have sundered the Zhu family bloodline.

Ayako, at night, when I am struck by the reality that I sinned against eight generations of the Zhu family, I am startled out of my sleep, soaked in a cold sweat, and unable to go back to sleep. Ayako, you can probably understand my feelings, since you have always been my favorite and have stayed with me the longest. You are grown up now, and have gained experience overseas. Can you tell me if the decisions I made for you and your brothers were right or wrong? Did I have the right to make such important decisions for your lives?

I imagine that your brothers, owing to work and lifestyle, will not return to make a life in Taiwan. Their children, the ninth generation of the Zhu family, will surely stay in the United States, which means that their children and grandchildren will never again be Taiwanese. Ayako, I cannot help but pin my selfish hopes on you. Though you are a girl, Zhu family blood does, after all, flow in your veins. I don't know why, but lately I have been possessed by the laughable idea that, as if arranged by an unknown force, you will be the one to revive the Zhu family. Don't laugh at your father for having such a notion; I am probably just getting old.

At the age of sixty with failing health, I have come to realize that what concerns me most, surprisingly, are the personal sentiments I was reluctant to talk about. Ayako, you are my favorite child. Have you given some thought to coming back to Taiwan to spend time with me before I die?

The letter had not been sent through the postal service, and had obviously been spirited out of Taiwan by someone trustworthy, in order to escape inspection. There was no envelope. All she received were a dozen or so pieces of red-bordered white cotton paper filled with his handwriting in blue ink. Tears streamed down her cheeks and dripped onto the blue words. The handwritten Japanese hiragana script was made up of few strokes, rendering the wet words recognizable only for a while. On the Chinese characters, with their complex strokes, the blue ink quickly began to spread as soon as it came into contact with her tears; the words bled into each other until they were so blurry they lost their shape, turning into round, blue, water marks dotting the white paper.

Snow still swirled outside the window, the result of the biggest snowstorm in New York in fifty years. As the night deepened, the darkening sky seemed to be under an assault by thousands of tons of snow, as if heaven and earth had broken apart and the sky was pressing down. Zhu Yinghong looked out the window, where flurries of snow were blurred by her teary vision. Her hometown would be visible only if she could see through a sky full of snow, across the American continent, and over the Pacific Ocean.

She shivered in her room, where the heater was turned all the way up.

She met him for the first time at a typical businessmen's dinner in Taipei.

They were introduced to one another as Mr. Lin, Chairman of the Board, Lin Xigeng, and Miss Zhu, Zhu Yinghong. She had been taken there by her uncle—her mother's only brother, who at the time was planning to sell a piece of land to Lin or looking to develop the land with him.

As "Special Assistant to the Chairman of the Board" at her uncle's company, Yinghong was occasionally required to attend banquets with her uncle, a well-known figure in the business world, who had a long-standing strategy: with one or two women around (and not just a lady of the night who sold her body), the men who got together to talk business would behave in a more gentlemanly way, which in turn helped reduce disputes.

From the surprised look in Lin's eyes, she knew the moment they were introduced that she had caught his attention.

"Ah, the Lucheng Zhu family," he said, following up with a name of an important figure in the financial world. "I think he's your—elder uncle. I know him."

She felt apprehensive. He obviously had some familiarity with her clan; she herself did not often get to see the elder uncle, an important figure in finance.

But she merely smiled and gracefully took her seat.

His youth and unexpected good looks surprised her. When he looked around, he had an arrogant, conceited expression, but his tall stature did make him stand out.

"You're younger than I thought," she said. He smiled indulgently, with obvious self-satisfaction. A hint of self-assurance graced the perfect outline of his lips, a sign that he had received more compliments than he could count. What should have followed was, "It's unusual to be so accomplished at such a young age," but instead, Yinghong continued in an off-handed manner:

"I've only read about you in the papers, and always thought you'd be a short, stocky businessman in his fifties or sixties." She laughed at her own words. "And that you were connected with the underworld."

She saw a subtle, shy look flit across his face; it was unquestionably a bashful look, no matter how quickly it faded. That stopped her.

Later they would, like many lovers, repeatedly return to when they first met. He would tease her about mentioning the underworld at their first encounter, and she would defend herself by saying that this was the impression she received from the news media, for he was a frequent subject for tabloid magazines, where he would be described this way:

REAL ESTATE TYCOON PLUCKS A STAR OUT OF THE FIRMAMENT

REAL ESTATE TYCOON ASSAULTED AT CONSTRUCTION SITE, TIES TO THE
    UNDERWORLD SUSPECTED
LIN XIGENG SPECULATES ON LAND, INCURS WRATH OF MAJOR INVEST-
    MENT COMPANY

Along with the spurt of economic growth in Taiwan, the number of tabloid magazines also grew substantially; in any given month several would appear to embellish and propagate wondrous stories about individuals who had accumulated great riches in the export business. The salacious stories were told in an erotic and exaggerated tone to highlight the tycoons' extravagances, including toilets made of gold in their houses, or how one was serviced simultaneously by a movie star and her mother, who was barely past prime.

Ever since Lin Xigeng was assaulted at a construction site, the magazine that claimed to have the inside scoop insisted that he had ties to the underworld, speculating that he had to have close relationships with local thugs to protect his massive enterprises, with construction sites all over the island. The magazine even offered a convincing analysis that his payoffs at every site each year were enough to support half of one particular gang, which was why he was on equal footing with the leader of that gang, which in turn made other gangs very unhappy.

At the time, a trade style unique to the island nation turned everything upside down and inside out; it was a time of anything goes and everything is possible. In an environment ripe for fanciful stories dealing with the underworld, a self-made man could become filthy rich almost overnight.

With the coquettish smile typical of a spoiled, naive girl, Yinghong repeated for Lin the gossip in a magazine, although, befitting her social status, she politely avoided the most sensational details.

Lin listened patiently, denying nothing, though with a perceptible show of shyness.

It was a banquet typical of Taipei businessmen, with one hostess per man, known as a "flower arrangement."

The five or six girls that night all looked about the same—lightly made up, they did not appear to have come from the red-light district, trying hard to convince everyone that they were just ordinary women.

At five feet three or taller, they had big bones and wide hips, thick arms and tall bodies; undressed, they would still display a full figure. Obviously, the highest-earning among their peers, these women, with their large frames, satisfied the demand for "good figures" by local men who were usually not particularly tall or their more important clients—Japanese men engaged in sex tourism.

Naturally, they were all young, in their twenties, pretty but not beautiful. They wore ready-made clothes common in Taiwan, a bit too frilly for Yinghong's taste, but in their view appropriate for evening wear. Some wore dresses with ruffled edges, some were in pencil skirts with side slits, and others had on layered-hem skirts that mimicked evening gowns. It was early spring, so not much flesh showed. Low waists with wide belts were in fashion, and, since the girls were large to begin with, six-inch-wide, bright, patent leather belts made them look even larger, their full-figured bodies overshadowing everything in sight.

They sat, absent-mindedly, nonchalantly, never taking the initiative to talk or strike up a conversation with anyone. The men ignored them as well. When Yinghong took her seat, she noticed nothing unusual, except that none of the women at the table were talking; she thought they were being neglected. Then she heard that the girl across from her was named Chen, so she greeted her politely and inquired:

"You're so young. Should I call you Miss Chen or Mrs. Chen?"

With a languid, scornful smile, the girl answered lightly:

"You can call me Fangfang."

What kind of woman would rather not use her family name? Yinghong wondered briefly before catching on.

Like so many lovers, they often talked about their first meeting. He loved to tease her in a tender, indulgent way, remarking how, as a woman who had seen the world, she could have mistaken professional hostesses as women from good families. Even ask the girl if she should call her Miss Chen or Mrs. Chen.

She would argue that they looked normal enough; they were just women. Later she realized that he enjoyed teasing her, for he obviously gained satisfaction from the fact that she was a pampered girl from a well-known family.

So she let him tease her, burying her face in his arms and pummeling him gently.

Like many typical banquets in Taipei's business circles, dishes were brought out one after another, usually twelve in all. Liquor followed the food. The quiet girls sitting with the men now got into action, pouring drinks and offering toasts. Raising their glasses, they offered unvarying greetings:

"My name is Manling (or Meilan, or Nancy, or Wawa, or Ziyan). I'm pleased to meet and learn from you. May I ask your honorable name, Sir?"

The sirs gave them their names.

"Mr. Lin (or Mr. Wang, or Mr. Li, or Mr. Wu, or Mr. Zhu). Here's to you."

Glasses were raised.

They poured drinks, they served food, and they passed out towelettes, all in a ritualistic, repetitive manner.

My name is Meilan. Cheers, Mr. Wang. I'm pleased to meet and learn from you. (This hot pot is made with shredded bamboo and locally grown chicken. The clear broth goes especially well with the liquor.)

My name is Nancy. Cheers, Mr. Li. I'm pleased to meet and learn from you. (Waiter, we're out of ice. Bring us some more.)

My name is Wawa. Cheers, Mr. Wu. I'm pleased to meet and learn from you. (Here's some lemon, freshly squeezed, real lemon juice. Add some to your glass to prevent dry mouth at night.)

My name is Ziyan. Cheers, Mr. Zhu. I'm pleased to meet and learn from you. (Towels. Do we have hot towels? Bring us some hot towels, waiter.)

The men drank and played the finger-guessing game. At first the game was played among the men only, but then the losers asked their assigned girls to play for them. As the girls joined in, the men picked up the speed of their drinking, to a point that they didn't even wait for the girls to pour. They did it themselves, half a glass for a finger-guessing round, one glass for three rounds or maybe four. Sometimes the losers were made to down the liquor in one drink.

> Why haven't we seen you here recently?
> Hey, fill up your glass. Look at mine, it's full.
> Go on, play this round for me.
> Here, give me a hug. It's been a long time since I last held you in my arms.
> Hey, you can't do that. A rain check on your turn to drink? When will you really drink it?

More and more XO Brandy was brought out and poured into a decanter with ice. The amber liquid was diluted after the ice melted, turning into a lusterless light brown and then an even lighter brown, with a tinge of lifeless white. Brandy that would normally overflow without dripping down the side of the glass could not withstand the added water; the liquid now oozed over the rims of the glasses.

They drained glasses of XO Brandy, dumping tumblers of the stuff into their open mouths. The brandy also figured in the guessing game, and it took little time for them to empty a case of twenty bottles.

The dinner, like all banquets in Taipei's business circles, was held in a small private restaurant room. A few dozen square meters in size, the room had only one door, which was tightly shut. The walls were decorated with red silk and satin on top and metal wainscoting. Spray painted in purple, the ceilings were sprinkled with gold dust. More than a dozen small light-bulbs shone from artistically designed lamps, their shiny metal shades inlaid with stained glass. These details were considered to represent grandeur and luxury, which was why they were all used here.

Their din echoed in the room, bouncing off the wainscoting up to the ceiling before careening back down to be absorbed by the silk fabric, giving off a muffled sound like someone chewing and gnawing on bones with the mouth closed.

Lin Xigeng sat there, the picture of idle ease, holding a cigarette in one hand. He looked at the men and women in front of him, playing games, drinking, and flirting, a barely perceptible smile on his face, as if he were outside what was a common scene for him.

On that early spring evening, sitting across the enormous round table from him, I thought I saw a weary look on the face of Lin Xigeng, a host who was remiss in getting his guests to eat.

He seemed to have seen it all, an impression that was particularly noticeable when he was not talking. As he looked down, the frames of his glasses masked the expression in his eyes and gave his face a glum look. His dark suit coat made him appear quite understated.

I'll never forget what he wore that night, for it was too casual for a banquet host. The tailoring was so-so, the color too dark; he was tieless and his suit was wrinkled. He must have been wearing the same clothes during the day and came over to entertain right after work.

It was on that early spring evening that I first met Lin Xigeng and the dinner guests around the table. His guests weren't necessarily unimportant figures, but he didn't make an effort to offer them drinks or supply topics for conversation. Instead, he just sat there, as if he were hiding most of himself somewhere inside. As a result, the glum understatement so typical of him left something undecided about a real estate tycoon who was rumored to be worth billions of dollars and who'd had love affairs with many women in the entertainment industry; he had an air about him that was unrelated to his business, an inclination akin to a need and desire for something else.

At that moment I had a profound sense that the successful man before me was quite different from other successful entrepreneurs I'd met. To be sure, he was accomplished, but he was brimming with a sense of imperfection, an uncertainty of which even he himself was likely unaware. It was precisely that deeply touching sense of uncertainty and dissatisfaction that convinced me that there was a place for a woman in this man's life.

Like most of the business dinners in Taipei, a nagashi team came in some time during the evening, a typical band with a man and a woman. The modish young man had shoulder-length hair and the woman, who was barely twenty, went without makeup. Dressed in common jeans and a blouse, she was obviously telling the audience that she was different from the other women of the trade.

The nagashi band brought their own electronic keyboard and a drum set, which, when turned all the way up, submerged the room in roaring, deafening music, making it impossible to talk to someone even across the table. The finger-guessing games came to a stop, and the men now slid into the girls' arms, holding them or resting their heads on their chests.

The nagashi woman began with a fast-tempo Mandarin song, after which she asked, microphone in hand, if any of the guests would like to sing. The men all fell into an act of feigned modesty and politeness, and in the end none of them went up. One of the girls then got up and sang a Taiwanese song, "Lingering Old Feelings." When she returned to her seat, one of Lin Xigeng's employees offered her a red, five-hundred-NT bill in front of everyone. It was a reward, which she accepted with ease; except for a "thank-you," she said nothing, did not even smile.

The girls now took turns singing, each song earning a reward of five hundred NT. One after another they went up, in an impressively orderly fashion. Most of their songs were sad, sentimental love songs; the singers were absorbed in their songs, in either Taiwanese or Mandarin, about being abandoned by heartless lovers. Accompanied by very loud music, their voices, amplified by the microphone, did not sound entirely human, resembling a collective effect created by a machine; it seemed that anyone who opened her mouth could be a singer, but it was impossible to tell just who was singing.

With the steadily loud music increasing the effects of alcohol, the men began to take off their ties and unbuttoned their shirts to reveal flabby chests and bellies. Their hands also got frisky, worming their way under the girls' clothes to reach for their breasts or under their skirts. Yinghong grabbed the purse on her knees, fighting the urge to get up and leave.

She wondered why her uncle had brought her to this dinner. Normally he wouldn't let her come if these girls were around. Was it because he was unaware this time or because he couldn't find someone else to accompany him? Or was it all involved with the land he was planning to sell to Lin? In any case, she couldn't leave. If she did, she would offend the host, for which her uncle would bear the consequences.

As she hesitated, the music paused, since no one went up to sing. One of the girls knocked over a chopstick when she tried to evade a man's face that had come too close to hers.

"My chopstick," she said with a flirty pout. "You have to get me another one."

"Do you really need to find another one? You can have mine. I promise it'll be big enough to fill you up and make you happy," the man said.

Laughter erupted in the room. Yinghong stood up with her purse, but her exit route was blocked by a tall figure. It was Lin Xigeng, who said calmly:

"Let's dance."

"Here?" She was unsure.

Before she could protest, he put his arm around her shoulder, forcefully moving her away from her seat into the area between the band and the tables.

At first she felt that the carpet under her feet was making it hard to move, as if her shoes were caught in the pile. Fortunately, Lin was barely moving his feet; they seemed to simply sway from side to side. Then she was relaxed enough to notice the music, a slow waltz.

"Is it really all right to dance here?" Unease caused her to blurt this out, but the moment she said it she realized that with the thunderous music, Lin couldn't have heard her even though they were practically pressed against each other. She could only turn her face toward him and shout into his ear, which made it natural for them to dance in each other's arms without worrying about how they looked to the others.

"Don't worry," he said, lowering his head and raising his voice slightly to speak into her ear, but most of what he said was lost amid loud music mixed with someone singing. She repeated her question, but only heard the second half of his answer:

". . . is there a better place to hold a girl in one's arms?"

Nodding, she relaxed her arm on his shoulder and held him lightly.

One by one, the other dinner guests got up to join them. Some of the drunken men were holding the girls, but it looked like they were hanging onto them as their hands roamed over their bodies. Others continued to dance, seemingly still sober, and pressed their bodies tightly up against those special areas of the women's bodies. Zhu frowned and gave Lin a smile, before looking away. She heard someone singing:

I never thought the feeling of separation could be so sad
It was not till today that I knew it takes so much strength to even say good-bye

Like most popular love songs, this one spoke of an honest sorrow, using simple words for longing to express heartbreak. The only difference was that the singer had a low voice, which meant she had to struggle to ring out the higher tones, creating the effect of undying love, as if every word were like crying through blood and tears. With a few turns on the dance floor, Yinghong was able to see the singer—one of the girls hired for that night's dinner, who was standing by the musicians, holding a microphone. Yinghong could not recall whether her name was Meilan or Fangfang, mainly because she held the microphone close to her mouth in big, bony hands that covered half her face.

Those were the hands of a woman traditionally considered born to a sad life in the entertainment industry. Eyes closed and head tilted slightly back, she presented a picture of self-degradation so typical of women in the red light district. As she sang, her head and shoulders swayed, her tightly knit brows painting her young face with the sorrow and bleakness of someone who had already suffered her fair share of a tough life.

If I'd known it would be like this, I wouldn't have agreed to let you go
I told you I wouldn't cry
I told you I give you my fond good wishes

Never once had a low-class popular song, especially one about nothing but love and hate bellowed out of a working girl's mouth on a night of heavy drinking and carnal pleasure, exerted such irresistible power. Yinghong first felt the effects of the alcohol surging vaguely inside; the slow-dance steps required little movement, but she began to feel dizzy.

Then there was the music, deafening music that made her feel as though she were sinking. The drum set was beating faster than her heart, each note thumping violently against her chest, while the fast-tempo keyboard was made to sound like flying arrows. On top of that was the girl's song about deep, boundless sorrow and bitterness that accompanied profound love, which was slowly seeping through the loud music and worming its way into her heart.

I want to hold back my tears but I can't keep my sorrow in check
I don't know when my face became covered in tears

Finally I understood the feeling of abandonment.

I rested my head on Lin Xigeng's shoulder, utterly disgusted by the unbearable banquet. For the first time in my life, I was at the same table as a group of working girls who drank and flirted with Taipei's nouveau riche, falling short only of having sex then and there. Worse yet, I was actually touched by the love and resentment in a sappy popular song sung by a woman of the trade.

In fact, it became clear to me that I was engaged in self-indulging abandonment; or to put it differently, in a degenerating indulgence. I experienced fierce, drunken pleasure, the enjoyment of letting myself go.

Which was how I finally comprehended feelings of abandonment.

For different reasons, our desire for love meant that we, as women—the working girl, the song, and I—were doomed to be underappreciated, for no one could truly understand or know how to cherish us; true reciprocal feelings would never be ours to enjoy.

Since we knew our fate, we—the working girl, the girl in the song, and I—would be better off if we abandoned love altogether. Then, after experiencing the helplessness and bitterness of regret, disenchantment with self-abandonment would lead us to endless degenerating and indulgent acts, the deprivation accompanied by wretched resentment and decadent pursuits.

If I'd known it would be like this, I wouldn't have agreed to let you go
I told you I wouldn't cry
I told you I give you my fond good wishes

Zhu Yinghong felt that her body was drifting and disintegrating, inch by inch, as the thunderous drum continued to pound against the deepest recess of her heart. The song continued, with its sorrow and bitterness from the self-abnegation of love, roared and roared as it movingly depicted a drunken, frenzied, orgiastic sensation.

I was dazed, but I couldn't stop thinking that, if at that moment this tall, handsome man had understood, I'd have gone with him anywhere to do anything.

Never once had I experienced such a fierce desire for a man I'd known only for a few hours. I'd fallen for good-looking men before, but it was never quite like this. I couldn't control the intoxicating desire for carnal pleasure; I'd never felt such longing to be held, touched, and pressed down hard by a man.

I told myself that all I wanted was a feeling of being fulfilled and belonging to someone, the kind of contact I could not complete alone, a comforting sensation that could come only from a man's embrace and caresses.

But I immediately knew that no one could understand me, and that I was doomed to be hurt.

Leaning against Lin Xigeng, Zhu Yinghong maintained a level of self-control even under the influence of alcohol and the titillating ambience, but she was nevertheless shocked by her own reckless reactions. The tall man offered such comfortable arms, and the charming song expressed such intoxicating emotions, that she decided to let herself go and not worry about anything.

The song came to an end in her dazed state, but she kept her hand on his shoulder; it was only when he began to talk that she realized that the deafening music was over, replaced by a sudden emptiness and silence. Now she heard his every word.

"You look like you were born in the last century," he said. "You have a serene quality particular to women of that age."

Still recovering, she looked up at him but didn't respond.

"With the virtues of traditional Taiwanese women, who were chaste, submissive, well brought up, and well behaved."

She smiled faintly.

"You really look like you were born in the last century, the turn of the last century, to Taiwan's last gentry family," he continued.

"Like in the 1890s."

She said, more like a reflex, but she was surprised by how loud she was, with her body still very much draped over his, the way they had been dancing.

"Something like that."

He said with a nod, to which she responded with another smile. But perhaps because she had yet to recover from a drunken, sentimental state, her face quivered and that smile began to spread, uncontrollably, until she cracked open her mouth and began to laugh, accompanied by tears. Then she heard herself blurt out without thinking:

"Like I was born in the last year of the First Sino-Japanese War."

A blanket of lotus flowers bloomed before her eyes, seemingly covering the sky.

In early summer the lotus leaves that had just sprouted were a pleasant green, each long, round leaf rippling like a green wave when a breeze blew past. After an occasional shower in the summer afternoon, the drops of rain remaining on the leaves rolled around and sparkled. The lotus grew abundant new leaves that were layered upon one another until they clamored over the bench into the center of Flowing Pillow Pavilion. Sometimes a red lotus stem would squeeze through the leaves and open its pink petals to reveal the tender yellow stamen.

Father was sitting on a rosewood lounge chair with mother-of-pearl inlay. His hair was showing some gray; the fineness of the hair gave it a light quality, so the pale gray hair, with its natural curl, fell gently around his face. Crow's-feet adorned his slightly sunken eyes, which looked large and pretty with their double folds, but there was a quiet liveliness in the expression.

Yinghong knocked on the open wooden door. Now in high school, she was tall enough to reach the top of the frame, and no longer had to experience the panicky fear whenever the tightly shut door wouldn't budge, even if she pushed hard. Over the years, Father had gradually dropped the habit of locking every door and window wherever he happened to be, and he no longer spent hours in bed.

"Ayako." Looking up from the book he was reading, Father called her Japanese name in an even more tender tone. He spoke to her in Japanese, as usual. "You came at the right time, Ayako. I'm going through some books that have been in our family for a long time. You know I haven't read these Chinese books for many years."

"Hai." With her hands on her knees, she leaned forward slightly to respond in Japanese, before squatting beside her father's rosewood lounge chair.

"I happened to open to the page in the *History of Jin* where Wang Ji wrote about 'using the flowing water as a pillow and rinsing his mouth with rocks.' Who among the intellectuals, particularly those in present-day Taiwan, has the strength of character befitting the spirit of 'using the flowing water as a pillow in order to wash the ears and rinsing the mouth with rocks in order to sharpen the teeth'?"

Father read the lines in Mandarin, but switched back to Japanese as he continued:

"Think about it. How many of the intellectuals these days could really pillow their heads on water to wash their ears and willingly listen to the truth and face reality? Or to rinse their teeth with rocks and willingly speak the truth to demand changes and progress?"

With her head down, she listened carefully while Father continued in a gloomy voice:

"Those Taiwanese were killed off a long time ago. The ones remaining are just like me, utterly useless, the dregs of society."

The yellowed paper of the book was double-fold, and the thin pages were showing their age. Some were breaking at the folds, but the cotton fiber managed to keep them together, as if bound by some emotional connection. One of the cracked pages displayed half a line of text that was still recognizable: "Biography 26, Volume 56 of the History of the Jin, Sun Chu."

"Do you still remember, Ayako, when you were little you once wrote that you were born in the last year of the Sino-Japanese War?" Father changed the subject, but remained pensive. Obviously he had been thinking about this. "It's now finally become clear to me that the Sino-Japanese War had a profound effect on the Taiwanese."

Her upbringing dictated that she keep her head bowed to listen, but she was nevertheless apprehensive, particularly because Father had never touched upon topics like this. He was quiet for a while before continuing in his deep, gloomy voice:

"I've been thinking lately that I myself am one of those Taiwanese born in the last years of the Sino-Japanese War, those who were oppressed and suffering but unable to speak up." Misgivings about what he was saying made him stop in mid sentence, but he managed to continue: "I still hold out hope. The Taiwanese may still have some backbone, even if just a little..."

His voice seemed to be breaking up, prompting her to look up in fear. She saw instead that the dark-green lotus leaves dotted with red flowers were swaying in the wind, rolling and roiling like undulating ocean waves.

TWO

"What's your name, little girl?"

In the main, the men who asked this question were middle-aged. They dressed in tunics of the Sun Yat-sen style, the blue fabric turning white from too many washings, the cuffs worn to the point of being threadbare. The pant legs were wide, loose, and shapeless, with no sign of a crease down the middle. They spoke the Beijing dialect, but with accents from other provinces, which made it hard for Zhu Yinghong to understand everything they said.

At first she answered politely:

"My name is Zhu Yinghong."

"Zhu Yinghong?" The questioner repeated her answer with a friendly smile. "That's a good girl. You're very smart. Would you mind telling me your father's name?"

"Zhu Zuyan."

"And your mother?"

"Ye Yuzhen."

She stood with her feet together, her back straight. Her teacher had taught her to be respectful to her elders, to answer their questions clearly, and to always wear a smile.

"Does your father often take you places?"

"Father isn't well. He stays in bed." She answered in a soft voice; her smile was fading, but she struggled to hold on to it.

"Does he have any frequent visitors?"

"No."

"Are you sure?"

"Yes, I'm sure. No one comes to visit us, not even the uncles from the Upper House. Ah-shu and Ah-xiong don't come to play with me either."

The questioner listened attentively and paused before continuing.

"What does your father usually talk to you about?"

"Nothing." Tears began to well in her eyes. "Mother said Father mustn't tire himself out."

The man cut her off to ask urgently:

"Has he ever talked to you about who's a bad person, or said down with someone, or that someone should be taken out and shot?"

"No."

"Really?"

"No. Father never says anything bad about anyone," she answered forcefully before adding, "What does 'down with someone' mean?"

The man turned and left without answering her question.

On her way home, she wondered why the questioner hadn't even said "good-bye." At night, when Mudan was washing Yinghong's feet in a little red lacquered pail, she stretched out her pudgy legs to kick up some water and sprayed Mudan, who grumbled unhappily. Yinghong had planned to tell her about the man who'd asked about her father, as she was reminded of how, since her father had returned after his sudden disappearance, everyone else in the family was whispering about what had happened to him but immediately shut up if she was around. The look on Mudan's face made her decide not to say anything now.

When the incident occurred, Zhu Yinghong was startled out of a deep sleep by a commotion somewhere in the house. The moment she opened her eyes she had a feeling that neither of her parents was in bed. As usual, she reached out to touch the thin blanket covering the plank bed, and felt nothing but a cold chill. Years later, she would piece together what little she remembered of that night with what she'd heard here and there, and concluded that it had happened sometime in April or May.

Amid the sounds of people talking and running feet slapping against the floor, she stood on the purple sandalwood armchair at her Lotus Tower second-story window to look down into the garden, where dim sixty-watt bulbs were lit. There were also circles of light held in people's hands; though not very bright, they moved around the garden and shone on everything. It was pitch black out there, and people—there were many people, all strangers—blended into the dark night as flickering shadows. They were talking in a language unfamiliar to her, amid cries and shouts and the sounds of heavy objects falling and doors opening.

With her eyes now open wide, though she did not cry, she felt the clamor go on and on, as if it might never end. It was morning the next time she awoke, with bright light bathing Lotus Tower. The sun's rays streaming in through the window made her face tingle. She realized that she'd fallen asleep in the armchair.

Father was gone, and Mother said she was going to see Yinghong's maternal grandfather in Taipei. Then Mother abruptly reappeared in Lotus Garden but disappeared a few days later. Mudan was busy with one thing or another the whole time. All of a sudden, no one paid any attention to Yinghong, so she began sneaking out of the house to play at Lucheng's Number Three Elementary School.

School was not in session. During the sweltering summer days, it was pretty much deserted. So she had the big, wooden elephant-shaped slide all to herself, and had a great time climbing up and sliding down. Cicadas in the banyan tree above were singing their drawn-out, monotonous, seemingly never-ending songs. Beyond the shade of the tree, the sun beat down on the ground, turning the dry, hard surface a withered gray that reflected the blinding white sun, like the glint of a knife. The reflected glow added to the sun's direct simmering light in creating a miasma that enshrouded the gray playground in a white steam.

The quiet was broken by two soldiers in khaki uniforms, each carrying a rifle over his shoulder. Gray leggings above their black cloth shoes were coming loose in places. They shuffled along, scraping the dry ground as they entered the school compound from a side gate and passed her on the slide before meeting an old janitor at the door to the staff office. The old man, who was holding a dustpan and a long-handled bamboo broom, pointed to the staff office in response to a question. He was still bowing even after the soldiers had gone inside.

The soldiers reemerged with a third person in front of them. Yinghong vaguely recalled that he was one of the teachers she'd seen around school quite often. The only reason he'd have been on campus during summer break was to be on duty.

Heading back the way the soldiers had come, the three men were quickly alongside the slide, giving Yinghong a glimpse of the teacher, a robust man in his thirties. He wore a grimly anxious look, seemingly shrouded in a dark cloud of worry, the sight of which would recur in her dreams for years afterward. As they walked past, she saw that his hands were tied behind him with a Boy Scout rope as thick as a man's finger. Wound around his wrists several times, each of its ends was held by a soldier.

After they exited through the side gate, from her perch high atop the slide Yinghong saw the three men get into a Jeep and roar off, trailing a column of dust.

When the Jeep disappeared from sight, she was ready, as always, to slide down the elephant's trunk, but this time, for some reason, a casual look downward sent her into a sudden panic over the terrifying height and rendered her immobile. She squatted down. The cicadas in the banyan tree continued to chirp away, the tiresome notes raising a seemingly endless din. Other sounds mingled with the cicadas' chirps: running footsteps, the thump of heavy objects, and frightened shouts. She began to wail.

She must have cried for a very long time, without pause, for her eyes were nearly swollen shut by the time the old janitor found her and carried her down off the slide on his back.

The memory of that night at the Lotus Tower, when she'd been startled awake by the chaotic situation and terrified shouts, remained with her long after her father returned and she started elementary school, even after she entered high school. She could recall how she had stood on the purple sandalwood armchair by the window looking down through a classic barrel-shaped ornamental window and seen two soldiers dressed in wrinkled, faded khaki uniforms. She saw that they were carrying rifles over their shoulders, and that their gray, mud-spattered leggings were coming loose as they marched her father past Lotus Tower. His hands were tied behind his back with a Boy Scout rope as thick as a man's finger. Wound around his pale wrists several times, each of its ends was held by a soldier.

She also vividly recalled the look of grim anxiety on his face. Compassionate sadness and heartfelt pity filled his beautiful, sunken, double-fold dark eyes. He held his head high as he walked in an unhurried manner, flanked by the two soldiers, who looked more like bodyguards. The profound worry on her father's face continued to appear before her eyes for many years.

She also remembered how the soldiers marched him out of Lotus Garden and stopped at the entrance arch to climb into a Jeep parked by a low lattice wall. Then the Jeep started up and drove away soundlessly into the dark night.

When she was about to leave for college in Japan after graduating from high school, Father finally broke his habit of not talking politics with her and revealed what had happened.

He told her that he'd been fully prepared once the net began to be cast wider and wider. Usually, after everyone in Lotus Tower was asleep, he'd get out of bed to spend the night alone in a bedroom in the Upper House. On that night, he'd heard the sound of people outside and a pounding at the door, and he'd known that his time had come. Her mother had rushed over from Lotus Garden to pack a few pieces of clothing into a small bundle for him. Bundle in hand, he'd gotten into the car and left, without waking up many people.

Father also mentioned that since her Great Uncle Lin Boting, an anti-Japanese war hero back in Shanghai, was present, the Upper House and Lotus Garden had been spared the usual ransacking, though unavoidably some items had gone missing after an extensive search.

Having been taught that she should never question or argue with her elders, she simply listened quietly, head down. Later that night she went up to Lotus Tower alone. By then she was old enough to look out through the barrel window without having to stand on the armchair.

It was the 1960s, and dim sixty-watt bulbs no longer illuminated Lotus Garden. Based on Father's design, the garden had been wired for bright florescent lights. Turning them all on, she stood at the Lotus Tower window looking south down at the pond whose surface was covered with lotus flowers. From where she stood, it turned out, she could not possibly have seen the garden entrance or the low lattice wall.

Which meant she could not have seen Father being taken away in a Jeep. As she stood at the window that summer night, she shuddered despite the warmth of the winds.

But there was absolutely no denying the existence of a man who, in his Sun Yat-sen suit, had come to question her about Father from time to time, because his last visit caused a bit of a stir. She was a third-grader, and had just written the line, "I was born in the last year of the First Sino-Japanese War . . . ," which had made her teacher, Keiko, laugh out loud.

The first time the man came and asked about Father hadn't meant much to Yinghong, who had planned to tell Mudan about it, but then Mudan had grumbled when she'd kicked her feet in the little red-lacquered pail and splashed water on her. Then Yinghong recalled how it always frightened her when someone in the family mentioned her father in a soft, strange voice, and she'd decided not to say anything.

Soon afterward, the man started showing up frequently, and always when she was on her way home after school. She'd be walking down Lucheng's main thoroughfare, the newly named Zhongshan Road. The crowd would begin to thin out after she passed the small-gauge train stop. The man would materialize from a corner, always dressed in the suit that had turned white from too many washings, the sleeves worn to the point of being threadbare. The pant legs were wide, loose, and shapeless, with no sign of a crease down the middle. He asked pretty much the same questions each time, whether Father had any frequent visitors, if he'd ever said down with someone. Over and over, nothing new. She grew used to him after he'd shown up a few times.

Then he stopped coming. When the new semester began after the winter break, another man appeared. Similar appearance, same questions, the only differences were, he was younger than the other man, with a gentler voice and a smile. Once he even brought her a bag of sweets, a common treat available in just about every little general store. They were bright orange round candies sprinkled with sugar crystals. He'd wrapped them in a piece of paper torn from a school notebook, which he must have been holding for quite some time, because the sugar crystals had melted and turned the paper into a warm sticky mess. When he opened the packet to show her, all she saw were orange pieces of candy.

Yinghong giggled and ran away. She returned home to tell Mudan that someone had offered her some cheap, filthy candy. Amita Buddha! Mudan grumbled, scolding her for her poor attitude toward things. The God of Thunder will punish you, Mudan said, before warning her to watch out for bad people who lured little kids with candy and then sold them. She told Yinghong to never take food from a stranger.

"I wouldn't have eaten that candy if he'd given it to me."

Yinghong pouted while she unwrapped a piece of candy wrapped in colorful paper that her father had asked someone to bring back from Taipei.

The young man came a few more times and then was replaced by the previous, older man, who had grown visibly thinner. His faded blue Sun

Yat-sen outfit was hopelessly wrinkled, now looking much too big on his slight body.

"Good little girl—"

"My name is Zhu Yinghong and my father is Zhu Zuyan."

She cut him off impatiently and supplied an answer to the same old questions, which she could recite backward and forward, before he even began.

Caught off guard, the man didn't know how to continue, now that the order had been disrupted. A look of displeasure flickered across his face, but he struggled to control his temper. He had to think a moment before finding the questions in the right sequence.

"Does your father have any frequent visitors?" he asked.

"No." Her answer was short.

"What does your father usually talk to you about?"

"Nothing."

She began by answering him in her usual casual manner, but then she recalled the young man who'd wanted to give her candy. The recollection led her to believe that the whole process could be a game, so she decided to make fun of the older man by imitating his accent and tone of voice:

"Has he ever talked to you about who's a bad person, or said down with someone, or that someone should be taken out and shot?" she asked with mock seriousness.

The man reddened, his swarthy face suddenly a murky dark red that extended all the way down to the exposed part of his neck above the tunic collar. Pointing a shaky finger at her, he shouted in a shrill, husky voice:

"All right, you fucking little girl. How dare you mock me? Why aren't you fighting the communists like me? Well, fuck your ancestors, all eight generations of them!"

She didn't quite understand what he was saying, but she instinctively backed away at the sight of his red face and the sound of his screaming voice.

"I'm going to get to the bottom of things right now. Your father has secret friends and he's planning a rebellion. He's going to rebel. Isn't that right?

Tell me!" The irate man advanced menacingly. "I'll kill you if you don't. Don't think I won't."

Too frightened to move, she began to wail.

"Tell me. Tell me your father plans to rebel. If you don't, I'll arrest you and throw you in jail. There'll be ghosts, headless ghosts and hanging ghosts, that'll come to get you at night."

He bent down, his big, dark-red face right in front of her, stuck out his tongue, and rolled his eyes to show only the white. Instinctive self-preservation made her forget that she was crying. She took off running.

"Run all you want, but you can't get away. Go ahead, show me where you're running to."

She quickened her pace as the heavy footsteps behind her drew closer.

It was dusk on a school day, and Lotus Garden, being on the outskirts of town, seldom saw much foot traffic. At this hour there wasn't another soul in sight. Tears returned to her eyes, and she could hear the man's shouts behind her:

"It's all because of you communists that I can't go home. I'm going to kill all of you, you damned communists!"

She was panting hard by now, after running and crying at the same time, so she slowed down, but when she looked back, she saw, to her horror, that he was gaining on her. At that moment, a woman with a bamboo basket on her arm ducked out of the small roadside Earth God temple. Yinghong instinctively exhausted her last bit of energy to run up and take refuge behind her.

Peeking out from behind the woman, she saw that the man had also stopped. His swarthy face had turned sickly pale and was crisscrossed with tears that flowed unstopped from under his puffy eyelids; two streams of sticky yellow snot ended at his upper lip. Not knowing what to do next, he stood still, his eyes staring straight ahead. Then he abruptly squatted down peasant-style, and began to howl. She heard him sniffle as he muttered:

"It's all . . . you communists . . . because of you I can't . . . can't go home . . . can't go home. Communists . . ."

She ran all the way home, face and body bathed in sweat in the bitter cold of late winter. That night she ran a high fever that came and went, keeping her home for nearly a month before she returned to school. By then everyone had finished the second semester's first monthly exam.

When she graduated from high school and was ready to leave for college in Japan, her father, believing she was old enough to know the truth, talked about his arrest years earlier. She sat with her head down; her hair, which had hardly grown from the required length for high-school girls, barely covered her earlobes, so her downy neck showed each time she lowered her head, forming elegant, graceful arcs that reached to her shoulders.

At one point she looked up and, after a momentary hesitation, asked in a firm, serious voice:

"What did Otosan do to warrant arrest?"

Her father's face darkened and he seemed lost in thought for a moment.

"What I did was never the issue. Ayako, you must keep in mind that throughout the course of human history, knowledge has repeatedly gotten people into trouble. I was guilty of the crime of being an intellectual, of being able to think, and not easily manipulated."

She began to tear up but forced the tears back. Father said in a feigned light tone:

"I was actually one of the lucky ones. They let me go because they thought I'd die from an infectious disease and wanted to show benevolence toward the Zhu family. They didn't expect me to survive." He paused, the lightness of a moment earlier vanishing. "But my life was over."

Still with tears in her eyes, Yinghong managed a smile. She thought quietly for a while before venturing to ask:

"If, I mean if, someone said that Otosan was a communist, how would Otosan respond to that?"

"Why is Ayako asking such a question?" he asked, keeping his voice low. Visibly apprehensive, he looked around to make sure they were alone.

"Does Otosan remember the time when I was just a kid and fell ill from a scare by a waishengren?" To put his mind at ease, she quickly went on, "He was crying and calling Otosan a communist who was the reason they had to leave their hometown and flee to Taiwan.'"

Father smiled bitterly.

"Want to hear a story?"

She hadn't expected that, but acquiesced with a nod.

"I heard this story when I was in prison. An especially patriotic soldier who came from one of China's backwaters saw his very first electric light when he was stationed at a new place. Being obsessively loyal, he was always vigilant against anyone who harbored ill will toward the country."

Father continued in Japanese, as always, but now with a detectable hint of sorrow.

"Shortly after the soldier began at his new post, he noticed that every day at dusk, across from where he lived, a light would flicker a few times and then stop, like a signal. After careful observation, he reported this to his superior and had a young student arrested."

At this point, Father stopped; Yinghong, clearly puzzled, looked up at him.

"It turned out that the flickering light, which was mistaken by the soldier as a secret code to the enemy, was caused by the student turning on the light to study." He added, "Back then, electric lights always flickered a few times when you turned them on."

Father's weighty gaze shifted to the scene outside the window, reminding Yinghong of the worry-laden face that kept recurring in her dream, a look of profound concern mingled with compassion and pity.

"Otosan . . ."

She wanted to say something but no sound emerged, as the recollection of Father upon his return flashed through her mind.

He had likely returned in the spring. Yinghong recalled that not long after he came home she started going to the neighborhood Number Three Elementary School, a schoolbag over her shoulder.

She'd been playing in Lotus Garden when Mudan found her. Back then Mudan called her Ah-hong. "Ah-hong, Ah-hong!" Mudan was running as she called her out of frustration, making her name sound more like hurried breathing. Yinghong wasn't having much fun playing alone, so she stepped out from behind a Yinghong Pavilion pillar. Mudan grabbed her arm and dragged her toward the Upper House. Yinghong was wearing Japanese geta, whose wooden soles knocked crisply against the garden's flagstones. The heels made running difficult, and she had to struggle to keep them on, but they were her favorite red clogs and she refused to take them off.

She heard a din in the Upper House when they drew near. Mingled with sounds of footsteps were whispered comments like "get the sacrifice ready," "offer up the incense," and "pig's feet and rice noodles."

When she entered the main room, which had always been dark and gloomy, she saw that the dozen or so formal armchairs on both sides of the room were all taken. Women were standing to the sides, while serving women were shuttling back and forth. And yet the room was deathly quiet. Mudan led her forward, where she heard her mother's soft, tender voice:

"Say 'Papa.' Papa's back." Her voice quivered.

She did what she was told, but kept her head down.

Then someone came up to help Father out of his chair. In what she could see with her head down, she spotted a pair of geta in front of the armchair's horse-hoof feet. They were the wooden clogs Father had always worn at home, Japanese-style, some three or four inches high. Moving slowly down into the clogs were two ghostly white feet so thin they were virtually shapeless, and so weak he fell forward before they reached the clogs.

Yinghong jerked her head up and saw Father's face. Over that puffy, deathly ashen face lay a profound melancholy, so sorrow-laden it kept appearing in her memory from that day on.

Father was laid up in Flowing Pillow Pavilion. She could not get in to see him for the longest time, and all she saw was Mudan going in and out with an enamel basin filled with water.

They owned several enamel basins like that, with similar patterns. Mudan used one of them to bathe her.

The thick white enamel, which had the look of spilled condensed milk, was spread evenly over the surface, a solid, opaque white. A large bouquet of hand-painted red flowers adorned the bottom of the basin—layer upon layer of bright red petals interspersed with orange stamens and high-lighted by a few green leaves. The flowers seemed to dance in the ripples when water was poured over them, and appeared to float up to the surface, at which moment she would step on them so they would stop moving and stay at the bottom, where they belonged.

She always had secret thoughts of her father when she did that. His enamel basin had the same red flowers, making that basin her only con-crete connection to him. For some peculiar reason, she was convinced that with her feet on those red flowers she could keep him around. But in no time she'd be frightened by the possibility that the flowers, though solid under her feet, might disappear completely, so she'd remove one foot and see, in the rippling water, the flowers floating at the bottom; then she'd hastily step on them again, now with a sense of relief over having verified that they were still there and that she had the power to keep them there.

Father was laid up for more than two years, during which Yinghong se-cretly continued to repeat her foot ritual. Sometimes, when Mudan was oc-cupied with other chores and forgot to get her to finish up, Yinghong would leave her feet in the water for as long as two hours, even in the depth of winter, long after it had turned icy cold.

Over the years that followed, up until she was a third-grader and wrote "I was born in the last year of the First Sino-Japanese War . . . ," she often saw Father, who was on the mend. But she was constantly plagued by the deeply affecting fear that she'd be awakened late one night by unidentified noises, then get up the next morning and never see him again. Then, after a long time, he would return and yet she still couldn't get to see him; his som-ber, worry-laden face alone kept reappearing in her dreams.

The next time she met him was at a similar social event for Taipei's busi-nessmen at a piano bar called "Elixir."

It was more of an accidental meeting.

As Elixir was one of the few bars without hostesses, Yinghong's uncle recommended the place to his friends for an after-dinner drink and chat. When they got there, Lin Xigeng was already drinking with his friends in the largest room. So after brief greetings, the two groups joined up and sat together.

Socializing for Taipei businessmen followed a typical formula—an early evening dinner, say, around 6:30, leaving plenty of time for after-dinner entertainment. Dinner was open to all, men and women, but after dinner, the women excused themselves if the men had other plans.

If only men were invited to dinner, then women from the entertainment industry were hired and the guests drank, flirted, and made plenty of noise at dinner. But no matter what the format, the host was considered inadequate if they stayed at one place all night; they had to go to a drinking establishment or piano bar afterward.

Wherever they went, they carried on pretty much the same, drinking, playing finger-guessing games, singing karaoke, dancing, and flirting. Come late night, the men would take the girls, now off duty, for a midnight snack, after which they could decide on their own what to do next. They hardly ever took the girls home; most likely their final activity of the night would be going to a hotel to "rest."

Though Elixir did not supply hostesses, good-looking young women would come in and introduce themselves, passing out business cards with such job titles as "manager" or "deputy manager." They poured drinks, served food, handed out towelettes, and toasted the guests. On this particular night four or five such women came and went the whole time. They sat quietly; except for toasting, they never started a conversation.

Still sober, the guests maintained a decorous appearance; no one groped the girls, since the real transactions had to be conducted outside. That was the rule for such occasions, one familiar to insiders.

Seasoned guests would never consider intimate contact with the girls here, though they didn't mind having one they knew sit by them for a tête-à-tête. So after a "deputy manager" was asked to switch with someone else, Yinghong and Xigeng wound up sitting next to each other.

He sat smoking a cigarette, but failed to mask the smell of alcohol. Obviously, he'd had quite a bit to drink before coming to Elixir.

Focusing on their current location, he opened the conversation.

"In the past, nightclubs, singing halls, and drinking bars all had raised dance floors, creating a distance between the performers and the audience. Now, see how low the floor is? That's so people can mingle and guests can go up to sing."

She was at first disturbed by his familiarity with denizens of the red-light district, but he was so unpretentiously direct, with an ease that seemed to make any explanation unnecessary, that she turned to look.

They were in a private room, where the wall behind them was made of glass so the guests could look out at the dance floor. A degree of privacy, though, was maintained by frosted prints of long-tailed phoenixes.

Through the glass partition, she saw an ebony Steinway on the dance floor. A singer was leaning against the piano, singing a popular song that bemoaned a heart-rending romance in a soft, sad voice. Strobe lights in front of her twirled and spinned, creating a myriad of colors—soft pinks, greens, blues, and purples—as if enveloping a dream from which it was hard to awaken.

Obviously in high spirits, Lin went on and on about his latest project, a development along nearly two hundred feet of Dunhua South Road; it would be the classiest residential community in all of Taiwan, flats outfitted with imported, brand-name materials, from granite and flush toilets, to door handles and electric circuits.

He was dressed casually that night: tapered-leg blue jeans, a style that would soon be all the rage, and a green shirt with maroon stripes. A faint glint reflecting off the shirt told her that it was made of high-quality cotton, so exquisitely tailored that it had to have been created by a world-class designer. Highly animated, he couldn't stop talking, a stark contrast to his low-key attitude at their first meeting. Now that the weariness and glum mood no longer showed on his face, he looked quite young.

He told her he'd come to Taipei before the age of twenty, with no money. He'd accepted an internship at an ad agency, where he'd worked on ads for real estate, which, he felt, was where Taiwan's development potential lay. He put together some capital and, with the knowledge that land was the island's most valuable resource, undertook some housing construction in Zhonghe, Xinzhuang, and Wanhua, before taking on the prized market of Taipei City.

She asked him how he had turned from real estate advertising to housing development.

"I witnessed a transformation in landowners who brought in builders to develop their land. In the beginning, they rode their bicycles to watch me create the ads. When the development was finished and they received their share of the flats, they came back to see me in their Mercedes."

She looked up in surprise, her gaze falling on the phoenixes on the glass partition. Their layered tails, as recorded in legend, trailed behind them, free flowing and soaring. But the transparent glass rendered their original vibrant colors as misty white outlines. The pristine white of the phoenixes left room for imagination, lending a sense of wonder to the birds.

He chain-smoked as he talked about his past in the same casual tone he used to talk of his successes. While differing in content, they were equally unique.

He said he'd come from the countryside in the south, a place called Pujiao, probably known to few people in Taiwan. He was the oldest of seven kids. Reduced to extreme poverty during the early postwar era, like so many country folks, the family converted to Christianity.

It was never clear to him whether it was Catholic or Protestant Christianity, or the particular denomination; all he recalled was that there was a Jesus and the Virgin Mary. His mother took him to church to hear sermons and returned home with sacks of flour, which was why the villagers called their religion "Flour Christianity."

He remembered how, when they returned home from the church, his mother would burn incense in front of the spirit tablets of their ancestors. Back then, Catholics, Protestants, and other religious adherents were allowed to keep the tablets of their ancestors; later, when there were enough believers, the rules changed and the practice was banned.

Their family also offered incense to a portrait, but he couldn't tell whether it was the Guanyin Bodhisattva or Mazu, the fisherman's patron saint. The portrait was carefully stashed in back of the spirit tablet, taken out only for worship, behind a closed door. They did not want the pastor or his wife to see them doing it.

He told her about the pants he'd worn as a child, made from American Aid flour sacks. There were blue symbols on them, but they were of no concern to him until he started school and learned that the blue symbols were a string of Arabic numbers and other unintelligible writing—serial numbers.

Taiwan's economy stabilized slowly after the war; his family was still on the verge of starvation, but his parents insisted that he go on to middle school. Having no interest in studying, he dropped out of a senior vocational school and came to Taipei to seek his fortune.

Separated by the glass wall and the misty white phoenixes, the dance floor looked blurry and unreal under the lights. When she looked away, the twirling strobe lights stayed with her, giving her the impression that the glass wall was gone and leaving the pristine white phoenixes to fly in a void and float in the soft, bewitching lights. Though white phoenixes existed only in legend, amid the exquisite artificial ambience of Elixir, the wondrous could become real. The phoenixes seemed to stop in mid flight when she turned her head, before they faded into the pink miasma.

Yet in that small room infused with soft, pink light, where white phoenixes took flight, the typical business dinner went on, with men drinking and flirting and playing finger-guessing games with the girls next to them, while others displayed their talent at karaoke. It was the sort of entertainment that required no conversation, except for the occasional exchange of business information or political news, which needed few words. Since there was no need for talk, the host and guests did not have to interact, as they carried on with their unique way of socializing—bantering with girls or singing karaoke to amuse themselves. Xigeng and Yinghong were ignored, so they continued their talk with no concern for the others.

They had the ideal backdrop for their conversation—karaoke, alcohol, working girls, man-made soft lights and ambience, cool, perfume-infused air created for the occasion, and the elegant decor of the glass-partitioned room. Uninhibited enjoyment, so characteristic of these businessmen, and a direct arousal of the senses, provided a constant stimulant for drunken indulgence. The legend of white phoenixes seemed possible, even appropriate for a business dinner saturated with wondrous sounds, sensuality, alcohol, and women.

When she was ready to leave, Lin offered to take her home. The decadent entertainment had yet to reach its apex, even at two in the morning. On that misty spring night, on a street devoid of traffic, she spotted his snow-white, long-body Rolls Royce, a behemoth of a car that, under the silent night sky, seemed to take up the whole block.

As if the spell had been broken, the fancy car did not come equipped with an elaborate ritual—Lin opened the rear door for her and followed her in. When he shut the door, she noticed the luxuriously appointed interior as well as the driver, who looked to be in his forties, with a crew cut like a worker from the countryside. Wearing a flashy patterned shirt made of synthetic fabric, he placed his large, brown laborer's hands on the leather-wrapped steering wheel.

She laughed despite herself as the car began to glide forward, the windows shutting out all outside noise. A soundless world existed beyond the window on late-night deserted streets, removing all sense of the real; what flashed past her eyes was more like a moving stage set. The car rolled on smoothly, at a steady speed; she felt no bumps in the road. Everything before and around her was a silent declaration of an imposing air that left no room for questions, the thought of which made her somewhat lightheaded, as if caught up in a strange dream.

Her place was in a one-way alley off Zhongshan North Road in the Yuanshan District. It looked to be too narrow for the Rolls, but that, in fact, provided a moment for the driver to show off his skill. She told him to stop in front of the red gate of a two-story building. Lin showed no sign of opening the door for her, nor did the driver, who was sitting comfortably in the front seat. She reached out for the handle, opened the door, and pushed out;

it was unexpectedly heavy, like the car itself, as if its express purpose were to impress.

"Such a heavy door," she said.

Lin followed her out.

"It's late and I don't want to wake up Mudan. I have to walk all the way across the yard." She knew she was being incoherent. "It's late, I . . . I'm kind of scared. Could you wait by the gate until I open the door?"

Wordlessly he moved to the side.

She opened the gate, revealing a large yard with a red-brick path flanked by lush vegetation several feet tall. The overgrown greenery had gone wild, trees layering on top of and into each other, an untamed mass that was overtaking the path.

The lush foliage had migrated into a grove of dark and light greens, over-crowding as it reached upward, displaying its indomitable vitality, a force to be reckoned with. It took him a while to realize that a patch of dark-green vegetation was, in fact, overgrown weeds. But, with its powerful urge to grow, it spread all over the place, filling every possible space, wild and disorderly. But when he realized that it was only untamed weeds, the patch of green emitted a sense of extreme degradation, a sort of ruin from prolonged neglect.

By then she had passed through tall, dark-green weeds that brushed against the hem of her long skirt, and reached the far side of the yard, where she stopped beside a small red door.

Like many lovers, they often repeated the story of how they had fallen in love. Naturally, she wanted to hear him talk about it; he was quiet at first, and she detected the same shyness on his face as before. He even looked away to avoid her gaze.

"It was that night when I took you home and you said you were afraid to walk across the yard," he said evasively, obviously uncomfortable with revealing his emotion, like most Taiwanese men at the time.

She brought it up again when they knew each other better, for she needed more verbal assurance. Now that they were so much closer, he was increasingly at ease and direct:

"Didn't I say you looked like someone born in the last century? Few girls these days have your demeanor, an air of competence instilled by growing up in an established family. I always thought you were so strong, capable of anything," he said in a soft, tender voice, "so I was surprised to know you weren't as brave as I thought, even frightened sometimes."

A few days later he called her at work, asking about her schedule. He was in such a hurry he hung up after she managed to say that she went to bed late.

At eleven that night he called from Los Angeles, where it was seven in the morning; the shades in his hotel room were drawn and his wristwatch still showed Taipei time.

He'd gone to L.A. on real estate business. Over the past thirty years, a large number of Taiwanese had emigrated with the fruits of Taiwan's economic growth; it was no longer just a dream to create a high-end residential area for Taiwanese immigrants in L.A. This was exactly what he'd always wanted—a global empire.

This was the first time they'd talked by phone. It was late, so every word he said in the quiet of the night seemed to go straight to her heart. She just listened. Though thousands of miles apart, his voice sounded as though they were in the same city; it was truly as the saying goes, far apart and yet so close.

She had picked up the phone in the living room, which had kept her from putting on something warmer. Now the cold spring-night air began to seep through her white silk pajamas, forcing her to cover herself with several cushions. The black satin cushions with their gold threads had been cold, but after coming in contact with her body, the cotton filling began to serve its function of warming her.

Gently she brought up the cost of international calls, especially because they had been talking for some time.

He went quiet for a while on the other end.

"You know what? I found your sense of decorum particularly endearing." He quickly added, "I never have time to make phone calls except when traveling. Back in Taiwan, I'm always busy with so many things it's impossible to have a good phone conversation. All my friends know I'll only call them when I'm on the road."

She laughed softly and said:

"An expensive hobby."

"I work so hard, traveling back and forth between Taiwan and the U.S. And for what, if not to be able to spend money whenever and however I like?"

Then his tone turned serious.

"I'm proud of being a Taiwanese now. Finally, we can afford to chat on international calls and fly first class on business trips or personal travel. Pretty soon, we'll own private jets, like the super rich in developed countries." He was getting animated. "I take great pride in the fact that, within a brief decade or two, we have amassed so much wealth that we can spend money however we want."

He quickly changed the subject, as he often did.

"Before I left, I sat in on a management forum at the Shangri-la Hotel. The speaker was a young M.B.A. who seemed to be following the trend of critiquing everything. He said that the flour sacks from the American Aid all had serial numbers. When we fashioned clothes out of those sacks, we each wore a number, like piglets raised on American flour. We were branded, just like the cattle in American Westerns."

"That was a time of pervasive poverty," she said gently.

"It sure was! Back then almost everyone was poor." He agreed casually, obviously unperturbed. "The M.B.A. also said that it began with the American Aid, followed by all sorts of special treatment by the American government, which steered Taiwan onto the road of a capitalist model we can never shake off. The multinational companies and our reliance on foreign capital give the Americans absolute control of Taiwan."

"What do you think?"

"I stood up and cut him off." There was still a hint of righteous indignation in his voice. "I told him I don't know a thing about multinational companies or capitalism, but I know that Taiwan's economy took off because many, many hardworking, diligent Taiwanese, like myself, worked tirelessly to make it happen."

She laughed softly again.

"Then what?"

"Everyone in the audience applauded."

Time passed quickly as they talked. She had wanted to remind him that it was getting late and, no matter what he had said, they really shouldn't be chatting on international calls. But then what he was saying caught her attention, until she was startled to sense that it must be very late, for all was quiet around her. She was feeling drowsy and her ear was getting numb from having the receiver pressed against it for so long. The voice on the other end sounded hoarse, deeper, fatigued even.

That reminded her of the first time they met, when he'd appeared reserved and weary.

She hurriedly offered an apology for keeping him on the phone for so long.

"What time is it? I don't have my watch."

"Mine is still on Taiwan time; it's 3:30."

So they'd talked for four and a half hours on a call between L.A. and Taipei. After she hung up, she remained curled up on the sofa, deluged by a weighty sense of fatigue in the late-night quiet. His voice was gone, but a buzzing sound lingered in her ear; she was tired beyond description and yet her mind was crystal clear. She was experiencing a dreamlike sensation, as if she were still riding in the Rolls Royce, with its seemingly unreal steady speed, or the carnal indulgence of Elixir with its sound, lights, and flesh, compounded by four-and-a-half hours of trans-Pacific conversation.

A few days later he called again at ten at night. He was back in Taipei and had just dealt with urgent matters at the company. All he said was he wanted to see her.

She recalled how since the first day, they'd always met in extravagant places, so she thought he'd take her to another, maybe even more exquisite, more expensive place. Instead what emerged from the familiar voice was:

"Let's go for a walk."

Caught off guard by her own erroneous assumption, she didn't react at once, but quickly recovered and laughed softly.

"It's raining."

"Walking in the rain, that's even better."

Looking at the soft spring rain, she wasn't sure she wanted to go. When was the last time she'd walked in the rain now that all indoor spaces in the city were air-conditioned? Then a sense of adventure made her agree with a laugh.

She opened the door when he rang the bell, only to see him standing in the dark in the rain, his white Rolls Royce nowhere in sight. That behemoth of a car was nearby wherever he went, so its absence that evening was confusing, as if he'd come out of nowhere.

They walked along Zhongshan North Road toward Yuanshan. Streetlights that glowed brilliant white in the rain illuminated a profusion of tender green leaves on red maples along the street, while those leaves threw the area beyond the light into a dark shadow.

A mist was rising. Strolling down the red-brick sidewalk, she looked around at the arboreal canopy that, in alternating light and darkness, looked as if green tips had been painted on the leaves before they sent their profusion of greenery down the street. It was like a man-made backdrop that had been beautified, so impossibly pretty it seemed unreal.

The rain increased as they walked and talked. He pointed to a small neighborhood watch booth.

"Let's go in there."

"I pass by here every day. Why haven't I ever noticed this little booth before?" She was surprised by her own lack of observation, then added, "That's for a neighborhood watchman. Can we go in there?"

"If we can't, then we must. On my way to L.A. this time, I saw a movie on the plane. I forget its name or what it was about, but I remember the male lead said to the female lead that he wanted to do something for her to remember him by."

He carried on with his usual confidence, which in turn made him sound more arrogant than ever. She recalled how much of his knowledge came from fragments of conversation or lectures; now he even had to take a page out of a romantic movie. She was about to tease him about that, but his self-assurance and his conviction in the rationality of his action changed her mind. Silently she followed him inside and sat down in the low, blue wooden booth.

Two makeshift planks were the only furniture; the lower one served as a chair and the higher one was obviously the desk. The cramped space made it natural for him to put his arm around her shoulder, and she leaned against him. He had a well-proportioned, powerful hand with clean, neatly trimmed nails.

A casual glance showed that he was wearing a plain-looking Patek Philippe watch, not the gold Rolex favored by Taipei businessmen. A bit surprised, she commented:

"Nice watch; good taste."

The comment only encouraged his smugness as he gestured at his clothes and gloated:

"The shirt is from Thierry Mugler, the suit is Claude Montana. Only a girl from old money would recognize these name brands."

She smiled vaguely, making him aware of how inappropriate that had been; it brought a moment of silence between them. Then he continued in his usual high spirits:

"There's a story about a gold watch making the rounds in Taipei business circles. Here's how it goes: there was this Shanghai textile tycoon, who was so big and tall that his Rolex already felt snug on his wrist when he

bought it. But then he put on some weight and had to have the gold watchband extended. Over the years that followed, his weight continued to go
up and his watchband got longer. When he died, his watch was so heavy it
couldn't be held in one hand."

She laughed, but by the time he finished, an eerie feeling made her
shudder.

It was getting late, so he walked her home. When they stopped outside
the gate, he spoke into her ear in a low, gentle voice:

"Still want me to wait for you here?"

With a smile, she shook her head and said in a shy, coquettish voice:

"No, but I'd like you to walk me to the door."

The weedy yard felt overpoweringly vibrant even in the dark, as it grew
and filled every available crevice, like a raging fire, lacking only green
flames. Pushing aside a knee-high weedy plant stretching across the path,
he frowned and said:

"I've never seen a stranger woman than you. Who lives in a house with
a weedy yard?"

"I once lived in a beautiful garden. It belonged to my father, in Lucheng.
It was called Lotus Garden. Maybe you've heard of it. Like the Lin Fam-
ily Garden of Taipei, it was one of the largest private garden compounds in
Taiwan."

She paused on the weedy path and turned to look at him. All he saw
was her dark, deep eyes on that rainy night, looking wild and mysterious
against the vegetation around her.

"After living in a big place like that, what do you think I could grow
here?"

She laughed softly.

"Besides, this isn't my house. It belongs to my uncle, who lets me live
here." She lowered her eyes, the long lids obscuring the light inside. "This
house was part of my mother's dowry."

"I could buy it from your uncle and you'd have it back."

He spoke in a confident, casual tone, obviously blurting it out without
thinking. Like a reflex, a reserved, aloof look immediately settled over her

face, with a hint of disdain and distance, effectively cutting him off. As if mute, he stood here, not knowing what to do or say next.

For the first time since they had met, she turned and leaned up to him; he wrapped his arms tightly around her for a long moment before saying good-bye.

Love came swiftly over me, like waves in a stormy sea. At first I was simply attracted to the dreamy sensation I received and everything surrounding him. In the midst of Taiwan's economic boom of the 1970s, I witnessed how this tall, handsome, arrogant middle-aged man forged ahead with full confidence, resolve, and hard work; it was how he took care of his business and dealt with love. In the 1970s, when anything and everything was possible, he was a model of innovation and vitality; it seemed as though everything he put his hand to was a success.

At that moment in time, I fell completely and hopelessly into a mystifying yet powerful love. I must admit that when I first met him, I was more attracted to his low-key attitude, so different from that of other Taipei businessmen. Drawn to his gloomy, enigmatic demeanor, I'd thought that an unstable, discontented self was hidden behind a facade of success.

Once we were together, I felt that he had completely conquered me, and that gave me a powerful sense of happiness. Years later, when I longed to return to the moment when we first met, I became dimly aware that he had always been the one talking, and usually about himself—Lin Xigeng, his past, his business empire, his innovations, and his dreams. And I had been happy to be his audience, cautiously following his topics of conversation.

At the time, I was submerged in a mysterious and powerful love. A mere shred of self-awareness told me that I was falling fast, little by little, inch by inch. On every night we saw each other to the following morning, he never ceased to induce nonstop, manic love in me.

I realized I was making fewer judgments and decisions of my own, as his imposing manner all but overpowered me. Now he became the center of my existence. My life revolved around him, as I thought about what he liked, self-consciously choosing what pleased him, and expressing myself in the way he preferred.

It was as if I were in a hazy dream, engulfed in a saccharine blur. My senses, all but the powerful feeling of love, were reduced to a bare minimum. A mist seemed to have shrouded everything external, creating a sense of distance that made it unreal yet omnipresent. I continued to work and go about my life, but nothing commanded my attention; now I was lethargic and languid. I lived for his phone calls and waited for him to come see me at night in his huge, dreamy, white Rolls Royce.

I'd been in love before, but never had there been a man like Lin, who seemed to take me back to my childhood, a girl who had everything arranged and decided for her. All that girl needed was to rely on others, to obey and follow orders, with few of her own ideas, as there was no need for her to have any. In fact, I was too lazy to make my own judgments and decisions.

Worse yet was the fact that I was happy, truly happy. I didn't have to think or worry, because there was someone to face the world on my behalf. What a carefree, indulgent happiness it is to be able to submit to a man you love, particularly if this man is so competent, reliable, and deserving of your wholehearted devotion.

But then I began to feel frightened.

Fear propelled Zhu Yinghong to try to learn everything she could about Lin Xigeng. It was easy enough; her uncle told her he had been married and that there were other women with whom he'd had intimate relationships.

Like every woman in love, she asked Lin about them.

"They were all before you," he said evasively.

"How do I know you're not still seeing them?"

She persisted coquettishly but stubbornly, reassured by the sweet feeling of being in love and confident of his love of her.

He was silent.

Later, when they'd been together long enough to know each other well, she brought up the women again.

"Do you think I'd let a woman control my life?" He continued in his usual arbitrary manner. "They listen to me; I don't listen to them."

When she finally became his legally wedded wife, they reserved several floors of Taipei's most luxurious hotel for a wedding that was viewed by socialites as "Taiwan's wedding of the century," and spent their first night as husband and wife in the presidential suite. As they exchanged rings, she thought back to the piercing heartache, despair, and fear she'd felt at the moment she'd learned that he had many women, and a wife.

He never made excuses in the face of her questions, nor even feeble attempts to defend himself, which naturally caused her concern and apprehension. But the sweet sensation of romantic love hung on, and she thought everything would stay as it was. Vaguely she sensed that, as long as she could be with him, in the end she would be willing to accept these other women in his life. She was so in love with him that she all but abandoned herself to him. She just knew she could come around to that; besides, it was too early to talk about such things.

He came to see her a few days after offering to buy the house. Contrary to his usual flair and directness, he was evasive:

"I'll be your big brother. If any of your boyfriends dare mistreat you after this, I'll settle scores with my fists."

"Thank you for telling me that," she replied softly.

It was too much like the dialogue in a third-rate novel or a sappy movie, formulaic and clichéd. But the foggy, dreamy feeling was still there. Absentmindedly she wondered if he had just watched another movie on an airplane trip.

When they reached her house, he stood at the door and asked abruptly, in the tone normally used on children, yet with total sincerity and the best of intentions:

"Want me to kiss you?"

They'd had many intimate moments in the past. She enjoyed leaning against his broad chest, her face close to his. On several occasions he'd made a move to kiss her, but she'd always managed to evade his advances, because romantic love meant too much to her. Delaying every stage in a relationship, she maintained the desired progress with great care, hoping to gain the ultimate experience at every stage so she could preserve all the perfect moments in her memory.

She never imagined that what she'd treasured for so long would turn out to be a sort of consolation from him when they parted. Though he was gentle and tender, he was clearly telling her that she would have less to regret if he kissed her.

With a shake of her head, she finally realized that they were saying good-bye for real.

She told him not to call her again so she could forget him.

"I can't do that," he replied calmly, showing a bit of hesitation for the first time that night. Then suddenly he moved closer, took her into his arms and continued in an even tone:

"I know it'll be wonderful being with you. You'll be small and tight. You'll grip me hard and bring me great pleasure . . ."

Lin Xigeng's tone of voice was unchanged and there was no hint of ambiguity in what he was saying. Nor was he trying to arouse her. They were saying good-bye, and this caught Yinghong completely by surprise; not until he'd had his say did some of the words get through, and she suddenly realized what he was talking about and exactly what those words referred to. Totally unprepared for what she was hearing, it dawned on her that the common, ordinary phrases he used were all about sex, and that, oddly enough, she was aroused.

Submissive as usual, she followed his signal and dutifully opened the gate; they went to the yard, where she let him lead her hand down to touch him. Without thinking about where her hand was going, she stroked him as he desired, her heart nearly breaking over the idea that he was about to leave her. But he had already deftly undone his trousers to expose himself and was standing there otherwise fully clothed. The skill with which he had accomplished this shocked her.

He must have known how to make love on various occasions, the only difference being the time, place, and the woman he was with.

He slid his hand under her clothes to touch her. Like so many woman in love, she shied away from, even rejected a sexual encounter out of the pain of imminent separation, and when he saw that it was not to be, he led her in a different direction. Yinghong sensed his arousal in her hand and knew that there was no going back. A masculine instinctive ability to convey dominance was part and parcel of Xigeng's personality. Confusion and admiration combined to prompt her to look down and gaze lovingly at what she held in her hand.

"It's so big."

Yet what filled her heart was the sorrow of the night, for when it was over she would never see him again, let alone the thing she was holding. With a mixture of what her rejection of a good-bye kiss had meant and the entangled emotions of loss in her mind, she looked down and stared dully at it. Then a pair of strong hands pressed down on her shoulders, and she knew what he wanted. So she bent down hesitantly as his hands brought her forcefully to the point where her lips touched it.

She remained crouching for a long moment before changing positions to kneel in front of it. Having her on her knees heightened his air of potency as he stood there, and highlighted her constant submissiveness and obedience toward him. Fascination and admiration engulfed her as he looked down from his prideful height and said:

"That is a man's prize possession and finest weapon, and it has to be used if it's brought out."

Then in a domineering tone of voice, he said:

"Do you still want to tell me not to call you?"

She was shocked into inaction and snapped her head up.

He was standing with his back to the house to avoid being seen. Now she looked up and saw nothing but a broad tangle of weeds behind him.

The grass looked even taller from where she knelt, and seemed to spread in all directions, claiming the whole yard. She saw that grass nearby had sprouted long stalks topped with green seeds. With no lamps to light up the area, shadows flitted through the darkness; the profusion of seedlings and green weeds had the power to crush everything in their path, which made the yard seem particularly dreary.

I didn't say good-bye when he finally left. Instead, I closed the door and went inside. But then I was seized by an urge to see him one last time. Overpowered by the desire, I ran up the stairs and stumbled into a second-story room facing the alley.

Perhaps I could still see him beyond the fence, where he could be getting ready to leave or hailing a taxi. I must have one more glance at him, no matter what, for I might never see him again; I couldn't let a man like him disappear from my life; I needed to see him one more time.

He hadn't gone beyond the fence, or maybe the fence blocked his outline. I stood on tiptoes, but couldn't see over the fence. I might never see him again.

At the age of six, Zhu Yinghong had stood on the purple sandalwood armchair in Lotus Pavilion and looked out the second-story window. The night was clotted dark. Round shafts of light held by invisible hands shone all over the garden, but the inky black held on. There were people, obviously many of them, all strangers, who melted into the darkness and turned into looming shadows.

One summer night when she was eighteen, just before she left for college in Japan, she went to Lotus Pavilion alone and turned on all the lights her father had recently fitted. She looked down through the window.

It was not the first time she'd stood at the window facing the pond that was overgrown with water lilies and lotus flowers, but she never could see the low fence and entrance arch to the east. And even if she could have seen it, it would have been too tall for her to see the vehicles parked beyond, even from her second-floor vantage point.

He might already have left. It is late, but there are plenty of taxis in the lane. Within seconds, one could have stopped and taken him away. Or he might be walking alongside the fence to hail a cab at the intersection, but the height of the fence blocks my view so I can't see him even from the second floor.

On the wooden elephant slide, Zhu Yinghong saw the teacher at Number Three Elementary School walking in front, followed by two rifle-toting soldiers. When they drew near, from the top of the slide she could see that the teacher's hands were tied behind his back by a thick Boy Scout rope, wound several times around his wrist, each end held by one of the soldiers. They walked toward the side door, where a Jeep was parked; all three climbed in and the Jeep drove off, leaving a small dust storm in its wake.

Worry was etched deeply on the teacher's face. A fairly stout man still in his thirties, he wore such a serious look that his face seemed masked in apprehension.

He left with firm resolve, perhaps because he was angry and frustrated that he could not finish what he was doing. Would that instill in him a sense of attachment that would bring him back to me? Maybe he'll ring the bell in a few minutes or call out to let me know he is standing outside but blocked by the tall fence.

I listened carefully to the deathly late-night silence. My head felt heavy from lack of sleep and the shedding of tears. My ears felt stuffed with loud, uncontrollable ringing.

Flanked by the two soldiers, Father walked past Lotus Pavilion. Thick Boy Scout cotton rope was wound round his fair wrists, each end held by one of the soldiers.

What appeared over and over was always Father's worry-laden face, a display of solemnity mingled with profound pity and compassion.

When I was finally aware that tears were blocking my view, everything was a blur. When had I started crying? Maybe at the very moment I missed my chance to see him one last time. I shut my eyes so the tears could flow down my face. Darkness reigned in the yard.

Could it be that the streetlight was too dim for me to see him, since the areas on both sides of the fence weren't bright enough? Maybe he was just beyond the fence pacing the whole time? Or, he didn't know I was still waiting, because the yard wasn't lit and it was pitch black inside the house.

I hurried to switch on the lights in the room and the yard.

Back then only dim sixty-watt bulbs illuminated Lotus Garden, and they had been put far apart, giving the place a weak but soft illumination. It was impossible to see Father's face clearly, let alone his worried look, even if I could have seen in the dark how he was taken away by the two soldiers, especially since I was standing high above him and the lighting was so muted.

The only possible explanation was I was deceived by my own childhood memories. I had merged two images, Father's arrest, which I had only heard about, and the teacher's arrest, which I had witnessed. Then I transferred and transposed them until what I was left with was an ironclad memory of seeing Father's arrest.

"Ah—" Zhu Yinghong cried out despite herself.

For many years her father's arrest had repeatedly made an appearance in her nightmares. When she recalled the scene, the deep worry creases on his face, compounded by the fear that she'd never see him again, tormented her. If all this had originated from unreliable memory, then wasn't it futile to have suffered over a decade-long premonition that she could not keep him around and would have to let him disappear before her eyes, not to mention the traumatic sorrow over all those years?

She sighed. She looked down at the yard, which was ablaze with light. After the early summer rains, the weedy expanse was a tangled profusion of dark green. Even late at night, she thought she could hear the weeds struggle upward and outward, in all directions, rising stubbornly with indomitable vitality, groaning to find a way through the assault of other weeds. Spreading their leaves and stalks, they hogged as much space as possible, noisily trampling on each other. The crackling sound of vital life rose like a snake spitting its forked tongue, as if attempting to witness its own endless upward growth.

A sense of relief and relaxation overtook her as she felt the shedding of a heavy load, but quickly a different kind of fear grabbed hold of her.

Is Lin Xigeng gone or is he still waiting beyond the fence?

When they were seeing each other often, she naturally paid a lot of attention to what she wore, hoping to leave him with a different impression each time with new clothes.

She missed and wished to recall what she was wearing when they first met, but never could. She was, however, able to recall what she was wearing the time he asked her out for a walk and they crowded into the small neighborhood watch booth.

Rain is a common feature of Taipei spring evenings. Now in late spring, an occasional rain produced a slight chill that slowly warmed up. Her new thin silk dress was like gossamer, the fabric cold to the touch, as if washed by water, when it first touched her skin.

But in that small booth, with its rain-soaked, stifling air, the dress was soft and warm because they were sitting shoulder to shoulder. When he reached out and took her in his arms, she leaned against his shoulder. The large warm hand on her back seemed to go straight through the thin silk fabric, as if the light dress had dissolved under their body heat.

It was a white dress in silk that gave off a delicate luster, but looked like flickering light on a cold day.

PART II

Lotus Garden underwent a major renovation when she was about to graduate from elementary school, two years after she'd written "I was born in the last year of the Sino-Japanese War."

By then Father had pretty much recovered his health. A hundred-year-old plane tree by the garden, with too many crisscrossing limbs overladen with branches and leaves, crushed the fish-scale tiles on a corner of Lotus Pavilion's eaves. After most of the branches were trimmed, a plan for a major renovation emerged.

The branches were trimmed in the middle of winter. Given central Taiwan's typical, subtropical weather, the plane tree was not deciduous, though its leaves were visibly sparser than in midsummer. Taiwan's plane tree leaves are smaller than the palm-sized leaves on French counterparts; they curl up on the edges in the cold of winter, reducing their size and altering their shape.

"The common name for the Taiwan plane tree is *citong*. Our ancestors planted them originally because on the Mainland the plane trees shed their leave; they needed sunlight on cold winter days and the plane trees did not block out the sun after the leaves had fallen. The leaves grow back in the summer to provide shade from the heat."

Father explained all this to her as he held her tiny hand in his. They were watching Luohan, whose former profession had been turning roosters into capons, as he directed workers in trimming branches.

"But the Taiwanese coral trees don't lose their leaves. So it would be pointless and ineffective to merely copy the Mainland practice of planting a tree by a building, wouldn't it?"

She nodded quietly.

"So should we take it down and replace it with an indigenous Taiwanese tree?" Father sounded vague and uncertain. "But it's more than a hundred years old and was planted by our ancestors. It's as old as Lotus Garden. I simply can't bring myself to do it."

Twenty years later, it was springtime when Zhu Yinghong decided to renovate Lotus Garden. The plane tree that had escaped the ax remained strong, even displaying a blanket of tiny red flowers. She had finally learned that it had a lovely name, Indian coral tree, or coral *citong*, which was why her father had called it *citong*. During the several years of renovation, she followed her father's habit of calling it that.

Unlike the *citong*, which underwent only a trimming, the pine and beech trees by Authenticity Studio were uprooted one by one.

Ignoring objections from the elders in the clan, Father went ahead with his plan. He disagreed with their practice of imitating Mainland garden architecture, including planting similar trees; the saplings they had taken so much trouble to find on the Mainland would not necessarily thrive in Taiwan.

"Why plant trees that won't do well in the local climate? It's better to grow indigenous trees and flowers," Father continued in Taiwanese. "Your children may be born in the year of the dog or the pig, but they're still your own flesh and blood."

Pines from the frigid zones baked in the harsh sun of central Taiwan for nearly half the year and lost the resilience of evergreens in the snow, where deciduous trees wither till the spring. They manage only to put forth anemic needles on shapeless branches. The pines were dug up and replaced by star fruit trees.

The star fruit trees came in mature forms, though many leafy branches were trimmed for the transplanting process. When spring arrived, tender, green, delicate leaves sprouted with impressive vitality. With the autumn wind came blankets of red flowers, so tiny they weren't particularly attractive by themselves, but the concentration of many shades of red presented an eye-catching yet sorrowful beauty, especially when blown off to the ground by strong winds. The ground was covered with small flowers, like blood-red tears.

With the arrival of winter, the flowers disappeared, as if they'd shed their last drops of blood, and were replaced by small star fruit hanging on the trees like tiny green stars. Yinghong had asked Mudan to pick some for her to play with, but each time was met with a stern refusal. Mudan said that they would grow to be delicious fruit and what she wanted was wasteful. But soon afterward, the starlike fruit began to fall, until not a single one was left. This time Mudan explained that the newly transplanted trees needed time to recover from the uprooting and branch trimming before they could properly nourish the fruit.

By the time she got around to renovating Lotus Garden, the star fruit trees near Authenticity Studio had all died. She wasn't sure what to do now, plant pines like her ancestors or grow star fruit trees like her father. Pines would be the obvious choice if she wanted to return the garden to its original design, but Father's plan seemed more practical and feasible. In the end, she opted for the latter, as the out-of-climate pines were frail and emaciated, in contrast to the star fruit trees, with their splendid and sorrowfully pretty red flowers, that left an indelible image in her mind.

She did exactly what her father had done by planting mature trees. One fall afternoon a few years later, when the renovation was near completion, she sat on her father's favorite Jiaping white stone terrace at Flowing Pillow Pavilion. A casual glance drew her attention to the red dots on the water in front of her. She scooped some up and saw that they were star fruit flowers, but there were no star-fruit trees nearby. So she followed the floating flowers, tracing them past several pavilions, terraces, and towers along the way, until she reached the small man-made waterfall, where she was surprised to find mature star fruit trees by Authenticity Studio. Their thick branches and dense leaves reached into the water, which was how the petals fell into the stream, past the artificial hills and winding paths and the pavilions and terraces, before appearing in every corner of Lotus Garden, with its crisscrossing waterways.

Tears blurred her vision.

> I have spent most of my life in Lotus Garden, but only recently, when I learned how to observe small things, did I find myself captivated by the many wondrous sights and minute occurrences in the garden. Our world is filled with endless surprises and mysteries; nothing is possible and everything is possible.

When Father wrote this letter, he must have seen flowers from the transplanted star fruit trees flowing down the waterways and reaching into every corner. The tiny teardrops of flowers traveled past pavilions and terraces, through the many ages of the human world and the vicissitudes of life in Lotus Garden.

In addition to planting star fruit trees, Father also cut down the original beech trees on the hill behind Authenticity Study and replaced them with flame trees.

"The ancients planted beech by their study because it portended good luck at the scholars' examination. Such feudal beliefs are not only outmoded but should be completely eliminated."

He turned solemn as he spoke:

"If one day democracy can be found in Taiwan, the Taiwanese will have a good life, even if it is the Western or Japanese type, even if it's just a semblance of democracy, so long as no one holds the idea of a mandate from heaven."

During the first few years after the transplanting, the flame trees looked rather ordinary, except for the leaves that littered the ground when winter came. The sparse-looking trees in turn brightened up the area near the study, allowing the warm winter sun to slant in and climb up the scrolls on the white walls, where the warmth from the sun remained, then dissipated as it began to set.

"The plane trees were planted so we could see their leaves fall, but the Taiwan coral planes never shed their leaves. Now we have flame trees with fallen leaves in the winter. Wouldn't you call this one action with multiple results?" Father said laughingly, obviously in high spirits.

When the flame trees began to bloom, the profusion of flowers over-shadowed the green leaves, bringing Father a different kind of pleasure. With the onset of summer, the leaves were small, but the buds were already showing their faces, in two shades of red—orange and bright red. As the temperature rose higher and higher, the flame flowers looked as though they had been bathed in fire and were reborn; like the phoenix, they spread their petals and bloomed, cradling the whiskerlike yellow stamens as if ready to soar into the air.

Any two of the flowers, which turned a fiery red with the arrival of each heat wave, could fit in the palm of your hand. Dozens of them formed clusters that hung high up on branches to create fire clouds against the clear blue sky of a summer day.

As the heat lost its intensity, flowers nurtured by the high temperature began to wither, even though it was still the height of summer; soon they would all be gone. But they showed a lingering affection for the world on branches that were now laden with delicate but fully grown leaves, like the tail of a phoenix, swaying and roiling in the wind, and that is how they got their local name: phoenix flowers.

Father was besotted with the flame trees to the point of obsessiveness.

"You can say that flame trees are typically Taiwanese. On an island nation at this latitude, with its high temperatures, the fiery trees are hardy and resilient, just like the Taiwanese, who maintain a fervent heart no matter what setbacks they encounter." Father continued, "Ayako, you know what I want most is to fill this garden with flame trees and change its name to Phoenix Garden. That would reflect a true Taiwanese flavor, don't you think? But ..."

Naturally, Father never did change the name of the garden. But every year, when the flowers bloomed in early summer, he spent all day under the trees, reading, even napping. She also liked to bring up a stool and sit by his side, still haunted by the fear that he'd abruptly disappear for a long time; then, when he returned, he would stay inside the Flowing Pillow Pavilion for years, not showing his face.

Most of the time, she could not manage to keep watch for long, and soon she'd lean against him and fall into a deep slumber in the lethargic summer air, forcing him to stay in his lounge chair for most of the afternoon. As he lay face up, distance was distorted, giving him the impression that the clusters of fiery red blooms were pressing down on him, filling every inch of his field of vision. By contrast, the azure blue sky of central Taiwan, now visible only through the leaves and flowers, seemed to spread out into the distance. The sky appeared to have never before been so far and so high.

When she was thirteen, Yinghong tested into a provincial girl's middle school in a town that was a thirty-minute bus ride from Lucheng. With the imminent beginning of the new semester, she had to cut off her long, fine hair and replace it with a uniform haircut that made her look like she was wearing half a watermelon rind. Father and Mother even had a fight over the haircut.

In the summer following the exam, Father began teaching her English, starting with the alphabet, pronunciation, and a few words. In addition, he began telling her about the Zhu ancestors, usually under the flame trees after she woke up from her afternoon nap.

"When we talk about our forebears, the Zhu clan likes to begin with Zhu Jiancheng. Our family lineage record begins with him. Some even say that Zhu was not our surname at first, but was given to us by the Zhu emperor of the Ming dynasty, to share the imperial surname."

With his eye on the fiery flowers, Father began casually:

"I disagree. I've looked through regional and county gazetteers and have found nothing to substantiate such a claim. I believe, fundamentally, that the Zhu family should not have considered it an honor to abandon their original surname and adopt the name of the ruling emperor. You must keep this in mind, Ayako."

Thirteen-year-old Yinghong had yet to see why it was not a good idea to adopt the emperor's surname, but she nodded obediently at what her father said.

"There's also a minor discrepancy in beginning the family lineage record with Zhu Jiancheng, who came to Taiwan during the reign of the Kangxi Emperor and developed Zhuluo County in central Taiwan, where he acquired a large quantity of land and property. One record shows that he harvested thousands of tons of rice to fill his storehouse, thus laying the foundation of the Zhu family fortune, and is deserving of our respect. But why wouldn't the record go back further to include his ancestors, such as his father or his grandfather? Do you know why, Ayako?"

She shook her head, for she did not understand everything he was saying.

"My speculation is that whoever began the lineage record decided to skip that part because Zhu Jiancheng's forebears must have done something dishonorable and shameful. As a child, I've heard elders whisper among themselves tales of our ancestors having been pirates."

Delighted by this, she giggled in a crisp voice that retained a hint of girlishness.

"That's wonderful, Otosan. Pirates! Were they like those in the stories you've told me, those who bury treasure on small islands?"

"Maybe," Father smiled. "I checked all the regional and county gazetteers until I finally discovered someone who may well be the first in our Zhu family to come to Taiwan. His name was Zhu Feng, and he ought to have been Zhu Jiancheng's grandfather. I went to the Upper House to ask Grand Uncle, who agreed that some people in our clan do accept Zhu Feng as our earliest recorded ancestor."

Looking at him with her beautiful, big eyes under long lashes, she asked:

"What did he do that was so bad that we have disowned him?"

"He was a pirate who killed and plundered, so it was unavoidable and reasonable that later generations would feel shame."

Father stared into the distance as he looked at the flowers.

"But we have to take note that Zhu Feng was no small-time pirate," he went on. "He is mentioned in the county gazetteer, where he is described as a brave, gallant, and righteous person who made great contributions to local development and was praised by later generations. Records also show that he helped smuggle residents from the Hokkien and Canton areas across the Taiwan Straits when the late-Ming government banned immigration to Taiwan. So he obviously wasn't just a murderous pirate."

"Then why was he dropped?" she asked anxiously.

"My sense is that it has to do with the piracy business of the time. It was late in the sixteenth century, when the Ming government had a policy of no contact with the outside world, which gave pirates an indispensible role to play in trade between Japan, the Chinese Mainland, Taiwan, and the South Pacific." Father spoke to her somberly in elegant Japanese. "Pirates being pirates, they would surely plunder and pillage along the coast. But, they also helped by transporting deerskins and sugar from Taiwan and silk and medicine from China, and facilitated trade with Japan and the Netherlands. So you can say that pirates were Taiwan's earliest global businessmen."

He began to slow down, and his tone turned despondent.

"But with the fall of the Ming, the Qing empire naturally wanted to contain the pirates and bring them into the fold. When the pirate leader Zheng Zhilong surrendered to the Qing, the pirates' enterprise came to an end."

He stopped and sighed softly.

"You can imagine how restricted Zhu Feng's maritime activities would have become by then. He probably faced two choices, either change his name and settle on land, or remain on the run with Qing soldiers after him."

"So which one did he choose?" She asked. "Was he killed?"

"No, but I think he was too used to the freedom of the ocean to settle on land and live out his years. He had to continue his old trade. The records of his last days all have him being chased by Qing ships all the way to Luzon."

Yinghong's large eyes darkened.

"But that still doesn't explain why our ancestors didn't include Zhu Feng's name in our lineage record," Father continued without looking at her. "That was reasonable and obvious: Zhu Feng refused to submit to the Qing imperial system, which probably displeased the local officials in Taiwan. Hence the Zhu family was worried that such an independent-spirited ancestor would have a negative impact on their accumulated wealth."

The thirteen-year-old girl had yet to fully comprehend what her father was saying, but she continued to listen attentively because pirates were involved and she wanted to hear more exciting stories.

"Now we have to talk about Zhu Feng's wife," Father said, changing the subject. "Our family records have very detailed descriptions of her. We know she was born a Chen, the offspring of a Hoklo immigrant, with indigenous and Dutch blood. She was pretty, tall with big eyes, but not those slanted, single-fold eyes typical of the yellow race. Hers were more like the indigenous or white people, big with double folds."

He reached out and touched her face with loving tenderness.

"Maybe big eyes like yours."

Ignoring the puzzled look on her face, he continued:

"I've been thinking that she must have encouraged him to stay on land, but he didn't listen to her. Worse yet, he abandoned her and their four young children. He ran off to the South Pacific with a Mainland Chinese concubine, a courtesan who had slanted eyes and bound feet. The woman from the Chen family, with her non-Chinese blood, must have had unbound feet."

With no more talk of pirates, Yinghong began to lose interest, but she remained seated, as required by her father's instruction.

"It was clearly difficult for the woman from the Chen family to raise four children all on her own, so they began to fall ill and three of them died. Only the second one survived, and he would be Zhu Jiancheng's father. He didn't live long either. Before his son was born, he died of lung disease from over-exhaustion as a carter. So Zhu Jiancheng was raised by his grandmother, the Chen woman. Zhu later made a name for himself and remained loyal to his grandmother, letting her control everything in the house. She died at the advanced age of ninety-four."

Noticing that her attention was flagging, he patted her on the head.

"The family lineage records show that she was a tireless, capable head of the family who was more decisive and powerful than any man. She established the many rules that the Zhu family followed over the next two hundred years. One of them was never in writing; it was passed down by word of mouth, dictating that no one in the Zhu family was to add Zhu Feng to the lineage record and reincorporate him into the family. Rumor has it that she made a brutal vow that the Zhu family would be ruined if anyone dared to do that."

It was the height of summer when she returned to Lotus Garden with him for the first time. Under a canopy of fiery, red flame blossoms, she told him about her distant ancestors, a pirate who was active along the coasts of Taiwan, China, and Japan three hundred years before, as well as his wife and her vow.

After she finished, he looked at her and said in a serious tone:

"Your father's views are very interesting. According to him, pirates were the progenitors of Taiwan's trade. If that's the case, then it was no coincidence that Taiwan rose three hundred years later in international trade."

He had always been cautious when the topic involved her father, and now he changed the subject and began to tease her:

"If I ran off with another woman, would you denounce me like your great-, great-, great-grandmother and deny me peace and quiet even after my death?"

She was quiet, smiling with her head down, before she teased him with a question of her own:

"Would you dare?"

Lin Xigeng roared in laughter.

"You do look as though you have pirate's blood in you," he said. "You have your great-, great-, great-grandmother's genes, and the day you murder me I won't know why."

She pummeled him with her fists, but then began to giggle and fell into his arms.

When the night deepened, they got up to return to Lotus Pavilion, where they would spend the night. It was so cool in the verdant Lotus Garden that he had a sudden urge to take her on the ground under the flame trees. She didn't say no. Outdoors sex was titillating to begin with, and the mysterious, abandoned garden added even more stimulation and excitement.

She lay on the ground in his arms. A bright, clear moon moved above them, making the phoenix flowers visible by its light. Only in spots heavy with layered flowers and leaves did dark shadows form to display a heaviness that seemed to hint at a bloody battle.

Under the red flower–laden trees, she waited, but he suddenly stopped moving.

"Why do I have the feeling that your pirate ancestor is somewhere nearby, lingering like a wronged ghost, watching us?"

In addition to Father, Yinghong had two additional sources for stories about pirates: Mudan and her husband, Luohan.

She begged Mudan for stories, but this time the maid slapped her thigh with her large, bony hand.

"How would someone like me know stories about pirates, those bad people who loot and burn?" Then she changed her tune. "But if you promise not to cause me any trouble or ruin the star fruit before it's ripe, I can tell you who's a source for pirate stories."

Naturally, Yinghong promised her anything.

"Go ask Luohan. One of his ancestors was an infamous evildoer in Water Ditch on the coast near Lucheng."

Luohan had a nickname, "The Caponer," because of what he used to do when he was young. A tall man with a refined look, he was bossed around by Mudan all day long, but nothing disagreeable ever showed on his agreeable face. He was a man of few words, and when he talked he was succinct and articulate, to which Mudan attributed his love of local drama. Whenever a show was put on in Lucheng, he wouldn't go home until he finished watching the entire play, no matter what was playing, an amateur Beiguan drama, a Nanguan play, Taiwanese opera, or a puppet show. One time, when the nearby Temple of the Zhu Patriarch put on a Taiwanese opera to celebrate the deity's birthday, Luohan took her along to watch, and didn't return until midnight, for which they both received a severe tongue-lashing from Mudan.

But it required Mudan's help to get Luohan to talk. Usually, after finishing his work in the garden, he would squat by the wall and smoke his pipe, the crackling the only audible sound around. On this day Yinghong squatted beside him to hear the stories.

Luohan began with the ocean, how the water was white when the boat first left the Mainland for Taiwan, but turned blue as the journey progressed. Then the boat would cross the "red ditch," where the water was as red as the rouge on women's faces. This was when the boatmen began tossing spirit money into the water in exchange for a safe passage. After the red ditch came the most treacherous black ditch, with rapid currents and deep gulches far below, where black water surged. If there was a southwesterly wind, the water turned into giant eddies, and the slightest error could send the boat wayward. The boatmen tossed in so much spirit money that the surface of the ocean was blanketed with paper; but once they were lucky enough to cross the ditch, Taiwan was not far off.

Luohan would usually follow the boat ride with stories of shipboard murders for the passengers' valuables. Transporting several hundred people in a leaky boat, the bandits, who were seasoned sailors, would order their passengers into the cabin and seal them inside. They would set off in the dead of the night and, when they were well into the ocean, the overcrowded leaky boat would naturally begin to sink. Another ruse was to take the passengers to a sandbar, which they claimed to be Taiwan, and tell them to get off. Not knowing what was happening, the travelers got off and drowned when the tides rose.

These were the scariest stories, which he told succinctly, but with terrifying effect, since his brief narration left so much room for her imagination to run wild. She came to fear the water in the Taiwan Straits, which, contrary to the clear blue described in books, was eerie red, like rouge, or black, like ink, both unusual ocean colors that were predictably strange and frightening.

After hearing these tales, she was afraid to get up at night and had to get Mudan to accompany her when she needed to use the toilet. When he got wind of that, Father would not allow Luohan and Mudan to tell her such stories again.

The last story she heard was about a battle between the pirates and Qing soldiers. Following his usual narrative style of few details, Luohan described how, when the people from both sides began to fight, the colors in the sky were clear, red on one side and blue on the other. Over the first few days, the sky quickly turned blood red, which lasted several days and nights, pressing down as if setting the land on fire as well. Now everyone knew that the pirates were winning, forcing the Qing soldiers back. Only a sliver of blue remained in the sky, on the verge of being swallowed up by red. But it was clear that the blue side was not destined for destruction yet, for the last shred of blue was able to hold off the attack and slowly gain ground inch by inch, restoring its blue dominance. Everyone knew that the Qing navy had regained control, and the sky was once again divided into red and blue. More battles, and the sky parted down the middle; the red would advance only to be beaten back by the blue. In the end the blue side won, and people knew that the pirates had been defeated.

Later, Father produced logical and reasonable explanations for everything. For instance, the water in the red and black ditches was not really red or black. The black current was affected by seasonal winds that produced eddies, altering the color of the waves. And the battle between the soldiers and the pirates did not change the colors of the sky. That was caused by burning cargo boats, setting the distant sky ablaze. Nonetheless, Yinghong could never get over her fears instilled by the eerie image of the sky divided down the middle, red on one side and blue on the other, as the combatants fought. Sometimes she dreamed about the destructive, frightening battle of colors in the sky, dreams that returned after Lin Xigeng told her he was leaving her.

Father's alternate explanation for the pirates helped eliminate her nagging concerns. At the time, he had just finished removing the pines and oaks in the garden, and their replacements, the flame trees, were in full bloom. He had also begun repairing the roofs of the several pavilions and towers, while planting smaller trees and flowering plants.

First he dug up plum trees by Long Rainbow Lying by the Moon. The plums were cold-weather flowers that showed off an ability to withstand the snow and frost, but in hot central Taiwan their withered branches were devoid of any sign of resilience. She had not once seen them bloom. So Father replaced them with Taiwanese magnolia and banana shrubs. The broad-leaved magnolia had fragrant flowers with long white jadelike petals, usually hidden among leaves. You could smell the flowers but couldn't find them, though their cool, subtle fragrance lingered for a long time on summer days. In contrast, the squat banana shrubs had smaller leaves, with beige, cone-shaped flower buds, called smile flowers, like almonds, easily within reach. On winter afternoons, they gave off a sweet aroma. She imitated her father in putting one in her pocket and letting it turn soft, with a sweet fragrance, warmed by her body.

Father planted the smile flowers by the path at the garden entrance.

"That way we welcome our guests with a smile." So Father had said, though they had few visitors when she was in elementary school, even up through early middle school.

In addition to Taiwanese magnolia and banana shrubs, Father also planted tree orchids and gardenias. In Taiwan fragrant flowers are normally white; tree orchids, however, had yellow blooms that sprouted from tiny green beads that were barely visible among the green leaves. When they bloomed, the flowers were half the size of a rice kernel, but bloomed in such profusion that they had a noticeable aroma and color.

Gardenias are small compared to other fragrant blooming trees. Yet when they bloom, the small, squat trees come alive with large, multipetalled white flowers, giving the impression of high density. With a tree full of fragrant flowers, they are typical aromatic tropical bloomers.

Father also planted cassia. Lucheng's autumn is often besieged by strong winds from the ocean that keep the number of cassia flowers low, but enough to produce a pervasive aroma. Hence, fragrant flowers graced Lotus Garden all year round, starting with the gardenias in late spring, the Taiwanese magnolia and tree orchids in the summer, cassias in the fall, and banana shrubs in the winter.

Besides blooming trees and flowers, Father planted fragrant shrubs, such as his favorite, jasmine, which bloomed in early summer. Mudan had a different name for the jasmine, whose tiny white flowers bloomed at dusk; she called them "maidservant flowers," her logic being that they must have been transformed maidservants or they would not bloom in the evening, when people do the dishes.

Father had stopped Mudan from telling her stories, but Mudan had a bad memory, and in her mouth the jasmine was the reincarnation of a wrongly accused maidservant, which, on summer evenings, reminded Yinghong of why such a delicate fragrant flower would bloom at a time when all other flowers were resting.

It was over the fragrant flowers of the subtropics that Father again brought up Zhu Feng, their pirate ancestor of more than three hundred years before.

"The pirates had large fleets, equipped with cannons and long guns. Their targets were large merchant ships loaded with goods for trade." He adopted a serious tone as he continued, "As for those who mistreated immigrating passengers or forced them onto the sandbar to drown, they weren't even eligible to be pirates. They were plain murderers."

She smiled with relief.

"So Zhu Feng didn't kill anyone," she said. "I'm going to tell Luohan and Mudan."

"That's not entirely true either." Father was searching for a good explanation. "The pirates were going after cargo, so it was unavoidable that weapons would be involved, and it was also inevitable that they would kill or be killed."

As he continued, his eyes began to sparkle.

"Ayako, I'm going to tell you a story passed down by our ancestors. Once, when Zhu Feng dispatched a dozen seafaring ships to surround a Dutch fleet, he dealt the redheaded Dutch such a resounding defeat that they had to abandon their ships. Just think, Ayako, back then he had a few dozen seafaring ships and the Dutch called him the China Captain."

Fragrant flowers blooming at various times year round filled the garden's terraces, pavilions, and towers. In hot and humid subtropical Taiwan, the heady fragrance of the many varieties of summer flowers and the subtly aromatic lilies from the big pond seemed even more redolent, as they fused with moist air until the combined effects of the flowers lingered in the air for a long time and created an intoxicating effect.

"China Captain, the Captain of China, Ayako. China Captain," Father continued in his usual Japanese. "We must remember that only a real man like Zhu Feng, who was used to riding the wind and sailing the ocean, who was not afraid to die, could be the ancestor of immigrants across the Taiwan Straits to open new routes and help maritime trade grow."

She nodded earnestly to show she would never forget what he had said.

"The early immigrants to Taiwan relied on the guidance of the pirates and even sailed in their ships for safe passage across the Straits. You must remember, Ayako, that not all the early immigrants were poor, nor were they all refugees. In fact, there were quite a few adventurers like Zhu Feng, who tried to find a paradise in a faraway place blocked by the ocean. Taiwan was their newfound paradise."

Father paused and asked solemnly:

"Ayako, do you know what Formosa means?"

"Beautiful Island."

She was able to answer promptly because of his instruction in the past.

"Yes, Beautiful Island, a rich island with fragrant flowers the year round, with emerald-green plains and snow-capped mountains."

Then, in the powerfully intoxicating aroma of flowers, Father began to speak slowly, looking at her in the utmost serious and solemn way:

"Ayako, you must remember that Taiwan is not a copy or microcosm of any other place on earth. Taiwan is Taiwan, a beautiful island."

It was early summer, after the spring rains, when gardenias began to spread their perfume, and Father began renovating the "dragon wall" behind Lotus Pavilion in order to separate the pavilion from the eastern side of the garden.

A "dragon wall" is a fence that follows the contours of the land; like other common walls, it is higher than a person of average height. The only difference is the dragon that sprawls along the top; the clay dragon's head is raised high, while its long body is made of semicircular roof tiles that are fitted to look like real dragon scales from the side. The scaly dragon body coils and spreads over the undulating wall, resembling a true, auspicious dragon.

"This kind of wall has a name; it's called 'cloud soaring dragon wall.' It's not commonly seen in ordinary people's houses because dragons are traditionally considered to be the symbol of the emperor and a taboo for commoners."

Standing by the wall and dwarfed by its height, Father looked frail owing to his medium build and his recent recovery from a long illness. The dragon wall helped create a square courtyard behind Lotus Pavilion, while also serving as a barrier for a copse of trees to the east. Like the average fence, there was a moon gate for passage, framed by the giant, clay dragon heads, with their fangs and claws circling the top of the gate, while their bodies extended away with the wall. Following the custom of garden architecture, their tails were hidden among the next rows of terraces and pavilion, a place where they could not be easily detected.

"The ancestors who built the garden wanted to use the 'cloud soaring dragons,' but were afraid to offend the emperor by using his symbol, which was why they created a creature that resembled a dragon, but wasn't one."

Father led her to a spot below the wall, where he pointed to a clay dragon head that had turned blurry from the elements.

"See, this dragon has fish scales, shrimp eyes, an ox nose, deer antlers, and eagle talons. At first glance it looks like a traditional dragon, but, Ayako, look carefully and you'll see that our dragons have only four talons, not the normal five."

Still a child at heart, Yinghong raised her slender index finger to count.

"One, two, three, four. It really has only four talons."

That drew a smile from Father.

"The ancestors who built the garden were the richest men in Taiwan back then. Taiwan was far from the Central Plain, a true manifestation of 'the sky is high and the emperor is far away.' They wanted to use the dragon, but didn't dare overdo it, and that is how our four-taloned dragon came into existence. With one less talon than the emperor's golden dragon, they showed they didn't dare consider themselves his equal, and if anything were to happen because of it, they would have a way out."

She nodded, not fully grasping the import of what he had just said.

"Ayako, we should be happy that we're no longer like our ancestors. Now we live in an era without an emperor, and we can create a golden dragon with five talons."

Then he sighed and his face darkened.

"Even so, when will Taiwan gain democracy?"

Despite his heavy heart, he was cheerful as he located an old master to renovate the cloud soaring dragon wall. The decaying dragon heads received a new coat of paint and the broken tiles of the bodies were replaced. He even asked the skillful master to give the dragons an additional talon each, making them true golden dragons.

"Let's consider the additional talon as the beginning of democracy for Taiwan. It's better than nothing."

He smiled bitterly as he examined the newly renovated dragon.

The garden was more or less fully renovated when masons finished repairing the cloud soaring dragon wall. The woodwork was repaired and repainted in the spring of her second year in junior high. On the day the work was completed, Father personally planted the last tree, a Cape lilac, in Lotus Garden.

The Cape lilac, called "bitter berry" by the locals, was planted in a wide-open space near Yinghong Pavilion. After watering it for the first time, Father said in his preferred language of Japanese:

"Bitter berry is the name I want; it means longing and experienced bitterness." Looking at the people around him, he continued, "I hope we'll never forget the bitterness or this experience."

A plant in the silk tree family, the Cape lilac, though having bitterness in its local name, grew into a tall tree with flowers so pretty they could only come from a dream when they bloom. Every spring and summer, it was covered in white flowers that gave off an unusual but pleasant fragrance, one with a hint of bitterness that wafted like lingering silk thread, as Father had said.

The tree covered with white flowers seemed shrouded in mist. Unlike flowers formed by petals, Cape lilacs have long, thin whiskerlike white stamens and pistils that radiate from the center, giving them a dreamy, puffy cloudlike appearance. When the tree is in bloom, it looks as though a patch of wayward clouds has temporarily stopped at the tips of the green leaves. Without the usual petals, the flowers, with their threadlike stamens and pistils, seem loosely connected and almost unreal, as if one of the island's frequent typhoons could blow them out of sight.

The Cape lilac flowers are particularly dense this year. The seemingly endless patch of white, for some reason, has instilled in me a feeling that everything will soon turn into nothing.

I picked this spot for the tree solely because only Yinghong Pavilion had a large-enough space for it; I didn't give it much thought or consideration. Now when I look at the misty, bitter white flowers serving to contrast "yinghong" in the name of the pavilion, I have to marvel at the coincidence and how everything seems to have been predestined. White bitter flowers against shadowy red. The flowers will bloom and fall to the ground. The flowers in the water are left in the shadowy red. Isn't everything an illusion, and won't it all turn to nothing?

Planting the Cape lilac by Yinghong Pavilion was a purely unintentional act, and it wasn't until just now that I finally understand the profound implication of its location. If everything in the past and in the future will turn into nothing, then won't even the "bitterness" also be an illusion? Wouldn't what I never managed to forget, and even planted a bitter berry tree as a reminder to myself, also be illusory and punctilious? It's easy to see through the prosperous side of life, for, if one can be at ease with bitterness, then what else should one pursue?

But, Ayako, do not be affected by my mentality, which is a result of old age, a time when I have learned to take everything lightly. You need to remember, however, the couplet from our ancestor at the lily pond closest to Yinghong Pavilion:

In a quite little garden, startled geese soar into the sky on the wind,
In the boundless green leaves, feathered friends frolic in shadowy red.

This is the real origin of your name. Just imagine how happy and bustling it is, with a pond filled with red water lilies serving as the backdrop for the startled geese, our feathered friends.

Speaking of bustling, I must tell you about the flame trees in the garden. Ayako, you must still remember when the garden was renovated, how I planted many flame trees in the garden because they were my favorite. I hadn't realized that they would continue to grow and, more than a decade later, tower over everything; their trunks are now so thick only an adult can wrap his arms around them. Their leaves and branches spread into all the terraces and pavilions, press down on eaves, and take up so much space that they have become an oddity, unfit for the overall look of the garden. But I did not want to trim them and turn them into dwarf trees. In the end, I had no choice but to move them elsewhere. Now even the small hill by Authenticity Studio has only three left, but that was the only way to keep the branches from crisscrossing so much they could crowd each other out of existence.

I planted the flame trees because they were my favorites. I never expected that one day I would have to move them out of Lotus Garden. You see, Ayako, how the world can be so mutable. Perhaps the only way to live a carefree life is not to care too much about love and hate.

It was May, but there was still snow on the streets of New York that year. A muddy gray was all anyone could see—an ashen sky and melting gray snow on the roadside. The only exception was some scrawny forsythia that kept up with the season and struggled to open a few sprigs of yellow flowers.

She thought she could hear her father saying:

"The flame trees can be considered typical Taiwanese flora. On an island nation with its high temperatures, the fiery red flowering trees, with their resilience, are just like the Taiwanese, who maintain a burning red heart no matter what setbacks they encounter."

There were sparkles of tears in the eyes of her father, who had just recovered from the long illness.

"Ayako, do you know that what I want to do most now is fill the garden with flame trees and change its name to Phoenix Garden? Wouldn't that be more Taiwanese? But..."

In the end Father never did change the name. In New York, where spring was so late in coming, she read the letter from her father and breathed a sigh of relief for him, though she couldn't stop herself from tearing up. Then a sudden, unusual idea dawned on her for the first time in her life.

Years ago, when Father was thinking about changing the name of the garden, in additional to personal reasons, could it also have been intended to commemorate Zhu Feng, the ancestor who made a fortune as a pirate, and whose name refers to a phoenix?

She would ask her father when she returned to Taiwan, Yinghong said to herself with a tearful smile.

But she never got the chance. Father didn't live to see the bitter berry bloom again the following year. The doctor said he died of liver disease caused by prolonged worry and unhappiness.

After Lin Xigeng left, Yinghong suffered pain the likes of which she hadn't experienced in a long time.

The idea that abstract, mental anguish that was impossible to measure could actually be transformed into real physical torment was new to her. For nearly a week, sound sleep eluded her, replaced by chaotic dreams bordering on the nightmarish. Feeling dimly awake, she was in fact in the grip of even more terrifying sleepy memories that had to be relived.

She was floating in a vast body of water, an endless aquamarine world. Water everywhere, and no sky. Suddenly the color around her darkened; instinct told her that sharks were nearing, but she could not see them. No waves, no tides, only a dense body of water that formed a solid mass and began to tilt and roil. After a series of violent tremors, she sensed that the invisible sharks had swum off, and she was finally freed from the water.

At first everything felt the same, as she was relieved to find her body uninjured; but when she pushed down to sit up, she discovered that her hands were powerless, and that thin blood was oozing out through bite marks. Her arms, which were lying flat, were sliced open down the middle, revealing zigzagging bite marks, clearly visible long lines of wounds caused by sharks' sharp teeth.

A further discovery showed that the sharks' teeth had bitten through her body, cutting it into horizontal halves separated by neat, visible rows of teeth marks.

Blood seeped out slowly, and the pain was not unbearable. But the injury was so utterly eerie, beyond understanding and imagination, that it caused a terrible fright.

That was followed by an even more terrifying scene: the blue sky, which had originally merged with the body of water, had at some point undergone sudden changes. It too was sliced down the middle, separated by two colors; one a ghastly blue and the other a bloody red.

A divided sky. Her childhood's worst fear came to mind. Father had vanished, and she woke up in the dead of the night; the bed in Lotus Garden retained no body warmth; she groped in the dark but there was no one, and she struggled to wake up. A long time later Father returned, only to lie in Flowing Pillow Pavilion for several years, virtually out of sight. After she was startled awake, her first thoughts were of Lin Xigeng, of his departure and the heartrending ache it produced.

After many sleepless nights she sank into a state of blurry wakefulness, in which she had but one wish: to hear from him. In the office and at home she waited day and night, turning down all invitations and seldom going out. Sometimes she'd wake up at night and grab the phone to see if it was working.

She held her breath and forced herself to be calm when answering the phone. At first, she feigned lethargy and indifference in how she said "hello." After a week of that, she began picking up the phone with a measured low voice so as to sound affectionate and seductive. She wanted him to hear her enchanting voice as soon as the call went through.

Two weeks went by, and then three. He didn't call. She abandoned the low, seductive voice, for the urgency in her heart made her tense. Now her "hello" sounded short and terse, with a hint of withering anxiety. She would immediately turn cold and unresponsive the moment she knew it wasn't him, afraid that the caller would keep the line tied up too long.

Naturally, she'd thought of calling him, but feelings of hurt and defeat were so powerful they overtook all her thought processes and left a permanent ache in her heart. In her confused state, she simply could not muster the physical and mental energy to do anything.

It would take a month and seventeen days, during which time she had seen him on several occasions, before the sense of permanent separation and suffocating pain subsided somewhat, and only then did she realize that he would eventually come back to her. He was not without feelings for her;

moreover, given his conceited nature, he would come back to observe the outcome, particularly after what he'd done when they broke up.

Besides, if he really did not want to get back together, it would be pointless for her to look him up, since all she would get in return would be humiliation and more hurt.

He had been the one to break up, so he would always have the upper hand if she were to seek him out first. He could always say:

"We agreed to break up. You're the one who changed your mind first."

He could even be downright cruel:

"I didn't come to you; you presented yourself to me."

Yinghong knew she would never let herself sink so low, no matter how much she loved him.

Finally, four weeks later, she was awakened by the phone late one night. It was a quarter past two in the morning, and she knew it was him.

He was in the habit of calling late at night. In the past, he'd sometimes call just to say a few words to her. He'd even defend his inconsiderate action by saying it was for her own good, since she must be longing to hear his voice, just as he wanted to hear hers.

After a prolonged wait, she felt nothing special now that he had actually phoned her. It was her uncle's voice on the phone; she could tell he was drunk when he told her that someone had asked him to make the call.

"Let me talk to him."

She could hear her uncle call out urgently:

Lin—Xi—geng.

She didn't realize until then that the hand holding the phone was shaking.

Her uncle sent his car to pick her up. The driver had been working for the family for over twenty years, and knew the proper behavior of not ringing the doorbell or sounding his horn late at night. Instead, he waited at the door. When she came out and saw that he had just about fallen asleep at the wheel, it dawned on her that she had made him wait a long time. She had been dressing in front of her mirror, trying on nearly all the clothes in her closet. In the end, she came out in a rather plain dress, under a light silk jacket, as it was late and drizzly.

Her uncle had called from a restaurant specializing in late-night snacks, in the basement of a building across from a police station. There was no sign at the entrance, but it looked like a restaurant nonetheless. She was well aware of the ins and outs of places like this; an illegal business staying open (facing a police station) until three or four in the morning for diners and girls leaving drinking establishments (who else would be snacking at such an hour?) had to have connections.

Bouncers were guarding the entrance. When she approached, they looked her over to make sure she wasn't a troublemaker before opening the door. She walked in and was immediately hit by an arctic blast of cold air mixed with the smell of cigarettes. Walking down a staircase carpeted in red, she heard her uncle call to her before she found her bearings in the dark.

It was a small room—no more than a hundred square feet—with a round table encircled by a large group of men and women. Since she was standing, the angle and her intuition quickly led her gaze over to Lin Xigeng, who was sitting between two girls. He knew she was there, but didn't look up, although he wore an awkward, even bashful smile.

He was clearly feeling uneasy, but that went undetected by the girls at his side, who continued toasting him and carrying food to his mouth. Though she was aware of the girls' profession, Yinghong still felt hurt, because it should have been her, not them, who was sitting next to him.

The girls were dressed in casual clothes, the sort they normally wore to go out with clients after drinking. That was an unwritten rule. Be they barmaids who wore *qipao* with long slits up the side, or waitresses from hostess bars who dressed in evening gowns, they always changed out of their work clothes before going out with clients. Replacing their "uniforms" with casual clothes sent a message that whatever occurred afterward was a private matter between the girl and the client, the significance of which was obviously important to both.

Any one of the dozen or so girls in a banquet room, where two dozen or so girls came and went all night, would consider herself lucky to be there, though of course the client had yet to decide whether to take her out for a "short chat" or to "spend the night." The two girls by Lin's side were apparently working hard to make something happen in the hope that they would earn the extra money.

At first she thought that Lin's embarrassment stemmed from the two girls' intimate gestures in front of her, but almost immediately she realized that was not the case. He was simply unsure how to greet her, so he continued to smile awkwardly, pretending to listen to a man who appeared to be in his mid fifties. The man looked flushed, after a long night of drinking and fooling around. It was late and he was tired, which was why a patina of steel gray lay across his red face; the corners of his eyes drooped. Even so, a gloomy sense of resolve shone in his eyes. He must have been quite tall, since even seated he towered over the other men. He filled his chair with his large body, a perfect illustration of the Taiwanese phrase, "fully in and fully out."

Sitting among men in suit and tie, he had a rustic air, particularly because of the contrast of the white folded sleeves against his dark-red, black-accented Taiwanese-style shirt, common attire among members of the underworld.

The demeanor of the tall, beefy middle-aged man caught Yinghong's attention, even as her heart was racing upon seeing Lin after so long. Years of attending social occasions like this had fostered in her an intuitive ability to judge people, and that ability told her that the man's eloquence, sounding as if he were talking to himself, was an effort to help Lin out. He obviously felt Lin's discomfort.

"Chairman Lin is very discerning," the man said. But he wasn't talking to Lin Xigeng; rather, he looked at the people around the table. His eyes skipped the girls but gave her a quick glance before looking away, as a way to show her that he knew she was different from the other girls.

"He was the real estate magnate who came up with the idea of preselling units."

Yinghong noticed that her uncle looked up at the man with great interest.

"Back at Taipei Construction, Chairman Lin here, with Zhenhui and Qidong, the three of them, proposed the idea of presale and created a real estate boom. Real estate is an engine of industry; without it, Taiwan would not have such a thriving economy."

"What presale was proposed by Chairman Lin?"

The question came from the girl to Lin's right; she waited openmouthed for the answer. Now that midnight had passed and her lipstick had gone, what had been a coquettish, seductive mouth gave her a somewhat dim-witted look.

Noticing the familiar way the man spoke to and about Lin Xigeng, Ying-hong leaned toward her uncle and signaled with her eyes. Understanding what she was asking about, her uncle answered with a smile, "Masao."

"You have sharp eyes," her uncle whispered. "He's Lin's right-hand man."

"The presale system was something completely new," Masao continued his explanation with a proud look. "In the past when you wanted to buy a house, you had to wait until the construction was completed before you made the purchase. The construction companies had to first buy a plot of land and the building materials, which in turn meant they needed a tre-mendous sum of cash before they could do anything. Now with the presale system, the houses are available for purchase even before the construction begins, and that is like taking the money from the home buyers to build their houses."

The man took a sip of his drink. "So what's the advantage of the sys-tem?" he asked.

"Yes, what is it?" the girl wanted to know.

"First of all, it reduces the buyer's financial burden. In the past you needed to save up all the money before you could buy a house. Now it takes about a year and a half to finish a new development and your payment is pegged to the construction schedule. The monthly payment is five or ten thousand, which is affordable for just about everyone. And the construction company doesn't need to put all its money into one site; instead, it can begin work on several sites at the same time. All this improves people's buying power and stimulates the economy."

Obviously wanting to ingratiate herself with Lin, the girl who asked the question was the only one who showed any interest in what the tall man was saying. It was very late, and all the other languid people around the table were too exhausted to pay attention, creating a lull in the conversation. Finally her uncle asked hoarsely:

"How come everyone credits Zhang Qidong for inventing the system?"

"That's because Chairman Lin did not want to take the credit," Masao said spiritedly. "After the partners at Taipei Construction split up, Zhang Qidong was left without money, and the presale system was his only capital. When Taiwan left the United Nations and all those who could manage moved away, Chairman Lin had the foresight to buy up land, which served as the foundation of his future success."

It was a night like so many others, and a long one at that. Everything proceeded as dictated by convention: a banquet, then visits to drinking establishments, followed by taking the girls out for "business." Since no one wanted to do that on an empty stomach, the custom of midnight snacking was formed. After the snacks, the men could go their separate ways, with their own girls.

Now that the eating was finished, everyone was waiting for the moment to do "business." Hence the lackluster conversation eventually lapsed into silence, which raised an alarm in Yinghong. She did not want everyone to leave too early, hoping they would stay a bit longer so she would have enough time to get reacquainted with Lin. But someone must have said "Let's go," because everyone at the table began to gather their things, while covering their mouths to stifle a yawn or stretch lazily.

She had to stand up with everyone else. Her uncle was saying something to Lin, who then walked up and said without looking at her:

"I invited you, so I should take you home."

In the drizzly late night, his Rolls Royce was an unwieldy mass of cold whiteness. As usual, he opened the door and slid in, followed by Yinghong, who struggled to close the heavy door, prompting him to lean over and shut it for her. But he immediately sat back and moved away from her.

She never realized that the back seat of a Rolls Royce could be so spacious. Even with her long skirt spread across the seat, there was still plenty of space between them.

This marked the first time she'd been unhappy with a spacious car. If they had been an ordinary couple, they'd have taken a local taxi, which would have forced him to sit close enough to touch the hem of her skirt, no matter how much he wanted to keep space between them.

He talked casually about how good business was, as if that was all he wanted to say to her. Gazing out at the passing scenery, he occasionally glanced at her, but quickly looked away. She responded in a calm voice that revealed nothing. The car soon arrived at her house; she didn't tell the driver to stop, wishing she lived farther away, like Tianmu or, better yet, Tamsui.

He was the one who noticed that the car had passed her place, and told the driver to turn around. Upset that he would not take the opportunity to stay awhile, she bid him a cold farewell and got out.

To his credit, he got out and waited until she had opened the gate and crossed the yard to reach the door. He was closing the gate for her when, separated by the overgrown wildness of the yard, he blurted out:

"There have been lots of ghosts recently, wandering, lonely ghosts."

Frightened by the sudden announcement, she instinctively moved closer to him, but the yard was so big, with dark-green, gloomy weeds, almost like an abyss on a dark, rainy night. A breeze brushed the tips of the grass, emitting a rustling noise that sounded like a strange object drifting by. She had goose bumps and felt a tingling on her spine.

"Isn't this the lunar seventh month?" he said.

She was well aware how he often had such flights of fancy; he was a fount of new ideas, a new zoning system for land use, or new sales techniques. At that moment he was standing in the gateway and must have been reminded that she was afraid of ghosts, which led to him to recall that it was the seventh lunar month, the ghost month.

When he finally said good night and left, I turned to shut the door behind me. I couldn't help wondering if he had been trying to frighten me so I would move closer to him. With the pride of a typical Taiwanese man, he would never try to make up with me after initiating the breakup.

As a woman, I could have taken advantage of that opportunity to lean on him; by showing how timid and frightened I was, I could erase the distance that had kept us apart all night. I wasn't totally inexperienced in regard to men and women, and I knew that with this contact, something that could not be accomplished by words might be started anew.

Besides, I wasn't entirely unafraid. His mention of ghosts had frightened me, and I'd felt like rushing into his arms. For all intents and purposes, that would have looked perfectly legitimate, and I wouldn't have appeared to be using feminine frailty as an excuse.

But I didn't do that.

My upbringing had taught me that girls should not display their emotions; I was told to pretend to be unfazed by events. So even at a moment like that, I deftly suppressed all my urges and desire, which gave rise to self-loathing.

Several months later, Yinghong was finally able to struggle out of the boundless sadness and hurt that had interfered with her ability to think clearly; now she realized that not only had Lin Xigeng not sent a car for her that night, but that he hadn't made the call. Her uncle had called her for him, so that Lin could not be accused of being the first to attempt reconciliation.

Many more days passed. Once she'd made up her mind to ensnare him and had devised the means to do so, she knew it would require tremendous effort to feign weakness, using a woman's frailty to get him back. It was not something she could have accomplished soon after they split up, since at the time she had been in great pain.

Besides, she was also troubled by a deep-seated fear of being hurt again, and that had stopped her from running into his arms that night. What had held her back and blocked an instinctive reaction was precisely this extreme fear.

She waited, biding her time till the acute fear of love receded from her heart.

But before that happened, she ran into Lin at a popular Taipei café.

It was like something out of a novel, a movie, or a TV drama. Taipei in the seventies had embarked upon a European style of interior decoration. Copies of European landscape paintings produced in Taiwan for export hung on the exquisitely carved mahogany posts and walls. Under soft lighting and amid a live performance, she looked up and spotted Lin walking in.

Though it resembled an ordinary gathering among friends, the purpose of the meeting was a billion NT loan that her uncle's company planned to apply for. The bank had valued a piece of land he was using as collateral at only 800,000,000, which meant that he would get about 600,000,000 if the bank were willing to approve a loan at 80 percent of its worth, much less than he needed.

Yinghong was seeking the assistance of a Ms. Lin, the fifth concubine of a high-ranking government official. If Ms. Lin was willing to speak with the official on their behalf, they would get what they needed, or, for that matter, any amount they desired, since no land had a set value.

Her uncle had invited the dinner guests, all young ladies and married women who often got together for dinner. After dinner, he excused himself, saying he had another banquet to attend; Yinghong was charged with the task of bringing the ladies, along with Ms. Lin, to the European-style café.

It was not the first time the subject of the loan had come up; Ms. Lin had already agreed to help, and everything seemed to be progressing nicely.

That night, Yinghong was there to give Ms. Lin a pay-to-bearer cashable check for two million NT. She looked up, and there he was. She knew from a single glance that it was him, knew it with a certainty that people often describe as being able to recognize your lover even if he or she had been burned to ashes. At first she didn't think much about it, but then she began to wonder how such a coincidence could be possible, something that happened only in novels or movies. She had been talking to Ms. Lin when she happened to look up, and was unnerved by the impossible coincidence. Wanting to make sure, she took a quick second look, only to realize that her eyes had lost focus and that everything was a blur.

Her eyes came back into focus before she could rub them, and Lin Xigeng's form immediately leaped into her consciousness.

She was momentarily shaken, but then she concentrated on how ridiculous the whole scene was, like a third-rate movie or TV melodrama. At such a moment, actors will rub their eyes to show that what they are witnessing is truly incredible. But then it dawned on her that even third-rate movies are based on reality.

Obviously Lin spotted her, and was surprised and somewhat incredulous; he returned her glance. They were separated by those mahogany posts decorated with dark mirrors intermixed with cheap, imitation European landscape paintings made in Taiwan for export. She was seated, he was standing, but the distance meant that she did not have to look up at his tall figure. Naturally, he walked straight up to her, but time seemed to stand still, giving the impression that it took a lifetime for him to get near her.

Feeling that she had been gazing at him for a long time made her uneasy. Finally she looked away, only to see multiple images of him in the dark mirrors on the posts: his back, one-quarter profile, half-profile, three-quarters profile. Each one was shown from only one angle, but there were so many of him from all directions that it seemed to be an endless image of him coming at her. It was so real and yet utterly unreal, and she had trouble telling the reflections from the real him. The mystifying sensation she'd had ever since their first meeting returned.

When he stood before her forcing her to look up, she was finally convinced that it was really him.

She greeted him casually and invited him to sit, but her heart was racing and her face was getting hot. As she rattled off a series of titles and introduced her friends to him, General Manager So-and-so's wife, Section Head So-and-so's daughter, etc., she could not keep from thinking that she should have changed out of her suit and blouse before coming to the café, because she knew that he had always liked her in more feminine clothes.

She tossed out one company and title after another, careful not to make mistakes. Mrs. Chen, whose husband was the Taiwan representative of an American fried chicken and hamburger firm; Mrs. Wu, whose husband was chairman of the board of a life insurance company; Miss Zhang, the youngest daughter of the chairman of the board of some enterprise, and so on. Her heartbeat quickened and she felt her smiling face beginning to quiver. Try as she might, she still got one title wrong; it should have been Dongqi Department Store, not Yuandong Department Store. Correcting herself, she quickly added that it was the first company to have a Japanese partner. At the grand opening the surge of shoppers had caused a huge traffic jam in the Eastern District, prompting the city to send more than a hundred traffic policemen to maintain order.

The women, married or not, all sat up and took notice. They knew he was the newest real estate tycoon, whose total worth was several billions; he would surely be the topic of conversation at their next social. To be sure, they would talk about him in a nonchalant manner—Lin Xigeng wasn't as imposing as people said; or, he was nice and polite, to which someone would be sure to respond by saying, Mrs. So-and-so, he was only nice to you. With others, he was a different person.

Lin nodded to each of them while handing out his business cards. Yinghong knew he wasn't paying much attention, until Ms. Lin was mentioned; then she detected something in his eyes and sensed that he must know who Ms. Lin was. But he just kept smiling, joining in the conversation every once in a while and never initiating any topics on his own. Yinghong thought he must be feeling awkward, and the odd discomfort he had displayed at that late-night snack joint was now turning into restlessness.

She was sitting so close to him she could hear him shift in his chair or change his posture. He crossed one leg, but quickly drew it back. Then he took out a cigarette and lit up, without even inquiring if the ladies would mind, totally ignoring etiquette. No one objected, but he quickly snubbed it out. Yinghong was too busy to notice if he'd switched to a different brand.

Equally uneasy, she began to talk, faster and faster, and even attempted a joke to erase the uneasiness. She was not unaware that she was saying too much and laughing too loudly at such an occasion, but she simply could not control herself.

Then he caught her off guard by suddenly standing up and saying he had business to attend to. The surprise sent stabbing pains through her heart, though she was still conscious of the popular romantic song being played on violin and piano by the live performers. She maintained her smile as he said good-bye to all the women before leaving.

Several years later, Yinghong would be entertaining guests in their luxurious home (Lin would be absent, as usual), at a time when the government official Ms. Lin had been living with would have just stepped down from his position, yet was still considered a force to be reckoned with in the complex political scene. Everyone present continued to treat Ms. Lin with special attention, but, of course, by now they were also flattering Yinghong.

She would smile as she listened to the pleasant and yet proper flattering words. It might have been the group of female guests, all with a similar background, or the languid air of the damp spring weather, or even the fragrance of lilies wafting through the house, but she was reminded of the day at the European style café and their chance encounter.

Sitting in her meticulously decorated house, she was forced to believe that it was precisely at the moment when he stood up to leave that she made up her mind. She wanted him, and would do anything and pay any price to have him, for that was the first time in her life that a man could repeatedly get up and walk away from her, and with such determination that nothing would change his mind.

TWO

Her first truly indelible memory of her mother was in the year she passed the exam for the provincial girl's middle school.

When the new students registered, the school conducted the customary hair-length inspection. School regulations stipulated that all female students must keep the length of their hair short, not reaching below their earlobes, which meant they would have newly shaven napes. For several days, Father had shown strong displeasure with the hair-length regulation. He was able to accept the requirement for school uniforms, but not the forced haircut that gave teenage girls an ugly appearance with the stubby ends in back looking like the rear end of a chicken. In fact, he was so upset he cursed repeatedly, using the Japanese word *bakayaro*, which was rare in his daily speech.

"I should have sent you to Japan earlier. With your two brothers there, and your Sixth Aunt in Tokyo, you'd have plenty of people to look after you. And you're not like me, who has to stay here as a hostage . . ."

Mother coughed to cut him off, and then went up to close the windows facing the lily pond, while telling Yinghong to return to Lotus Pavilion to review her English lessons. Yinghong acknowledged her mother's instruction and got up to leave, when Father said unhappily:

"If Ayako cuts her hair, Otosan won't want to see her again."

The moment she stepped out of Flowing Pillow Pavilion, Mother shut the doors behind her. Father had never said anything so severe to her before; she forced back her tears and, standing outside the door, was at a loss as to where to go. Then she heard her father complain in rapid Japanese about the educational system, with the names of some famous political figures thrown in.

When preparing for the entrance exam, all the students had been told that, in addition to the written test, there would be an oral exam that might involve current affairs. Having been told to memorize the names of important political figures, she had copied down all the names her teacher wrote on the blackboard, filling up a whole page of her notebook. Besides foreign officials such as the U.S. President Eisenhower and Secretary of State Dulles, she also had to memorize the names of domestic figures, President Chiang Kai-shek, Vice President Chen Cheng, and Premier Yan Jiagan.

She had committed their names to memory just as she had memorized all the subjects she'd be tested on, though it proved to be difficult, nearly impossible. She was only twelve, and in the town of Lucheng, like the rest of the island, there was no television, and newspapers were not commonly available. Furthermore, her father had often pointed at the papers and said:

"No need to read these useless things. They're all lies, made up to deceive people."

As a result, the politicians were new to her and, hence, completely meaningless; but because of the exam, she had forced herself to memorize the names, from the president to all his ministers.

She was surprised to hear the name of a minister she had memorized pop up in her father's tirade, so she stayed put and listened carefully. But he lowered his voice, and all she could hear through the heavy door of Flowing Pillow Pavilion was the angry tone in words she couldn't make out.

To everyone's surprise, Father had displayed such a strong objection to her new hairstyle that even her mother didn't dare take her to her favorite beauty shop, Eastman, on Zhongshan Road in town, for Mother's usual stylist, Lina, to cut off Yinghong's long hair. Many years later, in the United States, when Yinghong came across articles on modern Taiwanese history, she thought back to that day and realized that her father's objection at the time clearly was not limited to her haircut.

"If Ayako kept her hair, the school would not allow her to attend. Then Otosan would teach Ayako himself. Ayako would not learn the useless things they teach at school; instead Otosan would give Ayako real knowledge and there would be no need to believe in their lies."

Father kept repeating these words, in a calm but determined voice, and as the registration date drew near, Yinghong began to feel anxious, fearful even.

She had been taught to follow Father's every word. Back in elementary school, when her teacher had sometimes presented different views, she had always sided with her father. But with this matter regarding the hair, she knew she had no choice but to follow the school's rules.

On the night before registration, her mother brought Mudan over and wrapped her shoulders in a piece of navy-blue cloth printed with two large cranes with spread-wings. With a pair of scissors from Japan, Mother deftly cut off her long hair and then wrapped the shorn hair in a narrow white band of the type normally used to make elastic bands for pants, before handing the scissors to Mudan.

"Why don't you finish up and trim the hair?" Mother said with noticeable apprehension.

One summer afternoon shortly before she left for Japan, Mother took a bundle wrapped in navy-blue cloth from a black lacquered drawer with embossed human figures. After carefully laying the bundle out on the bed, she opened it to reveal prints of two giant cranes, whose white tails were tipped with yellow and green. On the white cranes was scattered a small cluster of long hair that had turned dark brown and lost its luster. Gathered in a yellowed band, the hair was a mess, with tangled fine ends.

"I cut your hair but had no confidence in myself, so I slept badly that night. The next day I asked Otosan how you would be able to study in Japan without middle and high school diplomas."

"Of course Otosan knew it had to be done; it was just that . . . you must understand how he felt, Ayako."

Yinghong remembered her long, beautiful hair, which Mudan had often praised, saying how a woman with fine hair like gold filigree was destined to live an easy life as the mistress of a wealthy family. Yinghong's was just like that—fine, satin-shiny hair that was soft when you held it in your hand. The hair, with a brown sheen, looked like threads of gold when the sun shone on it.

"Back then I was afraid Otosan would blame me for taking matters into my own hands. So after giving you the haircut, I explained to him that I'd just trimmed it shorter so you wouldn't look different from the others."

"When you came home with hair regulation length, short enough to show your earlobes, I told him it had been done by the school's military instructor."

Yinghong's hair had grown a bit by the time she graduated from high school; naturally wavy, it was black and thick, no longer golden and fine, as in her childhood, which prompted Mudan to complain that thick hair can suck away all of a woman's good fortune. Yinghong responded with a smile, for she liked her hair that way, and, besides, it was just like her mother's.

"I wasn't afraid of taking responsibility, nor did I want you to help me deceive your father. All I wanted was to give him an excuse to vent his anger. He could fault me or the military instructor, either one, which would give him a way out. It would have hurt his feelings if he'd known that I'd cut your hair and was not on his side. He'd suffered enough, and I simply couldn't bring myself to make him feel more alone. And this matter with the hair was a particularly touchy issue with him."

As she went on, Mother's voice regained its usual cheerfulness.

"You're a grown-up now, Ayako, so I can tell you this with a sense of relief."

"I understand, Okasan," Yinghong said with dutiful respect.

Shortly after they got back together, he left space between them in his Rolls Royce. On hot summer days, she was in the habit of wearing her long hair up, secured in the back with hairpins. But in the car, with its arctic air-conditioning blasting, she removed the pins and shook her head to let the long tresses cascade down like a waterfall. It now covered her exposed shoulders and back, and the inside of the car was infused with the clean orchid fragrance of the newly washed hair.

She knew he was fond of seeing her hair loose like that. As expected, he was unable to keep from reaching over to grasp her hair.

"I like women with unshaven underarms," he whispered almost incoherently. "Taiwanese women these days like to imitate the foreigners and shave the hair under their arms. They say that social etiquette demands it."

She responded with an alluring smile, which he took as an encouragement.

"You have so much black and soft hair," he continued. "I wonder what your body hair is like . . ."

Like him, she was becoming aroused, but she sat up with an exaggerated gesture of determination. He stopped touching her hair, which she gathered and pinned up again.

"My uncle says that sales are going well at the development project you two are working on," she said to change the subject, but leaned slightly into his arms.

"You've been clever ever since childhood, but a bit of a busybody. Your hands are good at learning whatever you want to do, and family and friends called you *jiapo*, meaning you like to meddle in others' business." Mother often said to her.

Mudan would not allow her to help with work around Lotus Garden, except when she had permission from her mother. But Yinghong enjoyed pitching in with household chores, particularly during holidays and festivals, when they needed to prepare sacrifices, slaughter chickens and ducks, steam rice cakes, and fry sweet desserts. Naturally she usually made a mess, which so annoyed Mudan that the maid felt like striking out, but couldn't, so she'd sit by the stove, stewing in her anger, ignoring Mother's summons.

Each year, when Mudan's husband, Luohan, returned from his hometown of Dingfanpo, a village not far from Lucheng, he brought back broods of chicks and ducklings. The fuzzy little birds would be kept in a small hilly spot outside Lotus Garden. Yinghong would check on them several times a day, each time secretly taking uncooked rice for them. The way she littered the place with rice, Mudan could not stop mumbling "Amita Buddha, what a crime!" over the wastefulness. When the chicks and ducklings grew bigger, their soft downy feather turning stiff until they were ugly, they no longer appealed to Yinghong, who stopped paying them any attention.

Some time passed before she was reminded of the chickens and ducks, so she strolled into the duck pens, where she was met by a large duck with a red head and crimson face, typical of the local breed. She reached out to touch it, but before she made contact, she was given a vicious peck. The shock and pain sent her scurrying, leaving the pen door unlatched and setting loose all the ducks, which now chased after her. Making a rumbling "heh-heh" sound, they waddled unrelenting on her heels.

All she could do was let out a loud wail.

The pecking had broken the skin but drew no blood, and soon it was just a painful bruise that took a week to disappear. With winter solstice came the season for tonics, and the ducks were slaughtered one by one. Most of the time, Luohan was in charge of slitting the throats to bleed the birds; Mudan would then dunk them in scalding water to make plucking them easier. That year Yinghong helped Mudan pluck the guilty bird clean, while cursing angrily:

"I'm going to pluck your feathers till you're dead and gone. Now do you feel like pecking me again?"

Her mother just smiled and let her be. That was how Yinghong earned the right to pluck feathers when they slaughtered chickens and ducks.

Mudan considered her an inconvenience, but could not chase her away, letting her play all she wanted, until her clothes were soaked. Mudan had to help her change, which naturally drew more complaints from the maid.

After New Year's came the next festival on the ninth day of the first lunar month, the birthday of the Heavenly King, a major festival in Lucheng that required five separate sacrificial items: two fish, two chickens, two ducks, a pig's head, and duck eggs. The preparation was too much for Mudan alone, who had to take care of other chores after fishing one of the ducks out of the scalding hot water. Later, when she returned to work on the duck, she found that Yinghong had beaten her to it by plucking the bird clean.

"You naughty girl! What a cursed girl. The duck for the Heavenly King's birthday must have tail feathers. You naughty, naughty girl. How are we supposed to offer it after you've plucked out all the feathers? What a cursed girl."

The enraged Mudan picked up a broom nearby and came after Yinghong, who froze on the spot, for she'd never seen Mudan so angry before. The maid raised the broom, but could not bring herself to beat Yinghong, so she let it fall from her hands, cursing her the whole time.

The clamor brought Mother, who was cleaning the sacrificial table upstairs. After hearing both sides, she said in a gentle tone but with a serious look:

"Make sure you ask for permission next time, understand?"

Yinghong nodded, but couldn't keep from defending herself.

"I'll just put the feathers back," she muttered.

"Put them back? Go ahead, see if you can!" Mudan said, her voice raised.

Yinghong squatted by the duck, picked up some of the feathers, and tried to stick them onto its tail. The pores on the warm duck had shrunk, making it impossible to stick in the feathers with their soft, thin, hollow quills.

"I've never heard of people sticking feathers back on a bird," Mudan muttered. "How can we offer a duck with a naked butt to the Heavenly King?"

Now Yinghong was in a true panic.

"It's all right. We'll try some others."

Mother crouched beside her and began to rummage through the pile of feathers. Soon she found some fierce-looking wing feathers, with solid quills, which were easily inserted into the duck's tail.

"Never in my life have I seen anyone replace tail feathers with wing feathers to offer to the Heavenly King. That's ridiculous." Mudan still would not let her off the hook.

"That's all right," Mother said to Mudan in a light-hearted tone. She smiled at Yinghong. "It's fine now."

By dusk, all the sacrificial items had been washed clean; the chickens, the pig's head, and the duck eggs, along with the ducks, were neatly placed in a large iron wok resting on a big stove, where they were parboiled and then fished out. With steam still rising from the birds, Mother removed the feathers she'd stuck in earlier and replaced them with several tail feathers she'd washed that afternoon. The tail feathers, which had been boiled in hot water, went in easily through pores now enlarged, once the duck was cooked through.

After a long afternoon of trepidation, Yinghong was finally able to smile. And she never again forgot to keep the tail feathers on sacrificial ducks for the Heavenly King's birthday. Her mother commented lightly:

"You won't make the same mistake next time," she said quietly. "Ayako needs to learn to do housework. If you're lucky, you may not need to do it yourself, but you should know how. That way, your servants won't try to show you up, and you'll have the authority over them. Understand?"

Yinghong nodded quietly and looked down at her hands.

She had small hands. A young girl in the process of turning into a woman, she still had the hands of a child. As she never had to do heavy work, her knuckles kept their size and shape and her hands remained soft and smooth. Even after she'd grown up, her hands remained the picture of "boneless soft."

On that afternoon, as they prepared the sacrifice, she looked down at her fair, slender hands and, with full knowledge that she was the favorite child, asked her mother in a childish voice:

"Okasan, can there be women who never have to do housework through-out their lives?" She paused and thought before continuing, "Or will there be people like Mudan, who do all the work for them?"

"Ayako," Mother fixed her gaze on her. "Life goes on for a long time, and you should never say anything with such certainty. No one knows what will happen in the future. You could live in a big house or a tall building one day, and have nothing left the next."

There was a hint of sorrow in her voice. At home, they followed Fa-ther's dictate to use only Taiwanese or Japanese. Mother spoke Japanese in a gentle, clear voice, and, with the usual *"a," "na," "ni," "ye,"* and *"hai,"* sounded tender and charming in the Tokyo accent prized by those who knew Japanese well. So at the moment, she seemed to be whispering a del-icate sense of sorrow.

On that afternoon, she was surprised to hear a different tone in her mother's voice, so Yinghong snapped her head up to look at her. The face must have displayed that sorrow, with a subtle frown and lowered eyes, but when Yinghong looked up, her mother was already returning to her usual bright, warm self, the frown replaced by a smile at the corners of her mouth.

It was past noon, and Mother had been busy all morning. She had combed her hair and tucked it behind her ears before wrapping her head in a dark blue triangular head scarf sprinkled with small flowers, not a single strand going astray. The loose dress she wore around the house was neat and spotless. Her face showed a tinge of red, from the busy work and the heat from the stove, but mother had maintained her composure and proper demeanor even at a busy time like this; she had quickly recovered from the sorrowful look when Yinghong scrutinized her face. All this proved un-usual to Yinghong, who couldn't stop staring at her mother as if in a trance.

"Let's go see how the sacrificial table is coming along," Mother sug-gested calmly.

In Yinghong's recollections, her mother had always looked gentle and reserved, rarely showing emotion, during all those years she was in ele-mentary school and even when Father was laid up in bed.

Her middle school summer uniform consisted of a white short-sleeve blouse and a black pleated skirt. The collar of the blouse was what Mother called a "komika collar," with pointed tips turning outward, while the skirt was made of coarse black cotton with inch-wide pleats created by tailoring and ironing. It required vigilance and constant ironing to maintain the pleats; otherwise, the hems would lose the pleat lines and spread out, like a puffy skirt.

When she wore the black skirt, Mother was adamant that she mustn't let the hem roll like waves when she walked. When she sat, she was to gather the pleats first, and mustn't shift her body too freely. That was the only way to keep the shape of the skirt after a day at school. After she took it off upon returning home, Mudan would hang it up immediately.

At night when Mudan finished all the household chores, she would take the skirt back to her own room, where she removed the straw mat and, after carefully gathering the pleats, place the skirt on the wooden bed planks. Then she'd replace the mat and lie down to sleep on it. The following day, when she got up, the pleats would be nice and sharp, as if ironed, each and every pleat retaining its shape.

"I want Ah-hong to be the best student on campus with the neatest uniform," Mudan said proudly.

It was an interesting novelty to discover that lying down to sleep helped preserve the pleats in her skirt, so Yinghong asked Mudan to let her try it. Imagine her surprise when Mudan pointed and mocked her with a hearty laugh:

"You're such a little unruly monkey! I've slept next to you before and, boy, you squirm like a fat worm all night long. If you slept on your skirt, you'd never be able to find it the next morning, let alone keep the pleats."

This effectively shut Yinghong up, since she could recall how Mudan could go to sleep in one position and wake up in the same one the next morning, not moving an inch.

The school had requirements for the winter uniform also, which included long pants, a jacket, and long-sleeve shirts. In addition, she came into possession of a few "chemises," which, according to her mother, meant underwear.

Sleeveless and collarless, the chemises were long enough to reach the knees, though shorter than her uniform black skirt. They were usually made of fine linen, with a slight curve around the waist. Mother instructed her to put the chemise on before her school uniform.

Her first day of middle school was in September, when it was still hot. Upon returning home, she immediately took off the uniform and unbuckled her Girl Scout belt, and, wearing only the chemise, was eager to go to Flowing Pillow Pavilion to tell Father what had happened at school that day. The moment she stepped out of her room, she ran into her mother, who said:

"You're not a little girl anymore and you can't run around in your chemise. Go put something over it."

Yinghong lowered her head. The sleeveless and collarless chemise exposed her skinny arms and bony shoulders. On the slender, flat body of an undeveloped twelve-year-old, she sensed the signs of femininity, which made her blush, and quickly went back inside to put on the dress she wore around the house.

Mother had her own chemises, and she never wore them outside. Yinghong liked to rummage through Mother's stuff. The drawers in the black-lacquered armoire painted green, light brown, and vermillion were filled with her mother's chemises. They were made of different fabrics—satin, silk, and poplin—all in white, but in different shades. With the satin, it was a bright milky white with a high sheen; the silk ones had a hint of beige, a light yellow showing through the white, and the poplin ones were a clean white, light and airy.

The chemises had layers of lace edging at the hems, the slits, and the necklines. Sleeveless and collarless, they had shoulder straps made of thin strips of horizontal fabric or lace, which were exquisitely embroidered with fine eyelets to hold up the low-cut, V-neck satin, silk, or poplin chemises, with or without a curved waist.

Yinghong liked to bury her face in the drawerful of chemises. The cool, fine fabrics always made her shudder when they touched her skin, as if brushed by a light breeze, accompanied by a subtle, nearly imperceptible fragrance. When she was older, she learned that that came from the empty perfume bottles her mother placed in the drawer, not from the chemises themselves.

Yet she'd never seen her mother in any of those gorgeous chemises. As a middle school girl, she didn't dare ask her mother about them, for she knew Mother would be unhappy with her if she learned that Yinghong rummaged through her drawers. Besides, she wanted to savor the pleasure of these wondrous pieces by herself. It wasn't until she was about to leave for college in Japan that she asked her mother in a feigned casual tone in one of their conversations. Why had she never seen her wearing those fancy chemises?

"Do I have any of those?" Mother thought hard before finally remembering. "I bought them overseas before I got married. I did wear them, before and shortly after I married your father. Then, what happened? I probably stopped wearing them after that incident with your Otosan."

Yinghong knew that Xigeng was besotted with anything refined and luxurious, partly because he had good taste, and partly because he understood that the greatest refinement and elegance meant something that could not be bought at any price.

She had let him touch her, little by little and only her arms, head, behind her ears and lips, all places usually not covered by clothes. When she decided to allow his hand under her clothes, she picked out satin underwear that had been washed once only to soften the fabric. The underwear had been called chemises before she grew into a woman, she recalled.

He had an 18,000-square-foot penthouse apartment that came with a living room decorated by a designer in the French style of pastel blue and lilac, and, yes, intersected with gray. It was in this room that she seduced him, though she made sure that he took the initiative of putting his hand under her clothes. She let him unbutton her blouse but would only allow him to touch her shoulders.

What was exposed was her white satin chemise, whose fabric was soft but thick enough to reveal nothing. She had made sure of that, and was certain he would not see anything, except for the lacy trim around the neck. To be sure, the eyelets on the lacy trim would betray her by revealing a bit of décolletage, and he could get a glimpse of her breasts. But would he see everything? No. She needn't worry; the dense satin fabric was the ideal cover-up. No one, not even an experienced man like him, could detect anything by simply looking.

She knew that he retained a degree of deference toward her; in fact he was even a bit in awe of her. He held himself back for the time being and acted decorously, because she came from the Lucheng Zhu family, and because the large amount of delicate lace decorating the fine satin underwear created a lavish impression. It was never her intention to give in to him, not yet, so at this stage she had only planned to let him see part of her body, along with her beautiful, lacy underwear. The trim wasn't handmade and not all that expensive, but she was certain that he had yet to learn, or might never learn, to tell handmade lace from one made by machine.

Under his gaze, she lowered her head bashfully, but let him gaze at her and her underwear. Naturally she had to stop his advances every once in a while. What went through her mind was how, given her current financial situation, she still could not afford underwear with real handmade lace, the chemise from her childhood.

"You're a grown-up now, not a little girl anymore," Mother had said.

Like most of the kids in Taiwan back then, she had been brought up on the instruction that "children have ears but no mouth," except that it was Mudan, not her parents, who told her that.

Rarely would Father instruct Yinghong with these rustic sayings, and Mother went out quite a bit after Yinghong began middle school. She knew she should never inquire after her parents' whereabouts, but it was clear to her that Mother was the one who ran the household.

And so, besides Father, Mudan was the person she saw most frequently after school; Mudan was also the one who took care of her.

Mudan had been Mother's maid before her marriage but she had forged a close relationship with other servants in Upper House. The first few years after Father's return, Lotus Garden saw few visitors. It was not until Yinghong was a third-grader, the year she wrote that she was born in the last year of the First Sino-Japanese War, that Father began to walk around the garden, and guests made visits.

The first group coming to get news was not her uncles from the Upper House but their maids and servants. Prompted by the country folk's tendency to gossip, they came to see what had been going on in Lotus Garden. Some had been good friends with Mudan and were not afraid to come see her, now that there had been no serious consequences. Soon all the maids and servants had resumed their former relationships with Mudan.

Before coming with Yinghong's mother to the Zhu family, Mudan grew up in Taipei's Dataocheng area, which meant she had lived a different life than the other Zhu family servants, who had been hired from areas near Lucheng. All the Zhu servants agreed on one thing about Mudan—she was a nice person, but she talked too much and was a show-off.

Her tendency to show off had been apparent back when the clan lived in the Upper House together. At the time, the large family shared wells and Mudan had to fetch water every day. The inconvenience often led her to complain:

"We used tap water when we lived in Dataocheng. You turn the faucet and the water flows freely."

It would take Lucheng more than two decades to get tap water, after Yinghong went to Japan and then to the United States to study. So when Mudan mentioned tap water to the other servants in the Upper House, it surely sounded wondrous and unusual, and Mudan did not stop there.

"There was once a soldier from China. When he saw in Dataocheng how we turned the faucet to get tap water to flow out of the wall, he went and bought a faucet and stuck it on his wall, but nothing came out."

When she reached this point of her story, she raised her head and sneered, tossing the bun behind her head around. She said with great contempt:

"What a rube that soldier was. He had no idea that he'd need pipes before he could get tap water. He actually believed he could just drill a hole in the wall and fit the faucet on."

Her audience naturally did not know how and where to bring the water over, so they peppered her with questions, which led to animated discussions.

Yinghong had heard plenty about tap water from Mudan ever since childhood and had asked her mother about details, but she still did not know how the water was brought over to turn into tap water. When she started middle school and gained a bit of basic knowledge, she finally understood, with an explanation from her mother, why Mudan had laughed at the soldier for fitting a faucet to the wall.

At the time, though Mother had been going out frequently, she never neglected Yinghong's education. Yinghong could still recall, many years later, that no matter how busy Mother was, she would never raise her soft, gentle voice, nor would she look hurried. Over those years, she often wore Western-style dresses, usually a short jacket with a long A-line or pencil skirt, occasionally four- or six-panel ones. The jackets and skirts would be made of the same materials with the same patterns, some with lace-trimmed collars, others with thin piping on the jacket pocket, which was definitely not meant for hands; instead, sometimes there would be a Japanese handkerchief made with fine linen and decorated with multiple flowers whose pink tips peeked out of the pocket.

Unlike the schoolteachers, particularly those from the Mainland, mother never wore *qipao*, nor would she wear Taiwanese-style clothes. Only Western one-piece dresses or a jacket-and-skirt combination. There sometimes were hats made of the same material as the dresses; they were tiny round or boat-shaped hats trimmed with lace or veils, which she would wear a bit to one side.

Mother wore a hat of the same material as her dress occasionally when she went out, and it was when she was securing the hat to her hair with a bobby pin that she laughed brightly over the stories about tap water that Yinghong had heard from Mudan.

"The tap water at your maternal grandpa's house wasn't that wondrous. It was not like the houses in the West, where you have faucets in the kitchen and bathroom and get water whenever you turn the faucet." Mother was still laughing as she continued: "Back at the house, the neighborhood families had to share a faucet. The water would come late in the afternoon, and each family had to fetch its water in a bucket and take it back to fill troughs and vats."

Then she turned from her mirror to face Yinghong, before saying in a serious tone, though still in her soft, gentle Tokyo Japanese:

"Don't mention this to Mudan or she will lose face."

Yinghong nodded, like a good girl.

"And don't bring it up with other servants either, all right? It doesn't matter how tap water flows out of the faucet. It's harmless. Never put everything out in the open, understand?"

Yinghong was not old enough to completely understand why Mother did not want her to explain things, but she was not too young to know that she should not give others the opportunity to laugh at Mudan. The strict rules she grew up with taught her to answer obediently in Japanese:

"I understand, Okasan."

Soon after that, Mother planned a trip back to Dataocheng and wanted Mudan to go along, which was a rare occurrence. With that trip back home, Mudan returned with more stories, this time about rice kernels.

"Someone from Dataocheng went to the South Sea, a long way away. I heard that the rice kernels over there were several hundred times larger than ours. Only one kernel is needed to cook a bowl of rice, no gruel but a regular rice meal."

Mudan gestured emphatically with her hands:

"Imagine how easy life would be. One kernel to make a bowl of rice. You'd only need several kernels each meal to make enough for the whole family."

A tiny person, Mudan had large hands and feet. When she gestured with her big bony hands, it looked as if a kernel of rice could truly make a giant bowl of rice.

Some people were amazed by her stories while others doubted their reliability and began spreading gossip about her. When she got wind of that, naturally she was unhappy and convinced that they didn't believe her because she wasn't a local. Often she would be heard to complain:

"I'm not from here, so I'm a stranger. Those Lucheng people have terrible customs, so many rules, and they're so hard to please. I never know what to do."

One time Yinghong happened to walk by when Mudan was airing her usual complaint, so Mudan started on her:

"Like you," she pointed at Yinghong, "you're a Lucheng local."

"So what if I'm a Lucheng local?" Yinghong retorted.

"You're just a Lucheng local." Mudan had not meant anything unpleasant by this comment, and did not know what to say next. Deflated, she could only repeat, "You're a Lucheng local, from the Zhu family, First Young Miss Zhu, with great learning."

The maids nearby all covered their mouths and giggled.

A month and seventeen days after Lin Xigeng left, the new construction project jointly developed by Yinghong's uncle and Lin was about to move to the sales phase, and, as a result, she and Lin saw each other frequently; it was not until after the extreme pain over the separation and the waiting began to subside that was she finally able to think straight, that her mind had begun to work again.

Finally she was able to evaluate how, on the night he left, he found an unusual way to say good-bye by having her submit to him by crouching down to kiss his erect penis. How had he managed to get her to do his bidding?

She had special feelings for that night; even during her most painful moments, when she couldn't think straight, she continued to cherish, and repeatedly savor, every minute of it. It was her way of establishing an intimate connection with him, one that had included bodily contact.

When he was about to leave, the pain in her heart forced her to refuse to let his hand under her clothes, even as she told herself that at a moment like this she would not be able to enjoy the pleasures of the flesh. She avoided and resisted his touch.

But then she'd let him guide her into touching him, as she believed that this most precious, this final connection, would help reduce the regret she would feel later.

She'd thought that his desire for bodily contact on that night had also stemmed from a similar wish to cherish the moment for future memory. But a month and seventeen days later she was finally clearheaded enough to realize that his actions had likely not derived from the same longing and love; instead it was probably all to gratify his male desire for possession and basic sexual needs. Gradually it became clear to her that the man who'd come to say good-bye was motivated by his characteristic desire for conquest, and that he would not leave until he'd gotten what he wanted from her.

She was then startled by an awareness that, because she still treasured the love they'd had, she'd denied him the ultimate pleasure, which in turn might be the very reason why he still had feelings for her and that their relationship might not be over after all. At the very least, she had denied him the opportunity to dismiss her casually when her name came up:

"What's the big deal with this woman? I already had my way with her."

No, he had not gotten what he wanted, because she had not consented, so at the moment, she had not lost everything.

But then, as her mind slowly cleared, the desire, the unmistakable bodily hunger returned with a vengeance. In her cherished recollections, she isolated her sorrow over the separation and focused solely on the sensation of his erect penis filling up her mouth, the memory of which produced in her a strong, irrepressible desire.

She began to search among the men who had shown interest in her; she wanted only one man, a married man who had no intention of getting a divorce and, like her, had to be concerned about reputation and would not babble about the relationship. Best, he should come from a different social circle, someone who wanted to be with her but would not create problems or an obstacle between her and Xigeng.

As a woman, she knew from the bottom of her heart that she was still blindly, deeply in love with him, even though she was now able to see that he had wanted her purely out of desire and a need to possess. One month and seventeen days after he left, she finally realized that there would be a prolonged battle between them and that she must not be betrayed by physical needs that came with her recovery.

To be able to wait without rushing into action, she must be sexually gratified, particularly by another man. Only that way could she not be easily overcome by desire, for she knew fully well that, like many other women, the moment she and Lin got back together, she would offer herself to him with gratitude, as a way to seek his promise and gain assurance.

Yinghong was a pretty woman to begin with, and now her desperation made her even more bewitching, for frenzied passion added flames to her large, enchanting eyes. The man responded to her needs as soon as she initiated their second meeting.

It was a man she knew already, nicknamed Teddy Zhang, who was married to the daughter of a textile tycoon. Now in his forties, Teddy was homely and short, but a girlfriend of hers had intimated that he was not only highly competent at work, but virile to the point of being insatiable. She was convinced that he would want more than she to keep it between the two of them, for he was no different than most men in Taiwan who treasured family wealth more than anything else.

Obviously an old hand at this, Teddy picked the most inconspicuous hotel out of the many "rest and recreation" places in a residential area in

Taipei. They arrived at different times and gave the reception desk false names. Everything was done in the dark, for they feared that the hotel might have installed a hidden camera or a peephole in the wall.

Even in the dark, she closed her eyes when she responded to his movements. He was clearly working hard to please her, and yet it was Lin's image that she saw, and she had to bite down hard on her lip to stop herself from calling out his name. Eventually, Teddy's persistent hard work paid off; the purely physical contact brought her enough pleasure that she responded accordingly, though it was not close to earth shattering.

Then, little by little, as they became more familiar with each other's body, she began to fully enjoy the carnal pleasure. She kept her eyes shut and called out Lin's name silently with lips tightly shut. When he brought her to orgasm time after time, she began to moan, and Lin's name escaped from between her teeth in a raspy sound.

They met once a week; the man wanted more, but was not put off when she said no. Yinghong knew that she was only one of his many women, a comforting fact to both of them. But he complained about how, when they were finished, she would get up and get dressed, not even spending a few extra minutes by his side.

She managed to explain why she could not stay at the hotel for long.

In a city crowded with people and endless events, a large number of hotels rose to meet their needs, appearing on every main street, sometimes even reaching into residential alleyways. They were like exploding red torches, each hotel an erotic sea with burning desire, crackling and raging all over the city.

In a medium-size hotel with a hundred or more rooms, there would be five to six hundred couples copulating every day. At their busiest hours, the hotel staff had to rush in to change sheets between couples, piling dirty sheets in the basement like a stack of white mourning couplets still dripping wet from the ink. Quickly another pair of naked bodies lay down on the new sheet, pushing, touching, and grabbing at each other, with nonstop moaning and groaning.

Sexual intercourse that cannot be performed at home is naturally different from the formulaic sex among married couples. Couples paid for the place because they had an urgent need to satisfy their bodily hunger. The hotels were where raging desires converged, creating a sexual vitality that was alluring to anyone who came for the pleasure.

To be expected, these hotels anticipated their customers' need by offering all sorts of stimulants: wall to ceiling mirrors on all sides, massage beds, as well as contraptions or exercise equipment to increase sexual pleasure. On the subtropical island of Taiwan, where summer lasts four months, with temperatures reaching 36 degrees Celsius, some hotels still offered Hawaiian tropical decor or Mediterranean furnishings, all to help arouse their customers.

To avoid the risk of recognition by hotel reception staff after frequenting the same hotel, the man took her to different places, and she went along with no qualms. In the dark, it did not matter if it was the Hawaiian or Mediterranean style; they came for sexual gratification and left after their needs were satisfied.

What she found unbearable was that the man, after getting off her, would want to cuddle. He was obviously a loyal reader of popular books on sex, for he wanted to hug and touch after they were finished. She abhorred such contact, just as she would never let him kiss her. For Yinghong, kissing, caressing, and hugging belonged to those with true love and real connections, while contacts of sexual organs were simply for the gratification of needs.

Of course she knew she couldn't tell him how she felt; no man would like to be reduced to a penis, even if it was a potent one that could give a woman so much pleasure.

She could sense that weekly intense gratification was calming her down; the distress and disquieting mood slowly left her, replaced by a sense of leisure, a serene ease. She knew now she could begin her hunt.

Now that her anxiety was gone and her skin had regained its luster from sexual satisfaction, she looked beautiful and graceful again, the dark circles under her eyes gone. She even devoted time to skin care and makeup, all in order to showcase herself at meetings, where they sat far across from each other.

The development that her uncle and Lin worked on together was nearing the sale stage, which meant nonstop meetings with the sales firm. They needed to position their product, settle on the price per *ping*, calculate the total sale price for each unit, design a promotion strategy, and more.

Lin's wild idea had been to construct a building with more than three hundred vacation homes on a hill outside the city. From his viewpoint, Taiwan's economy had developed to the point where some people would want to invest in a vacation home, a place where they could spend weekends and holidays. He believed that most homeowners could not yet afford to buy a single-family vacation home, and that management and maintenance could pose problems. But businessmen who had made a a fortune in foreign reserves would be interested in buying a second home, since, with a firm understanding that island land is limited, they had the typical Taiwanese penchant for buying. Why couldn't their second home be in a building in the outskirts of town? It would surely be cheaper than a single-family villa and a lot easier to maintain.

"I don't just deal in real estate; I also want to help Taiwan raise the standard of living and change people's views about housing," Lin said with customary confidence. "I want to teach the Taiwanese how to live a high-class lifestyle."

The meetings usually took place in Lin's office. True to his boastful nature, the table was a dozen meters long in his company headquarters, which occupied an entire building in Taipei's prized Eastern District. Yinghong's presence unsettled him somewhat, and that intensified his efforts to display everything—his decisiveness, his wealth, and his power—like putting on a show. But when he had to make a critical decision tied to the outcome of billions of dollars in real estate investments, he turned reserved and pragmatic, devoting all his energy and concentration to work and planning. In such situations, he would look glum and inscrutable, ignoring her to the point that she virtually ceased to exist.

Sitting at a distance from him, her heart beat violently, blood raced through her veins. As someone born with the natural talent of a leader, he would listen quietly and then quickly and accurately identify the central issues; when it came to final decisions, he rarely wavered and could convince anyone with his powers of persuasion. She felt the dreamlike sensation returning. They may have been worlds apart, yet she sat there, waiting with grace and beauty.

Once they were back together, her feminine side resurfaced and she could not stop commenting on his domineering stance and the resolve with which he made decisions during meetings, to which he responded with a loud, hearty laugh.

"I've got you fooled. Most of the time, I'm scared witless when I make decisions."

She looked up at him, incomprehension registering in her eyes.

"And I can't let my apprehension show; if I did, everyone in the company would lose their calm." Then his gaze turned cold. "Usually I feel like I'm a gambler, betting on data and analysis. I chalk up all my wins to mere luck."

Profound compassion and love led her to rest his head against her bosom, as sorrow and sweetness welled up inside.

Yinghong sat and waited at the long table that separated them as if they were worlds apart. When his gaze occasionally fell on her, she was poised, calmly flashing him a mysterious smile, though she knew she could not maintain that pose for long. He saw her frequently, easily, without having to make any special effort, so the torment of longing would be reduced, and when that happened, everything would become insignificant, pointless even.

She knew she could never be a rival to his career, and that she must wait till the vacation home project reached a certain stage before making her move.

Fifteen days and two months after they broke up, she drove back to Lotus Garden alone one late afternoon when the sky was painted with a brilliant sunset. She had told Mudan that she'd made last-minute plans to spend a few days in the south with a Mr. Huang; she left a stack of important documents about the building site, redesign certificates that would be needed the following day, with Mudan, telling her that if Mr. Lin, who had often phoned her in the past, called to ask about the certificates, she must remember to complain about how the young mistress had impulsively put everything aside and gone on a pleasure trip to the south with a Mr. Huang.

She was sure that only Lin had her home phone number, and that his natural course of action on such an urgent matter would be to call to express his displeasure. Then he would find out that she was vacationing with a Mr. Huang.

As predicted, Lin did hear all about her trip with Mr. Huang, but not via a phone call. It was the always responsible Mudan, who, believing that the documents were too important to hand over to someone from Lin's company, insisted that she needed him, someone she knew, to come to pick them up himself.

On the third day after she returned to work, she called to apologize for the unforeseen inconvenience she'd caused, making sure to add a languishing sweetness to her voice. Lin, who was holding a company meeting, asked that the call be transferred to his office, where he spent a quarter of an hour criticizing her for being irresponsible, indignantly mentioning Mr. Huang several times. He declared rudely that he would pick her up at eleven that night, before hanging up without waiting for her response.

That happened to be the day for her weekly tryst with Teddy. Yinghong and Teddy usually met during lunch or dinner for an hour to ninety minutes, long enough for their activity at the hotel, but not too long, in case his wife called his office and could not find him. That night Teddy had a dinner engagement. Taipei banquets were often set for 6:30, but a 7:00 arrival would not be considered late. Teddy could leave his office at five, which would give them two full hours.

But Lin would be coming to pick her up at eleven, a mere four hours after she had disentangled herself from Teddy's body. She hesitated, unsure if she ought to cancel her date with Teddy and, in fact, terminate their hotel meetings. The thought made her smile, a bleak smile that emerged from thin, tightly shut red lips, a soundless expression of what she was feeling.

Lin was jealous, and that put her in a state of heightened agitation; she was jittery all day, unable to settle down; losing her concentration, she frequently stopped working and stood up to pace her office. Luckily her uncle was abroad.

In her mind, the trysts with Teddy were her only chance of stopping the extreme tension and calming her down; the physical exhaustion temporarily counteracted her anxiety and unease. So she waited for the gratification that came with the sensation of being filled, her excitement now turning into waves of urgent need. She felt an eager, burning expansion somewhere deep inside, as if inhaling and exhaling one mouthful of hot air after another. Between the intake and expulsion of hot breaths, she would absorb satisfying penetration and movement, feeling fire, heat, and a throbbing sensation, in and out, waiting, lurking.

They knew each other well enough that, as soon as they were in the room, they began to take off their clothes. Even Teddy, a true believer in sexual theories, no longer felt the need for foreplay or taking off her clothes for her. On that late afternoon, she turned around and straddled him the moment they lay down.

It might have been the position that made her feel that she was on the offense. Her insides, moving in and out rhythmically, felt like a long narrow passage that compressed, pushed, advanced, and exposed the outside while awaiting the moment of penetration. She could feel that part of her body swell up and move forward, rising up as if to snatch the man's ready-for-action erection.

Then the prey was completely encircled; she breathed in deeply from the tight, filling sensation, but what happened next made her feel cheated.

The man was working harder because of her uncharacteristic eagerness, but she felt let down. It was like a sky full of exploding stars sinking into water, down to an unfathomable bottom, where the gratification of contact died off instantaneously. An urgent need remained inside, and it was not to be easily mollified by that thing between the man's legs.

So she became more demanding and the man responded accordingly. His familiarity with her body meant that he knew how to please her with the greatest result, but Yinghong felt like a beast with an unquenchable thirst, gulping down the source from the wellspring of life but never truly feeling sated.

To be sure, she felt sexual pleasure, and the resultant lethargy and exhaustion began to spread to every part of her body from that particular spot. She laid down her weighty body, as the comfort from the pleasure surged in waves, rushing against her. She split into two people, one moaning and enjoying herself, while the other lurked and waited with a hunger somewhere inside, like a beast lingering in the dark with glinting eyes, announcing an anxiety and desire that was purely physical but could not be satisfied by mere bodily contact.

Lin rang her doorbell that night at 11:05, and was greeted by the exquisite face of a languid woman who had just awakened from a nap. Her newly washed hair spread out loosely; she had pinned one side of the thick, unruly tresses to the back, leaving the curly hair on the other side to billow across an ivory shoulder exposed by her scanty summer dress. She had the lethargic look that came from a long soak in a tub; even without perfume she smelled refreshingly redolent, with a pleasant warmth.

He gave the driver a street name, but she was too flustered to get it. He turned and said, clearly wanting to explain:

"I've long wanted to take a break, so I flew to France, where I spent two days in Cannes and Nice alone. It wasn't all that interesting, so I flew to New York to spend a day there before coming back here."

She laughed, despite herself.

"Doesn't that mean you spent your vacation on airplanes?"

"That's right. I love flying, first class, of course. Who says travel can't be limited to flying in planes?"

His familiar bombast put her at ease. She was willing to accept that he hadn't come to see her for a while because he had been on vacation flying first class between Taiwan, France, and the United States. The Rolls Royce glided smoothly through the dark city with thinning traffic, the thick glass blocking out the noise outside, and she was feeling the same dreamy, unreal sensation again.

His short-sleeved shirt, she noticed, was clearly from a well-known Italian designer. The rolled-up sleeves were obviously intended to give the shirt a casual flair.

Streetlights and neon signs streamed into the car, painting his muscular arms in different colors. Those were not the chiseled muscles of an athlete who trained intensively, nor were they the strong arms of a young, inexperienced boy. They were simply the arms of a fully grown man, comfortable, mature, and solid.

Wanting to break the ice, Yinghong asked casually:

"Have you been exercising lately?"

"I've played a few rounds of golf, but with my workload, I couldn't gain weight if I tried."

He continued, as always, once he'd gotten into the mood of talking:

"I went to a sauna once. It was a club where the usual customers were CEOs, but all I saw was a roomful of ugly male bodies, not a single chairman of the board."

That made her laugh.

"So I told myself I can't be like them, at least for now; I couldn't stand it."

As the conversation continued, the car rolled out of the lit streets and entered darkness, while the ride got noticeably bumpy. Without turning around, the driver asked for more directions, and as he turned the wheel, she saw a large plot of quiet land under the brilliant moon and stars.

The car slowed down and drove around the edge of land that seemed to go on forever in the dark. Without streetlights, the inky night only intensified the feeling that the land was boundless, as if it continued to expand, rising up in the city where an inch of land was worth an ounce of gold. It had an absurd but imposing air about it.

Then Lin spoke up in the dark car, a note of agitation creeping into his voice:

"Land is meant to be walked on. Come on, let's get out and take a walk around."

They stepped out onto a flattened area that was still littered with crushed rock and chunks of sandy soil. She was wearing a pair of Italian sandals with thin, high heels, making her wobble as she walked and forcing her to hold on to Lin's arm with both hands. His powerful muscles and the sensation from his warm veins gave her the feeling that he was a man she could depend on.

As she steadied herself, she stood with him on the vast, newly paved land; he raised his head and said with smug satisfaction.

"On the land beneath your feet, I will build a real Taiwanese landmark, a plaza for the Taiwanese people, like the Arc de Triomph and the Champs Élysées in France, or the Empire State Building and Fifth Avenue in America. But it will have Taiwanese characteristics, fully representative of Taiwan."

The land that appeared boundless in the dark night did have the impressive potential for a grand dream. Lin continued expansively:

"This plaza will be surrounded by an eight-lane highway all around, with high rises lining each side. I don't want people to think that Taiwan can only afford to build seven-story apartment buildings or housing units. We Taiwanese can build skyscrapers like everyone else; we will have a structure with dozens of stories, with Taiwanese characteristics as well as international flair."

"What will that be, something that is both Taiwanese and modern?" Yinghong asked cautiously, in order not to dampen his enthusiasm. "That has been a cultural issue in dispute for some time."

"That's the architect's job. I'll give him the best working conditions, and if I can't do it, no one can."

She laughed softly over his confidence, before continuing with a bit of a taunt:

"Cultural issues can be hard to deal with, probably not things that money alone can solve; they need time to develop before you see results."

As she talked, she realized that Lin was not paying attention to what she was saying. Standing with his legs slightly apart under the evening sky, he planted his feet firmly on the land, looking determined, exact, and erect. They were surrounded by darkness, except for an occasional spot of light in the distance. It turned chilly on that late, midsummer night when a wind blew over the land, quietly and slowly flapping his light cotton shirt. When he took out his lighter to light a cigarette, she saw a different face in the flickering red flame. Behind the lenses of glasses that added a refined look to his face were eyes that betrayed a disturbing look of cold distance.

That scared her a bit, and made her lean gently toward him.

He reached out, spun her around and pressed her up against him. Before she had time to react, his lips were on hers.

He was obviously skilled at this; his predatory style of kissing completely won her over. In the meantime he began to expand his territory, moving to her ears and neck; she could not and did not put up any resistance, except for her vague awareness that no man could give her such a thrilling sensation with his lips alone.

I had just removed myself from under Teddy. After prolonged and violent movement, I felt somewhat raw down below; the physical gratification lingered. But under Lin Xigeng's touch, a different surge of desire came from somewhere and reared its head like a snake.

I shocked even myself. In the past I could not have imagined how bodily desire could be like a bottomless pit lying in wait somewhere in my body; as a woman, I had not known of its existence over the years, and it was only now, when aroused, that I knew it was there.

It was such a special feeling of being aroused, surrounded, and satisfied that, at the moment of exploding pleasure, I sensed another self scrutinizing every part of my body before its eyes came to rest on a woman's most private and secret part, attempting to find the inner source of that stirring.

I experienced a kind of pleasure that came from something other than genital contact; I was breathing hard and my face was flushed, as a driving heat enveloped me, raising tiny beads of sweat all over my body. I thought I must be drenched, but not so; the sweat seemed to exist only in my imagination.

So maybe the burning heat was not real either; the heat came from his palm. In Taiwan's summer heat, his body pressed tightly against mine like a blanket. As his hands, seemingly burning hot, moved across my skin, I shuddered and felt as if I would melt. The shudder and his violent kisses stirred me somewhere deep down, and a numbing pleasure spread throughout my body.

I went limp in his arms, as that other self examined and tested me with crystal clearness; in a flash I realized that the primal spot that had gone undiscovered and untouched, even under Teddy's prolonged movements, was now unfurling, spreading out under Lin's touch and his kisses. An anxious desire I'd thought could never be satisfied was finally soothed at that moment.

I knew it was all because of love, my everlasting, profound love for him.

Tears welled up in my eyes.

Yinghong could not wait to tell him that her trip down south with Mr. Huang had simply been a ruse. She also felt like telling him how much she loved him. But she didn't.

What she heard was Lin's self-satisfying boast:

"See how good I made you feel. I bet no man has ever done that to you."

Then he followed up, in his usual style of adding further explanation:

"I've not been doing so well in other areas lately. I guess I've played around too much in the past, so I have to work hard on this."

Still dazed, Yinghong disentangled herself from his arms and looked up at his face, only to be greeted by an impassive face devoid of sexual desire.

PART III

Father began taking photographs when he had nearly recovered, though he still needed time to mend. It was about a year after Yinghong had written "I was born in the last year of the First Sino-Japanese War" as a third-grader.

Starting out with a Leica III camera, which he'd bought in Germany during his student days, Father took pictures of anything near Flowing Pillow Pavilion that was worth photographing. Mostly it was common landscape photos, usually in medium or long shots, but after they were enlarged and developed, the details were all visible, including the multileveled, winding veranda by Long Rainbow Lying by the Moon, or the swallow eaves on Lotus Tower that soared into the sky, or the undulating green lotus leaves by Flowing Pillow Pavilion.

Back then Father had yet to develop his own film, and Lucheng had no photo studio with equipment good enough for him, so the negatives had to be sent to nearby Taichung, the largest city in central Taiwan. It took many days before they could be picked up.

All she could see on these enlarged black-and-white photographs was dust, grayish dust that seemed to show up everywhere.

She never could forget the dust. Fine grains of dusty sand traveled on the wind from the ocean near Lucheng the year long, roiling and flying around the small hill by Lotus Tower, like shifting sand, and turning into flying pebbles by the time they made their way to Lotus Garden. Winter was the worst, for it was the season of howling north winds, and the lack of rain turned the place dry and cold. Wind and dust were so strong and pervasive that you had to squint when stepping outside. You could never keep up with the dust that gathered on furniture and household items, and the garden seemed buried in layers of it.

It was through a veil of floating dust under fluctuating sunlight that she saw Father's lusterless face, gaunt after his long illness, looking as if gilded in a patina of gold, gloomy and melancholic.

The entire garden seemed buried in dust. When she came home from school, she was virtually alone, since her mother was busy caring for her father. She liked to wander over to Lotus Garden, with its tightly shut doors and windows, where she would pick out, among all the dust-covered spots, one blocked by less carved wood—usually a large pane of glass on the latticed window—reach out with a slender finger and slowly and carefully write her name. Her handwriting would make the pane look brighter, as if it had been wiped clean, revealing three large, unruly characters:

Zhu Ying Hong

Besides her own name, she liked to add Father's name, leaving "Zhu Zu Yan" on the dusty window. Sometimes, having to stay clear of the carved wood on the window frame, she was forced to allocate the strokes different sizes, and the last three strokes in "Yan" would be oversized, straying out of the normal frame, looking out of proportion.

She came once each day, at least once every other day, to tend to her calligraphy, so that new dust would not settle on the places laboriously cleaned by her finger and return them to their original, dusty state. When she returned each time, she would trace her earlier handwriting to reclaim some of the clean space. But her finger did not always fall on the exact same spot and the characters would be elongated or puffed up, seemingly floating on dust, like an ever-growing corpse nurtured and nourished by it.

One day Mudan happened to stop by the garden for some used items. She mocked Yinghong when she spotted her busily writing on the windowpanes.

"You'd need a barrel maker to loop your characters together. Otherwise they'll fall apart so easily you could never put them back together."

Mother had been the first to poke fun at her handwriting, and when Mudan overheard that, she'd memorized every word and repeated it, even though, as an illiterate, she could not know what was being written.

Upset, Yinghong reached out and erased the characters, spreading columns of floating dust, all but blocking out the light as it lingered in the air. The names had not completely disappeared; parts of the characters were still visible on the cleaner windowpanes, but now they were just fragments, an eerie sight reminiscent of broken limbs. Dust returned slowly and swallowed up the remnants until they were no longer visible. Yinghong ran off in a panic, never to return to trace the names again.

It was during this time, when she was in the fourth grade, that her father recovered enough from his illness to take up photography. She saw the pictures of Lotus Garden when they came home from Taichung—small, black-and-white, glossy photos in which overcrowded houses and scenery seemed to overlap. The inadequate contrast of black and white presented a gray, dusty mess of light and shadows.

The light-gray areas resembled the soft traces her fingers had made on the windowpanes when writing names. The grayish white spots in the middle were places where more dust had accumulated on the messier parts of her handwriting.

In junior high school she continued to hold the view that her father had seen the same dusty Lotus Garden and had been able to freeze the sight into images and retain it as memory. She was an admirer of her father's magic-like photographic skill.

Many years later when, with Lin Xigeng's help, she was ready to renovate Lotus Garden, she dug up those photos as a record of the past and the basis for the renovation. Whenever she saw them, she could almost smell the stifling, humid air from the dust stirred up by her fingers as she wiped away the handwriting. It assailed her face, seemingly suffocating her, as if she had in fact breathed it in. For the longest time, she'd thought it was the smell of death.

Father was apparently dissatisfied with the results of his first photographic endeavor, for a few weeks later, Japanese books on photography began to show up in the house. Most of the printed examples were neat and well proportioned, but lacked strong contrast, owing to soft lighting effects, and the human figures looked stiff. Names like Akiyama Shotaro often accompanied the books.

When Father showed her his Leica III camera, he would not let her hold it, telling her that it was the first handheld camera in the town of Lucheng. At the time, photo studios and families owned only primitive first-generation cameras. "Press cameras," he added in English.

"A press camera is not only heavy and clumsy but it lacks autofocus. So you have to judge the focus with your eyes or use a ruler."

He continued happily, a rare event:

"Ayako, do you remember the wedding of Zhenyuan, Seventh Grand Uncle's son, at the Upper House? The photographer measured each photo with a cloth ruler."

Yinghong smiled and nodded.

"My Leica III has a twin lens reflex," he said in English with a slight Japanese accent. "You can take a perfectly focused picture when the image overlaps the yellow frame in the lens."

As he explained, he let her look through the lens to see for herself. She started out looking with both eyes, and naturally saw nothing at all. Then following Father's instruction, she squeezed one eye shut and saw the yellow frame in the tiny glass frame. She tried for a long time yet failed to see how the images overlapped, despite Father's repeated explanation, though she nodded and smiled, so as not to disappoint him.

In high spirits, he did not notice her reactions.

"It was a freezing winter when I bought this camera in Germany," he explained. "Twenty or thirty degrees below zero. I took some pictures in the snow, and when I got inside, I noticed a thin layer of ice on the camera. I was worried that I'd ruined the fine machine."

"What happened?" She was so eager to know the answer she forgot the family rule of never interrupting one's elders.

"The camera was in perfect shape after the snow melted," Father replied in a soft voice, a warm glint reflected in his slightly sunken eyes. His gaze fell on a distant spot, as he was immersed in reminiscence.

"Another time I took pictures of a waterfall and the lens got wet because I was too close. Water is the great enemy of cameras, so I was worried. Fortunately it was dry in Germany and the moisture disappeared in a few days."

Touching the small, light camera, he continued slowly:

"There are many good things we get from advanced countries." He paused and then said sadly, "I'd thought I could learn something from these advanced countries and find a use for them in Taiwan, but..."

Then he turned sardonic:

"Now all I can do is use this device from an advanced country to take pictures of useless objects. There's nothing for me to do. I'm useless too."

Father enjoyed repeating stories of his life overseas, particularly focusing on cameras and photography, to the point that Yinghong could recite them from memory. But she still loved to hear him talk, for this marked the rare moments when his sad eyes glowed with vitality, even if it was short-lived.

After reading the books purchased from Japan, Father began to pay attention to the grid-of-gold structure, that is, making a grid with nine squares, like the one for a game of tic-tac-toe, placing what he wanted to shoot on the four points where the lines met. By using the grid, he took some well-formed pictures of scenes in Lotus Garden laden with trees and flowers.

In the black-and-white images, the pavilions, the towers, and the terraces were overshadowed by layers of green from the trees, and appeared to be cowering, usually with only the corner of a building, a few stone pillars, and some doors and windows left to struggle to break away from the verdant burial ground. It seemed to presage a not-distant future when everything would deteriorate until nothing was left; the structures and everything else would be gone, tragically swallowed up.

In addition to his Leica III, Father asked a friend to buy a Leica M3, a new model, for him. It came with three lenses, 50mm, 90mm, and 135mm.

Father waited in the garden daily from dawn to dusk with his two cameras and a set of lenses. As additional photos were developed, he grew more demanding of the quality. He tried to find the best balance between dark and light, which meant he'd spend a great deal of time waiting for the sun to move, for the weather to change, or for shadows to appear.

In terms of composition, he gradually broke away from the rigid grid; instead, he now formed a rectangle with his thumbs and index fingers and moved it nearer or farther away from him as he walked around to gauge the composition and arrangements of objects.

When Yinghong finished her homework after school, she would, with his permission, follow him around Lotus Garden, where she too formed rectangles with her fingers to observe the scenes around her.

On days when Father would not let her stick around she roamed the garden by herself. One evening in late spring, when she was in the fifth grade, she went to the Plucking Green Pavilion in the northeast corner of the compound. The pavilion was adjacent to a large grove of dense bamboo that had not been cut for a long time. Each bamboo plant was as thick around as a rice bowl. She saw an emerald-green snake, shorter than the length of her open palm. Pure green, it sparkled in the bright sunlight, but turned a deep, dark green in the shades, slithering in and out of the fallen bamboo leaves on the ground, visible one moment and out of sight the next. Captivated by the beautiful snake, she formed a rectangle with her hands and moved them around, trying to see it better. But before she had a chance, the snake vanished from her sight and was nowhere to be seen again.

It was such a pity that she babbled about the snake to Father at the dinner table, only to be shocked by his blanched face.

"Don't go to Plucking Green Pavilion again, or I'll give you a good spanking."

She froze from his loud voice and the unprecedented threat, tears welling up in her large eyes. Father then took her hand and changed to a gentle soothing tone:

"It's a poisonous 'green bamboo silk' snake. If it bites you you'll die on the spot." He paused and, as if to make sure she understood the severity of his warning, looked hard at her as he went on, "Do you know what death is?"

She nodded, holding back her tears.

"I know. Mudan told me that death means you can't see anything any more. Death means not being able to see Otosan, Okasan, and—"

She stopped and finished her sentence quickly:

"—and not being able to see Lotus Garden."

Father looked at her with loving tenderness as he continued:

"There's another poisonous snake in Taiwan called the 'hundred steps.' Why is it called that? Because once you're bitten, you'll die after taking a hundred steps. Green bamboo silk is even more venomous than hundred steps, for you'll die before taking a hundred steps."

She listened carefully and shuddered at the thought that a beautiful, emerald-green snake could be so lethal. Then all of a sudden, tears began streaming down her face and she burst into sobs, as another concern occurred to her.

On a warm late-spring evening, the fifth-grader, Yinghong, was struck by the thought that she need not worry if she were bitten by a green bamboo silk snake; as long as she stood still, she wouldn't die. Didn't Otosan say that she'd die after taking a hundred steps? So she wouldn't take a single step; instead she'd simply stand there, waiting for Otosan to save her.

She raised her hand to rub her eyes and dry her tears.

When she was a little older and had graduated from elementary school, Father's renovation of the Lotus Garden reached Plucking Green Pavilion, where most of the bamboo was cut down. Father made clear soup out of the small shoots that had just poked through the ground. When there was no more threat of the green bamboo silk snake, she brought it up with Father that even back then, she'd not been afraid of the snakes, for she had an effective solution of not moving if she were bitten. She wouldn't take a single step, let alone a hundred, which would spare her life.

Father burst out laughing uncharacteristically, lending his gaunt face a false image of fullness and adding vitality to his large, dark eyes.

"Ayako," Father spoke in Japanese, as usual. "When I said a hundred steps, I didn't mean the actually number of steps. I was talking about the time it takes to walk one hundred steps."

She was so shocked she broke into a cold sweat.

"Let's try to see how long it will take to walk a hundred steps."

Walking ahead of her, Father started from Plucking Green Pavilion and reached the little bridge by Moon Descending and Wind Arriving, where he stopped to look at his watch, and then continued to count:

"Ninety-seven, ninety-eight, ninety-nine, a hundred. Slightly over a minute."

Yinghong couldn't stifle a startled cry.

Shortly after she had spotted the green snake by Plucking Green Pavilion, Father's days of taking photographs stretched into months. When he'd finished photographing all the scenery in Lotus Garden, he was at a loss as to what to do next. It so happened that a hundred-year-old plane tree, with its many twisted branches laden with twigs and leaves, fell and crashed down on the soaring eaves on one side of Lotus Tower, giving Father the idea of beginning a large-scale renovation of Lotus Garden.

Removing withering plants that were meant for cold weather, he replaced them with flowers and trees indigenous to Taiwan, while the masons repaired the fences, roofs, and brick walls that were loosened or damaged by the roots of various plants. Father took detailed pictures of the renovation process.

Many years later, after marrying Lin Xigeng and deciding to renovate Lotus Garden again, she dug out the thousands of pictures Father had taken. She saw that his camera lens had captured the minute details of how the wood joints were connected and the roof tiles were laid down.

He had even made adjustments to Lotus Garden's structures to accommodate his photography work. Authenticity Studio had been the book storage and reading room in Lotus Garden, which was why it had windows high enough to take up nearly two-thirds of the wall, with pane after pane of glass on the four walls. Even the tall doors were made of carved frames fitted with glass panes, flooding the room with bright light. The latticed windows were decorated with the usual auspicious pictures and patterns, but the four corners had elaborate, exquisite wood carving and inlay to showcase the four botanic gentlemen—plum, orchid, bamboo, and chrysanthemum. The branches on the plum were resilient and robust, while the orchid leaves were lively and elegant, all giving the unique flair of an upright gentleman.

The small room by Authenticity Studio, originally used as a bedroom, had two small windows. Father told the carpenter renovating Lotus Garden to seal up the windows with large sheets of plywood and paste black paper over all openings.

"It's best to seal up the windows with bricks and mortar to prevent light from streaming in, but that would ruin the appearance of Authenticity Studio," Father said to her with a hint of regret.

Through a friend who was living in Germany, Father bought a Leitz enlarger and purchased other film-developing material from a photography equipment store in Taichung. Yinghong, who had just begun chemistry class in junior high, was intrigued by the various chemicals, photographic developers called Hydro Quinond and Elon, and a fixer called Hypo Fixing Bath. She thought they were wondrous novelties.

For a long time, she was convinced that darkness must have provided some kind of magical effects, since negatives could be developed only in a darkroom.

Father trimmed the negatives, which were made by Agfa and came in twenty and thirty-six sheets, in the darkroom himself. When he began taking large numbers of pictures, his need for negatives increased accordingly, so he copied other photographers by cutting large film negatives into smaller ones. A five-meter-long film could be cut into thirty-six small photographic negatives, and a hundred-meter-long film could be turned into twenty large negatives.

"This is what the *puluo* do, to save money on negatives." Father pronounced "professional" in the Japanese way, shortening it to *"puluo."*

For a while he was keen on developing film himself. When he reached the point where he could ensure good results, and the black-and-white pictures had a clear contrast, he stopped going to the darkroom so often. During that time, Yinghong, who wrote that she wanted to be a nurse, then an inventor, in her school essays, thought that her father wanted to be a photographer, so she asked him:

"Why does Otosan take pictures?"

"Indeed! Why do I take pictures?" A hint of alarm flickered in his deep, dark eyes. "What would I do if I didn't take pictures? How would I pass the days left to me?"

A second-year student in junior high, she did not know how to respond.

After losing interest in developing film himself, Father began collecting cameras.

The first one he bought was a Linhof, which he called a first-generation press camera. It was clunky, only partially made of metal, with an accordion-like folding section. What she liked most about this camera was that she didn't have to close one eye and strain to see through the tiny view window. Instead, the lens could be laid flat and, with her hand covering one eye, she could look down through the lens to see everything.

Moreover, the scene she saw was reversed, creating a magical effect, a mixed sense of the real and the unreal, which served to verify what had worried her all along—nothing was stable and changeless, whether seen through a lens or in a photograph. The impression of permanence was in fact created through the multitude of instantaneous changes beyond human control.

It was through this Linhof camera that she got to see the little hill by Lotus Garden being set on fire, though of course, the right and left sides were reversed.

Lotus Garden was located on a small hill in the western outskirts of Lucheng. Over a century earlier, the Zhu ancestor who completed the construction had hoped to look at the ocean from high up on the hill. But silt gradually blocked and filled up the port of Lucheng, which, as a result, lost its former glory as the Port of Taiwan for ships from the Chinese Mainland. The one-time beach was transformed into mulberry fields. The reclaimed land pushed the shore farther and farther into the ocean, until the Zhu family no longer saw the ocean even from Sea-gazing Tower in the northwest corner of Lotus Garden.

From the time Father fell ill until his recovery, Yinghong witnessed how the hill, which had nothing but a few trees, was gradually overtaken by dark-green tasselgrass and a wild pineapple plant called pandan, blanketed in a vibrant, aggressive green.

The pandan had thick trunks with spreading leaves. Long needles dotted the edges of hard leaves infused with milky starch, giving them a ferocious, menacing appearance that stopped anyone from getting too close. The tasselgrass, however, had a profusion of thin long leaves that swayed in the wind; though it appeared delicate, its clever tendrils spread out and fought the pineapple for space.

Most of the time the pandan and tasselgrass were a ferocious green; along with the vigorous flora, they seemed to surround and swallow up the garden, like a boundless green maze, cutting off all other life inside and outside the garden with its primitive verdant curtains.

Giving up on clearing the pandan and tasselgrass, Father decided he would set the hill on fire; that caused a panic in the Upper House. The uncles and grand uncles came to talk to him several times, but to no avail, and eventually they announced with determination that they would cut off all ties with a "prodigal son who would ruin the clan."

Father stubbornly held to his plan of a controlled burn in late spring. Lucheng, being a coastal town, suffered from fierce northeastern winds in fall and winter, when it was dry and unsuitable for anything to do with fire. Late spring was the right time, with spring rains, before the arrival of the dry summer weather. Besides, there was the southwestern wind from the ocean, with its hospitable moisture and wind direction.

In that spring, when the rains had ended and the soil was soft, Father told Luohan to hire a large group of workers, who were to cut down the primeval green pandan and tasselgrass around Lotus Garden, creating a fire wall that was over a dozen meters wide. Below the hill was nothing but paddy fields with irrigation water running along the ditches. Father estimated that the fire would stop there.

Even with detailed planning, he kept the workers around that day; buckets and any other containers they could think of were filled with water and scattered around the garden in case they were needed.

He, on the other hand, set up photographic equipment all around the garden, with Mother as his assistant to watch over the Leica III camera. The clunky old Linhof was placed on an outcropping between the hill and the garden. After adjusting the focus, Father stressed in no uncertain terms that the camera was not to be moved; he showed Yinghong how to press the button and advance the film. He even gave her permission to take twelve pictures any time she wanted during the burn.

A junior high student known in the clan to be smart and endowed with clever hands, she quickly learned how to operate the camera. Since he had given her such an important task, she used extreme caution to avoid mistakes. Overjoyed by the prospect of taking twelve pictures on her own, she kept her eyes close to the camera the whole time and saw most of the hill burn through its lens.

The pandan and tasselgrass were not tall vegetation. The latter caught fire quickly; shortly after Father threw in the torch, flames shot up and began to spread. The tongues of fire licked up, presenting a sad but captivating sight, but the pandan and the tasselgrass, about the same height as other shrubs, failed to create the expected terrifying sea of fire. Instead, the fire stayed low to the ground, rolling atop the wide open hill, and, with the boundless ocean and sky as a distant backdrop, lent a tragic beauty to its burning scene.

The large columns of churning smoke grew thicker as the fire spread. The pandan and tasselgrass had taken in so much water from the rain that they burned slowly, and, in the meantime, thick, dark smoke lingered above the bright red tongues of flame.

Yinghong waited, unsure when to press the button, her palm getting wet and slippery from perspiration, while beads of sweat seemed about to drip down onto the camera any moment. She could not tell if the sweat was caused by her anxiety or the rising temperature; all she could think of was the opportunity presented by the twelve shots. She shouldn't use them too soon or she might miss precious scenes later; nor should she be too slow and leave some negatives unused.

The wind took a sudden turn, aiding the crackling fire, which had stopped spreading on the low ground and had jumped toward Lotus Garden. Through the Linhof's lens, which reversed the images, she saw the fire continue to burn on her right, so she was sure it had spared Lotus Garden even though it was spreading fast and fiercely in the strong wind. To her, it was a sure thing that, no matter what happened, even if she were to lose consciousness, she would remember unerringly the direction of Lotus Garden—to her left from where she was standing.

The wind fanned the fire, sending flames higher and higher into the air, until a shocking red blanket of fire spread over the top of the hill and swallowed up most of its greenery. As the fire grew stronger, the thick smoke thinned out, increasing visibility. Through the lens, Yinghong witnessed the splendid sight of a hill burning, prompting her to change the negatives one after the other as she took a quick succession of pictures; she paid little attention to what might follow.

It was her mother who first threw down her camera and ran toward Lotus Garden, shouting for the workers to douse the fire by the fire wall. She was followed by Father, who, with his camera, lenses, and negatives slung over his shoulder, had been taking shots all over the place. Amid the shouts and screams, Mudan ran out of Lotus Garden banging an aluminum washbasin, claiming that it would scare away the fire god. Everyone was thrown into a frenzied panic as they tried to put out the fire, but the tongues of flame continued to follow the wind and licked at Lotus Garden. Bits of dry grass caught fire and sparks flew everywhere. It seemed that in a matter of seconds the flames would sail over the fire wall and land on Lotus Garden's terraces, towers, and pavilions.

Then as suddenly as it had first changed direction, the wind shifted again and weakened considerably, taking flames along as it raced down the hill, as if trying to catch up on extra work. Isolated small fires burned here and there for days before finally dying out. Father told Luohan and the workers to stand watch day and night; they were not allowed to leave until they'd emptied many buckets of water and were certain there were no more burning cinders.

From the moment the fire was set until the hill was covered in ashes, Father never stopped taking pictures, capturing everything through his lens. Since Mother rushed to help fight the fire, she left many of the thirty-six negative in her Leica unused. Yinghong, however, used up all twelve of her Linhof negatives.

When the negatives were developed, they saw that she was the only one who had captured the moment when the fire was at its most ferocious. Even with black-and-white photos, the leaping flames and flurries of sparks presented a terrifying and striking sight.

Before weeds began to sprout on the barren hill after the fire, Father had the workers plant cassia trees in neat rows, adding small canopies of green to the charred slopes.

"Your father was truly a man capable of squandering the family fortune. He spent all his days in the garden thinking up crazy ideas, so no wonder the family lost everything," Lin Xigeng commented in his usual willful way. "Whoever heard of someone nearly burning down an entire estate by setting fire to a hill just so he could take pictures?"

Her face darkened at his words.

"Father set fire to the hill because the pandan and the tasselgrass were too dense. We cut the plants down but they grew back, again and again. Besides, isn't it better now with the cassia trees?"

They were standing outside the garden under the cassia groves that had grown to a height of more than three meters. Their slender, pointed leaves were not dense enough to block out the sun, leaving spaces for the late-afternoon sunlight to slant in. Instead of the famous, blood-red forget-me-not peas, the cassia trees, also called forget-me-not in Taiwan, produced only tiny yellow flowers that sprinkled the area with colorful petals when each breeze swept past.

"I won't argue with you. I can't say anything negative when it comes to your father," he complained softly, then, in an abrupt change of attitude, said enthusiastically:

"Your father meant for you to be born and grow up in this garden, and I, I'm going to help you renovate it so you can move back to live here."

Caught off guard by his unexpected plan, she looked at him with worried eyes.

"And I want you to marry me," he declared in a hurried but customary decisive tone.

Under cassia trees laden with yellow flowers, tears welled up in Yinghong's eyes, only days after the planned abortion of his child.

Father continued his shopping spree for cameras. In the 1960s, before Japanese cameras made it into the international market, Father bought only cameras from Europe, even though he had studied in Japan. His favorite was naturally the Leica, and he could not wait to own each new model as soon as it came on the market.

Besides the latest models, he also began to collect old cameras, and ended up with a few old models of Linhof, Rolleiflex, and Contax. At first he frequented a photography equipment store that catered to professionals in Taichung. After several visits, he became friends with the owner, who, whenever a new shipment arrived, sent a man called Kozo to Lotus Garden with the cameras for Father to have the first pick. During the five or six years that Kozo made his visits, Father collected more than fifty cameras of various makes and models.

The man known by his Japanese name, Kozo, was in his forties and taller than most Taiwanese of the time. He was always dressed in Taiwanese-style shirt and pants that he apparently never changed out of, for the one-time blue fabric looked forever gray, as if it had never been washed clean. Mudan liked to gossip with Yinghong that Kozo was single and had no woman to take care of his needs.

What interested Yinghong most about Kozo was that he rarely wore shoes. He had big feet that were usually covered in dark mud. Yet the shoeless big feet never seemed steady on the ground; when he walked, his rear end swayed from side to side, as if he were walking on tiptoes. She had just learned the expression, "swaying gracefully back and forth," which reminded her of the way Kozo walked, yet that seemed somehow not to fit a full-grown man.

"Kozo has a sissy way of walking, swaying his hips this way and that," Mudan often commented.

Yinghong saw quite a bit of Kozo, since he often came to show Father the photography equipment. For years, he was the only visitor to Lotus Garden, and everyone liked him, everyone but Mudan.

Mudan began to ignore Kozo only after she learned that some of his cameras cost the price of one or two *jia* of land.

"What kind of camera costs that much? What trickery is that? Trading two *jia* of land for a metal box." Mudan spread one of her big bony hands. "Something not even as big as this requires one or two *jia* of the best paddy field. What a trick. If he keeps on like this, pretty soon everything will be tricked out of the family until it's all gone."

Mudan naturally refused to be photographed, even years later, when photos taken by Father were hung all over Lotus Garden, including pictures of Luohan.

"I'd be put in there if I had my picture taken."

By "there," she meant the camera, of course.

She did have a picture taken in order to get an identity card, but took pains to keep it and the negative, with careful instructions to Luohan and Yinghong that, when she died, the picture and the negative must be placed in her coffin so she could leave this world with every part of herself intact.

"I'll not have part of my soul missing, even if I go to hell," she said.

But what galled Mudan most at the time was the price—one or two *jia* of land. She'd even complained in front of Father that Kozo would one day trick him out of everything in the family. Father just smiled, never trying to offer her an explanation.

Kozo began his frequent visits when she was in the sixth grade. Once he came with a big black umbrella on a bright sunny day, and would not let go of it, even during lunch. After the meal, Kozo asked Father and Yinghong to take him to Flowing Pillow Pavilion, where he shut all the doors and windows before turning on the lights. Then he began to mutter after casting her a glance:

"I respectfully ask for the assistance of the Heavenly King, Grandma Mazu, Guanyin Bodhisattva, Prince Neza, and all other deities. By the throne of the Heavenly Palace I bring precious stones of seven colors . . . precious, precious, precious, truly rare treasures from the Heavenly Palace, with the help of Jesus and God, passing through Japan, Germany, England, America, to arrive in Taiwan."

Kozo was muttering in a soft voice, so she did not understand every word he said, but she recalled how Mudan loved to mock him about his swaying head and ears, and the sight nearly made her laugh out loud. Naturally she wouldn't dare, so she smiled secretly, covering her mouth with her slender, fair hands.

But Father was so pleased he burst out laughing.

Seemingly oblivious, Kozo continued his incantation by reaching out with his dark, coarse hands and making a dainty pose, gesticulating and gesturing as he shouted:

"Come. Come. Come. Change. Change. Change."

Then he raised the black umbrella and swung it around before blowing on it three times.

"Pu. Pu. Pu. Change. Change. Change."

Then he slapped the metal ribs of the umbrella and, lo and behold, the tip twisted and fell off to rain down two dozen colorful gemstones. He caught the stones in his palms to show Father and Yinghong, then balled his fist and blew three more times before laying the gemstones on the carved purple sandalwood tabletop.

There were red and green gems, as well as blue stones and a diamond encircled by several small ones, which amounted to two or three carats. Kozo's fingers, still in a dainty gesture, zeroed in on the diamond and picked it up.

"Only this one is good enough for Mr. Zhu."

He spoke in Japanese, thinking that Yinghong didn't understand the language.

"It was hidden in the umbrella ribs as it traveled across the ocean."

Father coughed and gave Kozo a look, effectively silencing him. Then he walked into the inner room, where he rummaged around and came out with a big diamond that looked to be over ten carats.

"What do you think of this?" Father said with a smile.

Kozo tapped his forehead.

"Fine. Fine. Fine."

He said while gathering all the gemstones on the table into the hollow umbrella ribs. He capped the umbrella, with an expression of nonchalance. Father, on the other hand, looked awkward and said:

"When I went abroad, Grandma wanted me to take this along for emergencies."

Later he continued in an intentional light tone, obviously regretting the showy display of the big diamond and unwilling to make Kozo feel that his trip was in vain.

"But, it's time to start getting Ayako's dowry ready."

He had Kozo bring out the gemstones again and picked out a few before thanking the man in a slightly abashed manner.

Besides the gemstones, Kozo also brought other items with him each time, including Mother's cosmetics from Japan, the latest fashions from Hong Kong, and perfume from Paris. Father made frequent purchases, until one day he realized that Mother rarely wore or used any of the items. Then he began buying trinkets for Yinghong.

By the time she started junior high and Father stopped buying her dolls, she already owned over thirty imported dolls in all shapes and sizes, from well-decked-out Japanese dolls in kimonos to princess dolls from Paris in full skirts to soft, huggable rag dolls. She was also given several music boxes that opened to reveal pretty girls in gauzy skirts dancing to soft music, as well as different kinds of candy and Japanese stationery. Even her hair clips were made in Japan.

Most of what Kozo brought was in the area of the latest camera and photography equipment Father required. Expensive items that cost a few *jia* of paddy land Kozo casually carried in a nondescript cotton cloth sack like those farmers used for rice.

Every time he came, Father had him stay for drinks and dinner. They would discuss the latest models and collections owned by professionals from all over.

One warm spring day during her second year in junior high, Kozo brought a big stack of white paper, and, in a secretive tone, asked Father to store it for him. Then the two of them were engaged in a whispered conversation. In the end, Kozo decided to hide the paper under the carved sandalwood curtained bed in Flowing Pillow Pavilion, to which Father raised no objection.

Yinghong was infatuated with painting that year, which all started when Father showed her some lovely albums from Japan. Father gave her a detailed explanation of the symmetry and beauty of classical painting, which emphasized the arrangement and use of space, as well as the Impressionists' focus on light and shadow, freedom and life.

Having made up her mind to be a painter, she spent much of her spare time out painting in Lotus Garden. She was partial to the bright, vibrant color scheme of the Impressionists, for Father had told her that Monet had made several paintings of the same lily pond, all with varying results because of the different times and lighting. So with the Japanese Moth-brand watercolor paint that Kozo brought over, she began to apply bright colors to scenes of Lotus Garden at different times.

Once, while painting the scene at "New Moon by the Small Bridge," with lotus leaves as a backdrop, she ran out of paper. Afraid she could not recreate the scene once sunlight shifted, she recalled the stack of white paper Kozo had placed under the carved bed in Flowing Pillow Pavilion. She went and selected a few sheets, with the idea that she'd ask Father to buy some to replace those she had taken.

The paper, not too thick but obviously of very high quality, was so dense that water barely seeped through it. Since she was using watercolors, the nonabsorbent paper presented a problem at first, but after a few tries she learned to add less water to the paint before applying it to the paper, creating an effect like an oil painting.

The innovative result piqued her interest so much that she got more of the same white paper and spent a whole day painting just about everything in Lotus Garden. Then she went to see Father for his assessment.

Kozo, who was drinking and chatting with Father in the main hall at Lotus Tower, came over to take a look and gave his approval before letting out a startled cry. He did not, however, forget to form the dainty gesture with his fingers before slapping the back of his head, as he yelled:

"Oh, no! I'm done for. All done for. That paper, it's for printing money."

Stunned, Yinghong asked without thinking:

"What do you mean, printing money?"

"Printing ten-dollar and hundred-dollar bills. The New Taiwan dollars. These, every single sheet is money, pretty, nice-smelling New Taiwan dollars. This is terrible! Every single one of the bills has grown wings and flown away from me. Half of my property is gone, all gone."

Despite continued signals from Father, this time Kozo could not hold back.

"The denomination hasn't been printed yet, but this is authentic paper used to print the new NT. Do you know how much trouble I had to go through to get this much paper? I didn't dare leave the stack at my house, and that's why I asked your Otosan to store it for me. Oh, this is awful, just awful. Such misery."

He continued yelling and screaming till he saw the frightened look on her face; then he slowly calmed down and adopted a lighthearted tone:

"The Young Miss is a fine representative of a wealthy, established family, with her uncommon style and flair. A painting by you is worth one, even two thousand NT. These paintings here are enough to buy a whole row of Lucheng houses and their storefronts. Young Miss is a fine artist."

Knowing that nothing could be changed, Kozo tried to make the best of a bad situation.

"Oh well," he said with a slight laugh, "what's done is done, so it's all right. But I wonder which family will be wealthy enough to gain you as daughter-in-law. See how you used up enough money to build Lotus Garden just by painting it."

After the initial outburst, Kozo let it pass, though he did take the remaining paper with him. Yinghong, of course, received a bit of scolding and punishment, but Father focused on not taking other people's property when you know it does not belong to you, and did not believe that she'd ruined Kozo's dream of becoming rich overnight.

"Kozo is crazy. He thinks about getting rich every day, and now he's going to print money. It's not that simple."

Later she overheard Father talking to Mother:

"All this government knows what to do is arrest and kill people; they are more ruthless than the Japanese. There are government spies everywhere. Do you think they would let anyone print fake money? If Kozo keeps this up, sooner or later something bad will happen to him."

Mother continued in a worried tone:

"Yes, indeed. Printing money is only part of it. Just look how he parades his smuggled items all the time. I'm afraid he's going to get into trouble." She paused and then added, "Could we get involved somehow?"

"We've experienced the worst already. What are we afraid of now?" Father snorted.

"It's that not simple. Printing money is interfering with the country's finances. It disrupts the social order and endangers national security. If the government takes it seriously, it could be really bad." Mother sounded anxious.

Father was quiet for a long time.

After graduating from junior high, Yinghong was preoccupied with her senior high school entrance exam. By that time, all the newly planted flame trees in Lotus Garden were blooming, and Kozo stopping showing up. She could not avoid a vague concern that he must have gotten into trouble.

Gone, also, was the old soldier from the Mainland whom the local Taiwanese called Old Taro, a man who had kept a lackluster watch over Lotus Garden. His place was taken by a shrewd-looking middle-aged Mainlander and a young Taiwanese man. The two of them kept a tight watch at the entrance to Lotus Garden. Father spent virtually every day inside, and even Mother, who had business to take care of, rarely went out. Yinghong was repeatedly told to come home directly from school.

The watch lasted about three months. Then one day, Mudan opened the gate early in the morning and saw that Old Taro was sitting on one of the granite steps, his reappearance as sudden as his earlier disappearance.

It would be years before Yinghong finally and truly understood what Kozo had done, and even then it was difficult to imagine someone like Kozo, a pantywaist, according to Mudan, being involved in that kind of business, particularly since he was so gutless that a loud noise made him jump out of his chair and thump his chest with his dainty fingers.

But from the bits and pieces revealed by Mudan, Yinghong learned that Kozo had come from a wealthy family in Gongzhailiao, in the countryside outside Lucheng. He'd gone to school, but several acres of family land had been seized by the government after the implementation of the Land to the

Tillers policy. Since he was no good at working the remaining plot of land, he had to find another way to make a living.

She stopped painting for such a long time that she gradually forgot her dream of becoming a painter, either because she had cost Kozo millions of NT with her painting or because she had to prepare for exams.

Now that Kozo no longer came to Lotus Garden to show Father the latest cameras and photography equipment, Father had to once again visit the store in Taichung. As he was always looking for something to do, it occurred to him to buy a car, since he had to make the trip so often.

At the time there was only one automobile in Lucheng, a black sedan belonging to the town head. If members of wealthy families who had worked away from Lucheng over the years bought a car, they naturally kept it for use in the city, occasionally driving it back on home visits; hence the town head's "Black Hood" was the only car Lucheng residents saw on a daily basis.

Rumor had it that the town head had colluded with the KMT government when it relocated to Taiwan, which was how he could suddenly transform himself from a local hooligan into a rich man overnight and become the local representative before serving as the town head. With such a background in an old town with lost glory, he had earned no respect from the locals. Now that he had bought the Japanese "Black Hood", it was pretty much settled that no self-respecting Lucheng family would follow his example and buy a second one. The established families were in the habit of competing with one another on who was better at "saving" money. With the motto that a single coin should be tied at four corners so it would not be spent too easily, they all believed that wasting money on superfluous objects was an act of the nouveau riche.

"Lucheng has one major thoroughfare, Zhongzheng Road. It doesn't take long to walk from one end to the other. Buying a car is truly the behavior of someone doomed to squander away the family fortune," people said.

Hence all eyes were on Father when he bought his car, particularly because he did not buy a Black Hood, one familiar to everyone in town. Instead, he bought a German car called a "Mercedes Benz," unheard of by anyone.

Finding "Mercedes Benz" too hard to say, the locals shortened it to Benz, which sounded more like Mens when pronounced in Japanese.

The "Mens" was sold to Father by a consul who was returning home after serving his term in Taiwan. A uniformed chauffeur drove the car to Lucheng, drawing the attention of people along the way, forming a human wall that was said to be the equal of a parade of the deities. The crowd forced the chauffeur to slow down, and he arrived in Lotus Garden with some local ragamuffins' hands on the car. They told Father they'd helped push it to his house, to which he responded with a pleasant smile and some tips.

The 1953 Mercedes came in a cobalt blue, made before car designers had begun to worry about the wind factor, so it did not have an aerodynamic body. Instead, the car was all angles, with a rounded tail that was smooth and well textured, while the platinum logo on the hood displayed an extraordinarily luxurious elegance.

The consul's chauffer stayed on at Lotus Garden for more than two weeks, helping Father get reacquainted with driving a car. During those days, she often saw Father, accompanied by the driver, leave early in the morning to hone his driving skills, not returning till dusk. Unable to resist her request, he agreed to let her be his first passenger, but he also insisted that the chauffer do the driving. He wanted to wait, once the driver had left, to practice on his own for ten days or so before he'd let Yinghong and her mother ride with him.

As they were driven around by the consul's chauffer, Yinghong and Father, who were both sitting in the back, began to chat in Japanese, after Father explained to the young man, who didn't know the language, that Japanese was their daily language at home.

"When I was little, your grandfather drove a Japanese Black Hood, and he was actually the one who taught his chauffer how to drive. He was well mannered."

Father spoke slowly, but as always, when he talked about something important, his laconic eloquence showed how well read and knowledgeable he was. She listened quietly and carefully.

"I remember when I was a child, the driver at our house didn't wear a uniform, because your grandfather was a considerate man who didn't want people to determine the driver's status from his clothes. He often told us that ours was a large family that made no distinction between employer and the employee. This I learned in childhood, and, later, when I went to study in Japan, it played a significant role in my eventual decision to major in political science, instead of the more popular field of medicine."

Father paused before continuing:

"Your grandfather did not allow me to be driven to and from my Japanese elementary and junior high schools because he did not want me to think I was different from the other kids. It didn't bother me until one day, when an arrogant and aggressive Japanese classmate who had moved to Taipei returned to Lucheng for a visit. I didn't want him to look down upon us Taiwanese, so I told the driver to take me to the train station to pick him up. Your grandfather gave me a severe tongue lashing after the classmate left."

Yinghong frowned as a sudden anxiety rose up in her, but she quickly relaxed her brows when she sensed it was not the right thing to do.

"Young people are always full of pride. I remember that at the time I pretended to listen to your grandfather, but in fact I did not agree with him. So when other Japanese classmates came to visit, I made a deal with the driver for him to bring me to a street outside the Upper House and we'd walk home from there. The driver, who was fond of me, went along each time. I felt I'd gained enough prestige and the Japanese classmates would not dare look down upon me."

Father smiled at Yinghong as he talked.

"The driver's name was Ah-bing. He was in his forties. He was fluent in Japanese, but your grandfather was strict about not using Japanese at home. Only Taiwanese was allowed. So we called him Ah-bing. Your grandfather had taught us early on that the Japanese were an alien race, invaders, and I never forget that."

Father turned to look out the window. Yinghong followed his gaze to see how the autumn scene near Lucheng, typical of central Taiwan, receded slowly as the car moved along. The rice had been harvested, and the field was blanketed by a riot of bright yellow flowers from newly planted rape. Row upon row of purple hemp ready for fiber extraction appeared quiet and peaceful under a bright autumn sun, interrupted only by tires going over a stone path that years later would be paved in asphalt.

"The funny thing is, one day I realized that there were people who were not from an alien race, yet were more ruthless than the aliens, not invaders but more bloodthirsty than invaders. So I began to use the alien's language to teach my own children."

Still with his gaze fixed out the window, he continued quietly without turning to look at her.

After Father began driving, Old Taro, who guarded Lotus Garden, got a bicycle from God-knows-where and began to follow the Mercedes. Back then there were no stoplights in Lucheng, and people rarely paid attention when they crossed the street. As a result, Father drove slowly in town, and Old Taro was able to keep up for a while along Zhongshan Road.

But once Father left town, he'd step down on the gas pedal, sending the powerful Mercedes flying down the road, and leaving Old Taro in his dust. Underestimating the power of the car, he actually pedaled to catch up as if his life depended on it. It only took a few minutes for the Mercedes to disappear into the distance, forcing him to give up the chase; he was panting hard but shook his head incredulously.

That happened several times, until he was convinced that he'd never catch up with the Mercedes on his rickety bike. After that, he'd give chase in a lackluster fashion and follow along for a while, just for show, of course. When the Mercedes sped up, he kept at his own speed, and Father had no idea when he stopped following.

Father never hired a driver, preferring to drive himself around and enjoy the scenery. When Yinghong passed the exam to enter the senior-high division of a top-tiered girl's high school in the provincial capital, it was his daily duty to pick her up at school.

A late riser, Father rarely got her to school in time for the morning study session at seven, so Yinghong caught a local train on her own. When school let out, she lined up with other students to leave the campus together, then walked off alone onto a main street by the school, where Father would be waiting for her.

Even at home in Lotus Garden, Father maintained the habit of dressing up before leaving his bedroom. He was an even more meticulous dresser when he was leaving the house in his car. At the time, Western suit pants with suspenders were in vogue, and they became father's usual attire, along with shirts from Hong Kong or Japan, a bow tie, wing-tip oxfords, his hair parted on the side and sleeked back with hair oil.

For years, Father was known in Lucheng as a good-looking man, in addition to his reputation as a prodigal son. Behind his back, people used a slangy nickname, the Black Hound of the Zhu Family, as a way to separate him from other prodigal sons. He always looked elegant and refined, and never visited the red-light district or other unsavory businesses, which gained him some grudging respect from the townsfolk, who would not dare call him "Black Hound" to his face.

But he never paid attention to any of this. No matter whether he went out for a ride or to pick up Yinghong, he usually chose a less-traveled route. When he got home to Lotus Garden, he drove into a newly built car park. He also washed and waxed the car himself.

In the beginning, when he was gung-ho about washing the car, he was so meticulous that toothpicks and cotton swabs were his usual tools. The toothpicks were used to remove sand and dirt from crevices, while the cotton swabs were for a detailed polishing job. Back then not even hospitals in Taiwan used cotton swabs; instead they rolled wads of cotton on medical equipment. In order to care for his Mercedes, Father asked friends to bring him cotton swabs when they returned from abroad, as he'd used them when traveling overseas.

Washing and polishing the car obviously helped Father kill a substantial amount of time. But like everything else, he soon lost interest in it and turned the chore over to Luohan, who was so fond of the vehicle that, whenever there was a wind and the weather turned cold, he'd run over to protect it with a canvas cover, as if afraid it might catch cold.

However, Father kept up his custom of going out for a ride just about every day. He frequently drove to Taichung, where he would buy stereo equipment—his new hobby. His Mercedes served as perfect transport to bring the turntables and speakers back to Lotus Garden and back to Taichung for repair if there was a problem with the system. By the time Yinghong started senior high, Father would pepper his discussion with the stereo shop owner with references to loudspeakers from England's Vitavox, or 300B amplifiers from W.E., all with a Japanese accent, of course. Buying stereo magazines from Japan and putting together a stereo system became a major task in his daily life.

The stereo equipment volume could be turned up all the way in Lotus Garden with no concern for neighbors. Father taught Yinghong how to listen to music played on 78 and 33 1/3 speeds, to understand the simple installation step of putting a vacuum tube on the outside for ventilation, and to know all about the advanced setup of assembling the arms and turntable. She also learned to appreciate various composers, from Bach to Dvorak; Father's favorite was "Pathétique" by Tchaikovsky.

Father's interpretation of classical music was heavily influenced by articles in the current music magazines; for instance, this is how he explained "Twilight of the Gods," the last movement of Wagner's *The Ring of the Nibelung*, to Yinghong:

"As with the arrival of twilight, ripples of light flicker on the surface of the water. The strings, like a bleak winter scene, descend in gloomy darkness, symbolizing the frustration one experiences and the desolation of life."

Accompanied by classical music, particularly the soft, subtle movements of lingering, unending sorrow, or the echoes of regret after a resounding performance of strings and winds, the four seasons in Lotus Garden changed dramatically and affectively with the unspeakable anguish conveyed by Father's interpretation.

Cape lilacs were overtaken by a blanket of misty white flowers in the spring, like a lost cloud pausing at the green leaves; it was the kind of mysterious illusion that could only be embodied by a string of lithe, tinkling notes plucked by the nimble fingers of a harpist.

In the summer, flowers on the flame trees were best represented by the powerful pounding of brass and string instruments, roaring and exploding with trees filled with red phoenixes ready to take wing. Amid the cacophony of the brass and strings, the fiery clouds vanished, leaving only the sadness of unfulfilled dreams. That was followed by tiny star fruit flowers in the fall; with the weeping and supplicating violin and the twisting and winding flute, the dots of red, like tears, flowed across the water in the garden, crossing the artificial hills and covered paths, and passing by the pavilions, terraces, and towers, year in and year out.

The tiger claw trees did not shed all their leaves in the winter; some withered branches seemed to hold on to their last life force, with a suppressed gloom, as if they held no hope nor any future, like the moment before the thunderous musical movement comes to an end.

With the sound of classical music flowing throughout Lotus Garden, Father continued to buy equipment for his stereo system. He soon had turntable sets from two different companies, three sets of speakers, and three amplifiers, which he considered to be the standard setup to mix and match for appreciating different types of music.

By the time Yinghong graduated from high school and left for college in Japan, Japanese cameras had made successful inroads into the international market. Nikon was now as good as the best European camera, and Father began to collect a large number of Japanese models.

He no longer studied and examined cameras before selecting one; instead, he would look at the row of Japanese cameras on display and, pointing at those that struck his fancy, buy them all. His record purchase was six in one day.

And he kept at his passion for cars as well. His second car was another Mercedes, which was then a new design with aerodynamic lines, though he was still partial to his 1953 model. When he went to Taichung on trips to purchase camera and stereo equipment, he always drove the old car, which was in pretty good shape.

Then she graduated from college in Japan and Father insisted that she go directly to the United States for postgraduate work.

If you were to return, I'm afraid I could not bear to let you leave again. I would prefer Ayako to be like me; with a Japanese and American education, you can maintain the foundation of Eastern cultural traditions while absorbing the modern spirit of Western civilization. This is the kind of basic education I would like you to have.

When Ayako is studying overseas, you will naturally witness all sorts of novel and unusual sights and objects. Your letters often remind me of my ambitious plans when I left Taiwan as a youngster, seeing many wondrous and interesting things in these countries and feeling free and unfettered. I was brought to tears by these recollections; it is indeed true when people say it is hard to look back at the past.

The ambition of my younger days died many years ago; what remains are depression and a meaningless life. Since you left, days seem to go by even more slowly in Lotus Garden. The abyss of despair truly feels like an endless descent into a bottomless pit, a feeling that has followed me like a shadow for decades. There is no end; no matter how far or how deep I fall, there is still no end to the descent.

Ayako, you are still young, so you will not and should not understand the feelings of a useless man like me, confronted by the senselessness of a wasted life filled with despair. But Ayako, don't worry too much; I am just . . .

This letter did not reach Yinghong until years later, when she rushed home from New York after receiving the news of Father's death. She found it in his personal correspondence when going through his things.

Tears blurred her eyes again and again, no matter how hard she tried to stop them from falling.

For months, Yinghong was in a state of ecstasy. Once she was back together with Lin Xigeng, she ignored all the designs and plans she had made, for she realized that he was the one she wanted, and that she actually loathed all other men.

She made a sudden, clean break with Teddy, refusing to continue their secret rendezvous, and began to avoid him. He was so upset he threatened to make their relationship public, though in the end he did not, out of concern for his wife. Still, during their last phone call, he declared:

"You'll come back to me one day. I know all about women like you, sex-craved and needy, and I'm the only man who can truly satisfy you. You'll beg me to come back."

Yinghong angrily slammed down the phone, but then she laughed softly.

When she and Lin first got back together, she was able to tease him and let him have his way only within limits; she would not allow him what he really wanted. But along with the growing emotional ties from all the time they spent together, she knew she would not able to put him off for long, though she was aware that she must not let him have the one thing she had been depending on too quickly.

She finally gave in when he insisted. Like any woman in love who had held out for a long time, she happily and willingly let him have his way, and often reminisced about the first night with fondness.

It took not years but months before his love for her begin to fade. She soon realized that their sex life was not as wonderful as she had thought it would be. Lin lacked Teddy's stamina and was not as considerate; it would take her a long while to understand Lin's way with women, and she learned that there was practically nothing she could do to change that.

At first Lin tried hard to please her, employing all his passion to work on her, the way he worked on his real estate business. Even during the deliriously happy moments of lovemaking, Yinghong could still tell that he was most sexually needy when he was confronted with an important decision or when work piled up.

He wanted to know where she was every minute. In the same way he came up with sudden, innovative ideas, he wanted her at all sorts of unusual times and places. After a long, boring meeting or during a free moment at work, he would send his driver for her or tell her to take a taxi to have sex with him in different parts of Taipei, where he seemed to have a multitude of residences.

Those places were usually splendidly decorated, spacious, high-rise units; it could be in the up-and-coming Eastern District or along declining Zhongshan North Road, even in an old residential area like Wanhua. It took her a while to realize that when he called to tell her where to meet, it depended on where he was having a meeting or doing something work related. He would choose the closest spot to avoid the increasingly heavy traffic in the city and save travel time for himself.

As a man who had made his fortune in real estate, Lin appeared to have already scouted out spots separated by equal distances and reserved them as his pleasure dens in a city he had helped to build. Even after they were married, Yinghong still was not sure how many such units he had reserved in these buildings.

But no matter which district or which floor of a new building it was, he would quickly pick a place where he'd come for daytime sex before dashing off to another meeting or business meal, or he would fall asleep as soon as it was over. It was only at night that he would come to her place, and not always for sex. Just to be able to fall asleep with you in my arms, he whispered to her, with a bashful look.

He arrived at different times. Sometimes at three or four in the morning, after leaving a banquet he had hosted at some drinking establishment. He'd be so drunk he'd slur his words as he told her how he missed her, even though he'd been surrounded by dozens of barmaids who wanted to spend the night with him for a little extra cash.

She was only dimly aware that cool autumn had been replaced by early winter. As the island's economy experienced exponential growth through international trade, streets in the biggest city, Taipei, were expanded for ten lanes of traffic. In the process of making the city green, a tree called "sudden golden shower" was widely planted along these streets. A typical subtropical tree, it was not tall, with compound leaves that were thin and tender, creating a lovely sea of greenery. With the arrival of early winter, the leaves remained on the trees, while strings of yellow flowers burst onto the tips of the branches. The flowers were light yellow at first, but the cooler the weather got, the more the flowers bloomed, and more golden yellow they turned, until the tree was virtually covered in bright yellow petals. The clusters of flowers looked like a sudden shower of golden raindrops, giving the illusion that the city of nouveaux riches was paved in gold.

In a rapidly developing city that could boast the timely planting of "sudden golden showers," Yinghong would travel in the Rolls Royce, which was steady as in a dream, on her way to a tryst with Lin Xigeng in a unit located in a high rise somewhere in the city. She would look out the window as the car glided past densely planted sudden golden showers, bathed in the glow of warm winter sunshine. Everything was so brilliantly lit it seemed unreal.

It was also during the seasonal change from cool autumn to cold winter that an unprecedented shift in Taiwan's real estate market took place. Business owners, using Japan's economic development as an example, estimated that an increase in real estate value would occur every five to seven years, and assumed that the same was about to happen in Taiwan. How big a jump and for how long, no one could say for sure, considering how Taiwan's economy had just experienced its first prodigious growth.

Lin's real estate business was also entering a new era. He worked day and night, gathering nearly every one of Taipei's competent brokers to talk about possible sales or joint developments with landowners. Accompanying these brokers, who chewed betel nut and wore plastic sandals, he would go to restaurants with bar girls and get so drunk he could barely stand. These people could call to wake him up in the dead of the night or early morning if it was about a piece of beautiful land.

They talked about land as if it were a living thing; in particular, they sounded like they were discussing women, not only using similar terms, but also insinuating something erotic.

"Square and proper, such a pretty piece."

"Skinny and slender, but with a good style."

"With land like this, you have to 'possess' it right away."

Lin needed large amounts of cash to buy land and build on it. So he took bank loan officers to bars, where they flirted with the girls and followed the custom of taking them out. Of course, construction company owners who wanted his business, building-material salesmen who wanted to sell him material, and brokerages who wanted to promote the units also frequently invited him to banquets. Everyone did their best to flatter and fawn over him, and they went only to bars or restaurants with girls.

Then Yinghong began to notice the difference in bed.

At first, when she gave in to him after she could no longer put him off, he would spend time kissing and touching to arouse her, which was not new to her, though it still gave her indescribable pleasure. His foreplay, like his professional strokes of genius, frequently brought her unexpected stimulation and increased her sexual appetite.

But when they really got down to business, his actual performance paled in comparison with foreplay, which could be controlled by his wit, experience, and competence. At moments like this, he would look frustrated but would tell her, in his usual boastful tone, that when he was younger, he often had sex with several women in a single night. Sometimes the women were all there together; sometimes one would arrive right after another. There were times when he did not sleep a wink; he had just started his business, and could last nearly an hour with no problem at all. And now?

"Maybe I overdid it when I was young," he said, dejected, as he continued to please her in his own ways.

He did not want sex with her too often, and, unlike Teddy, he could not keep at it for very long, but Yinghong never felt unfulfilled. Her love for him made his every touch feel like an electric shock; every contact had an effect like fireworks or a lightning strike. Even she was surprised at her ability to adapt, but she was so madly in love that she rarely reflected upon the differences between the two men.

As cool autumn turned into cold winter, endless rain started up again in Taipei, as usual. At its worst, it could rain day and night for weeks on end. It rarely stopped throughout the winter, and sometimes even lasted into late spring, followed by the "plum rains." These were usually just drizzles, but they went on and on, the raindrops forming a gray curtain to shroud the

Taipei Basin. Compared with stirring earthquakes and typhoons, which could level the island, the rain had an everlasting, stubborn quality, a kind of entanglement that would end only in death.

With continuous rain adding to the humidity, the island seemed to be wet everywhere and everything took on a mist. No one noticed how the flowers disappeared from "sudden golden showers" along the roadsides; like their name, they vanished after a sudden shower, leaving behind a verdant canopy that looked even greener in the rain.

I almost immediately sensed the change in him. Now he was always in a hurry and seemed perfunctory, no longer taking time to please me. He still kissed and touched me, but he looked hurried. He would quickly get what he wanted and fall asleep as soon as it was over. Obviously, he too noticed the difference, for he looked abashed and defended himself in a somewhat uncertain tone:

"The doctor told me, three minutes. If I can do it more than three minutes, it's not premature ejaculation."

He repeated that to reassure himself, but after a few times he stopped bothering to explain.

A terrifying fear rose from the bottom of my heart; it gripped me and refused to let go.

What came to mind right away was that there was another woman. I suffered the same sort of pain and dismay as the last time he left me. But this time, with the intimate relationship between us, the thought of him with another woman brought me a strong and totally unexpected desire that gnawed on me daily amid jealous rage.

I could not keep from thinking that he hurried away from my body in order to satisfy another woman and make her moan with pleasure beneath him. I also realized that whenever I did not know where he was, whenever I felt his detachment, my doubts, worries, jealous anger, and pain would surface to highlight his recent perfunctory performance and hurried behavior. And the feeling that I had not been truly satisfied for a long time intensified and appeared nakedly in my body.

The desire felt like a burning, shuddering sensation, accumulating and swelling somewhere inside, refusing to be eliminated. It pestered me day and night, complaining loudly that it had not been satisfied; it was a stubborn desire that went beyond pain. However, because of our intimate contact, the desire was concrete and solid evidence that we'd been together, and it continued to bring me basic faith and comfort.

It was clear to me now that the fear of pain from this love would not drag me down and make me cower and wait passively, as it had the last time; instead I knew it would make me fearlessly fight for what I wanted.

And all this, I told myself, was because of my abiding love for him.

Zhu Yinghong began to work on the people in Lin Xigeng's office.

She worked on them not to ingratiate herself. Lin was given to parading their relationship at the office and among close friends. "She's from the Lucheng Zhu family," is how he usually referred to her. "Her uncle is chairman of the board of Huatai Trust." Yinghong knew he hoped to benefit from this connection.

Her focus was on Lin's personal assistant, the director of the accounting office, and his driver, making sure they received special treatment because of her. She had a way of letting them know that she cared about those who worked for Lin, for she was, after all, the young lady from the Lucheng Zhu family.

Lin's drivers seldom stayed for long; he often entertained at bars late into the night and had to race to a construction site in central Taiwan at eight the following morning. Most drivers could not keep up with that kind of schedule; they complained that the boss could catch up on sleep in the car so he didn't care how late he stayed at the bars. The salary they received wasn't high enough to risk their lives on the highway.

When one of the drivers quit, Yinghong, using Xigeng's safety as an excuse, replaced him with a young man who had just been discharged from the military, a country boy Mudan had helped her find in Lucheng. With the assistance of the director of accounting, who had just written off a large sum of unaccounted-for money with her help, Yinghong slowly increased the driver's salary to an amount he could not possibly get anywhere else. Back when few private drivers in Taipei wore uniforms, Yinghong took it upon herself to design a simple uniform in a dark color and teach him protocols befitting a chauffeur.

In the end, everyone was happy. At first, Lin didn't know how to deal with a driver who knew the proper etiquette, but his flair and his confidence—he was, after all, paying the man—quickly led him to act as if he'd been using a driver like that all along. Sometimes he even used his driver as an example to criticize other drivers' lack of manners. Yinghong now had Xigeng's whereabouts under total control, unless, of course, he took the company car or hailed a taxi.

She was aware that, except under extraordinary circumstances, Lin was too impatient to wait for a taxi or for his assistant to arrange for a company car. His conceit and arrogance would not allow him to scheme to avoid her tracking; besides, he was convinced that he could handle her even if she knew what he was up to.

"Women. They're all alike," she could almost hear him say.

From the driver, she learned that Lin had no steady female companion over a period of time, though sometimes he took one of the bar girls to a hotel after a banquet.

"They left the hotel quickly," the driver would say.

Little by little, she got to know everything regarding his daily schedule and activities. It was apparent that, in order to avoid potential problems, he would not take any of his one-night stands to any of his apartments throughout the city. She was aware that men in Lin's position did not casually show their business cards at entertainment locations, for they would not want the girls to call them. What she had to watch out for were the women he took to the apartments.

Cold and unending rain is typical of winter in the Taipei Basin. Blooms on the "sudden golden showers" had turned into the proverbial yellow flowers of yesterday. On the rare occasions when the rain stopped for a day or two, the sun would show its elusive face only in the afternoon, and it usually had to peek through cloud layers. It was at such a time that she made an important decision—to resign as special assistant to the chairman of the board at her uncle's company.

The rise in real estate value was cyclical, and everyone knew that the next upward trend was on the horizon. At each new project, model houses would be crammed full of brokers and buyers who were serious about purchasing; there was no need to advertise or to populate construction site shows with pretty, scantily clad girls. The sales prices might even jump several times a day, so if a buyer hesitated for even an hour, the new price might have increased by a factor of ten. Too rich for your blood, please feel free to leave, because there are more buyers waiting to take your place, since no one can predict how much the price will increase by that afternoon.

At first Lin promoted several sites that had been planned for quite some time, which led the other construction companies to follow suit. But when the real estate business turned white hot, Lin decided to halt most of the sales, despite the puzzling looks from others. Knowing that another rise was just around the corner, he was going to wait until prices surged before selling the remaining units.

That presented him with some uncommonly free time, just as the island's trade-based economy took off and the real estate business enjoyed an unprecedented boom. He played a few rounds of golf before complaining about too much free time. Yinghong saved the day with a timely suggestion for him to run for the Construction Guild directorship; he agreed, under the urging of friends and with the support of his staff.

In order to mediate the intricate interpersonal relationships among factions and smooth over the election process, Yinghong convinced Lin that she should begin working in his company as his special assistant. Naturally, he was aware that, once she was in his company, there would be another pair of eyes watching him, thus decreasing his personal freedom. But the title of guild director apparently was more attractive than anything else; with that title, he knew that he would be seeing the genesis of a new business.

Yinghong also began to accompany him to the endless banquets for guild members, as well as for officials assigned to supervise the election. There had been no change in entertainment and banquets among Taipei's businessmen; it was still the same formula of a relatively early dinner, during which they drank and fooled around. The real pleasure was still visits to bars, including piano bars, where they drank, played finger-guessing names, sang karaoke, danced, and flirted. As usual, the presence of "girls" was what made these outings lively. As the nights wore on, the men would take the "girls" out for a snack before making individual arrangements. A "short stay" at a hotel cost five thousand NT, while eight thousand would get her to stay the night; this was the origin of "long eight, short five."

With her family connections, Yinghong was able to host banquets that drew important government officials and heads of major enterprises, though she knew that without Lin Xigeng, she alone could not have managed the invitations so easily.

She was particularly adept at mixing politicians with businessmen, knowing that the best way to make connections was to bring people with different needs together so they could exchange interests to achieve mutual benefits. She understood the intricacies of nouveau riche social circles.

"Without concrete interests and real benefits, public relations are a waste," she said to Lin with a broad smile; he listened attentively, with a degree of indulgence.

Yinghong usually attended lunch and dinner meetings, and told people at the company not to arrange for girls to join them. If they needed the presence of women, she would invite female real estate agents or office staff. Sometimes, she asked guests to bring their wives along, which went against the norm of the husband-only practice, but achieved unexpected results. A few of the more active wives even urged Yinghong to form a lady's club so they could get together regularly.

She saw, from these wives, a solidifying base for Lin's election.

In addition to inviting wives to join the men's banquets, Yinghong also insisted on not joining the men when they went to bars after dinner. Everything was fine at the various Taipei restaurants, where there remained a clear distinction between dinner and men's entertainment; the line was blurred once the men went to Beitou, particularly because hotels there provided all services, from meals to banquets, to drinking and flirting, to rooms for other activities.

Beitou, located on a small hill on the edge of the Taipei Basin, was developed as early as the colonial era, thanks to its high concentration of sulfur springs. Interspersed in the verdant hill were hot springs hotels in the Japanese style, all with such elegant names as Singing Wind Pavilion, Carefree Garden, and the like. It had been a pleasure den for all sorts of people: poets, literati, wealthy merchants, and entrepreneurs.

When the island's economy took off, the omnipresent real estate business, the so-called engine of all business, had also spread its tentacles into this beautiful hill. With real estate's tendency to destroy anything old, the traditional, secluded Japanese hotels were leveled and the greenery on the hill was slowly overwhelmed by high rises in concrete and steel, hotels with up to two hundred rooms, and, as dictated by current style, imported bathroom tiles laid on the outside, the more vulgar the better.

Gaudy new hotels spread Beitou's reputation as a town that never sleeps. As for the few remaining Japanese-style hotels, a different kind of eroticism and lewd desire were hidden in tatami-filled rooms inside zenlike pavilions and gardens characterized by gray roof tiles. After newly developed real estate razed most of the traditional buildings, nostalgia returned people to these elegant, old-style hotels for pleasure.

Singing Wind Pavilion, situated at mid-hill, had a driveway that led to stone steps framed by nicely maintained Japanese gardens, with small ponds encircled by fine white sand, pine trees, and osmanthus. In the fall and winter, the osmanthus sent its subtle fragrance into the air, giving the illusion that it floated above the damp, heavy smell of sulfur. If you inhaled, you smelled the pleasant fragrance of osmanthus first before the sulfur hit you.

The elaborate Japanese structure had a large entranceway with wind chimes hanging from the outstretched eaves. In the lobby were a reception desk, sofas, and long cabinets for shoes. Middle-aged women came up, bent at the waist to offer slippers, which were laid out in neat rows on a floor made of long strips of dark brown wood. The straw slippers were identical, except for size—larger for men and smaller for women. Some customers considered shared slippers unclean and left them behind.

Guests followed winding hallways to their rooms, where paper doors were opened to reveal a ten-tatami room in which there were low, round tables high enough for the guests to sit with legs crossed or knees bent. One rainy night in early spring Yinghong and Lin arrived to be greeted by more than a dozen people around one of the tables. Unlike chairs at restaurants, tatami floors offered diners the chance to press up against each other. One man was already straddling a bar girl, while they fed each other liquor through their mouths.

The host that night was Mr. Chen, the owner of Big and Wide Construction, and, like Lin, a real estate tycoon with considerable influence. He got up when they entered and greeted them attentively. During the brief pause in the noisy singing, he introduced Lin and Yinghong. Most of the men were too drunk to stop their raucous bantering.

The young woman who opened the paper door and walked in got everyone's attention after someone welcomed her with cheers and applause. She walked in slowly, in a composed manner. On that early spring night, she was wearing a colorful pullover top over a black patent-leather skirt that wrapped tightly around her full, round behind. The wrinkled leather showed it had been worn many times, which was why it fit so nicely; it was not long enough to cover knees on long legs clad in black fishnet stockings.

Her long, permed hair was a tangled, puffed-up mess that framed a pair of sleepy, limpid eyes offset by rouged cheeks. She zeroed in on her target and slipped in the space beside Lin Xigeng. With a flirtatious glance, she called him Brother Lin in a honeyed voice.

Before she had a chance to say another word, Lin introduced Yinghong to the woman, who lowered her eyes, and, with no perceptible change in demeanor and posture, shifted her body and glued herself to the host, who was seated next to Lin, toasting him and threatening his original companion, a tall girl whose expression changed, though she sat quietly, impassively raising her glass. While fully aware of the intention of the new girl, she could do nothing but look upset.

At that moment, the door that the girl in the leather skirt had pulled shut was opened again, to reveal a tall, potbellied, middle-aged man with an oily sheen on his red face. He swaggered in to sit beside the girl in the leather skirt and blurted out proudly:

"Let me show you the good stuff."

With a swift movement, he yanked the girl's top out of the leather skirt, unzipped it and pulled it down the shoulders. Before anyone realized what was going on, the girl's chest was in full view; a pair of large, natural breasts under a transparent, unpadded lacy bra.

"See. Guaranteed real. There's no match."

As the man continued talking, he opened the black bra to expose a pair of fleshy, arching breasts that jiggled in front of the guests.

Everyone's gaze was fixed on her breasts, which, so rare among Asian girls, projected a degree of self-assurance. Big and full, they looked proud and imposing, with a healthy, pink-tinged paleness. The dark, red nipples were erect, probably from the man's hands when he pulled her bra open.

With a quiet gasp, Yinghong looked instead at the two canines through the girl's parted lips. Those were teeth adored by Japanese men, who saw them as standing for the purity and innocence of young girls. But this girl wore a smug smile. The other girls looked at her with disdain, but the knowledge that they could not match what she had added unhappiness to their faces.

The man reached out and pushed the girl's head toward his chest. She then stuck out her pink tongue to slowly and carefully lick every inch of his exposed chest.

Saliva oozed from the corners of her slightly opened mouth; she had no chance to swallow, for her mouth was all over his chest, smearing her lipstick at the corners and staining the edges of her lips with thick, irregular bloodlike smudges. The man's chest was also covered in red spots, like bloodied wounds, as if he'd just been bitten.

Sticky saliva stuck to the man's black chest hair, wet and twisted, as if a snail or a worm had just crawled over it.

Instinctively, Yinghong wanted to get up to leave, but a pair of powerful hands pressed down on her waist. They were Lin's hands, and she gave up. She was reminded of the first time they met, at one of those typical banquets with the businessmen fooling around; Lin had also gotten her to stay by asking her to dance when she felt insulted.

With flirtation continuing at the table, the host watched quietly for a while before turning to Lin and beginning a casual conversation about a hillside plot with great potential.

They could open an amusement park on this plot of land, which was on the outskirts of Taipei, but reachable within an hour by car via the highway. It would be like Magic Mountain in the United States, with a roller coaster and other recreational features; it would please the Taiwanese, who were now rich enough to enjoy such leisure activities. It could be a new direction in their investment.

Yinghong had first brought up the idea. Though they might not manage a joint venture with an American amusement park, such as Disneyland, it could work with a smaller company as the first step toward international cooperation. Lin himself did not entertain any big ambitions for an amusement park, but with the development of a park like that, the land around it would rise in value, which would generate substantial profits, and this was what interested the two real estate tycoons.

They were making a preliminary evaluation of their financial investment, risk, and profits. It was not the first, nor would it be the last time they discussed the feasibility of the plan, for there would be endless, prolonged meetings. For the two major players, consensus on the fundamental issues needed to be reached first, and the raucous gathering in Beitou provided them with an opportunity to chat, during which they touched upon issues casually in order to get to know one another better and make an initial plan.

The flirting continued at the table, but by this time the man had stood up and pulled the woman over to fondle her full breasts. They were then all over each other, as they moved toward the paper door, which the man freed up one of his hands to open. Now Yinghong had a clear view of the next room, a smaller room with a tatami floor; bedding and pillows were strewn all over, an indication that they had already been used. She realized the convenience a simple paper door provided, which could be why Beitou had enjoyed popularity for such a long time.

"Impressive. Good going. He can go right back and do it again," someone at the table jeered, but it was impossible to know who that was over all that noise.

The paper door was still open, but the man was already on top of the woman, who struggled to free one of her hands with red-lacquered fingernails to pull the two doors together, but failed to close them completely; from where she was sitting, Yinghong could no longer see what went on inside the next room.

Loud laughter erupted at the table, a sign that everyone was used to it, as they continued to drink and sing. Perhaps taunted by the fact that the girl could earn her fee twice in such a short period of time, the other girls took turns going up to sing popular love songs about waiting faithfully for their lovers to return, or "flowers opening up waiting to be plucked," or "bees flying off after taking nectar from the flowers," or "flowers waiting to bloom in the rain."

One by one, the men took girls into another room with a paper door, and the racket at the table began to die down, until the drinking, finger guessing, and flirting came to an end. Lin seized that moment to say good-bye before leaving with Yinghong.

They were not the last couple to leave, but the owner walked them out to the entrance, where Yinghong cast a quick glance at the wall clock. It was past two in the morning. As they walked down the stone steps, the early spring night seemed to be much colder in the hot springs district. In the misty night, damp with dew and fog, he reached out and grabbed her hand.

"Come on, let's go back inside."

Though confused, she walked up the stairs with him and reached the reception desk, where Lin asked, with noticeable familiarity, for a room on the west. The mama-san, who obviously knew him well, replied with a big smile:

"Director Lin, the previous guests have only just left, but the room has been cleaned."

They walked along the hardwood floor of the winding hallway to the room. When the paper door was opened, Yinghong let out a cry of wonder.

It was a twin of the previous room, but this one faced a corner of the courtyard, where ground-level lights in the Japanese garden softly illuminated an old cherry tree with many branches, all laden with flowers in full bloom. A tree full of red flowers evoked a dream that would be hard to wake up from.

He kissed her the minute they stepped inside. She closed her eyes, but the sea of red flowers seemed to remain before her eyes and crowded around her from all sides.

While kissing her, he began to undress her, but instead of taking her right away, he led her into a side room with a small pool filled with water from a hot spring. As they soaked in the water, he bit on her ears and whispered in a slurred voice:

"Let's get a masseuse."

Yinghong's heart skipped a beat. She'd heard stories about young women giving massages in the nude and then sleeping with their clients, so she hesitated. But the heat of the bath created a different kind of dizziness; as the misty air enshrouded them, she felt that anything was possible, so long as it was a professional masseuse. Relaxed in the comfortable setting, she nodded.

The knock at the door came later than she had anticipated. Obviously, contrary to what she had thought, not every hotel had a masseuse waiting to be summoned. As she waited, she began to regret her decision, but she knew that Lin would be upset if she had a change of heart, and she didn't want to displease him.

It was half an hour later when the mama-san came in with a blind, middle-aged masseuse.

"I'm sorry to make you wait so long," the mama-san apologized in Japanese. "I wanted to get you the best, the master masseuse."

She paused and glanced at Yinghong.

"Would the young lady like a massage also?"

Lin smiled and took out a thousand NT, which sent the mama-san away with a broad smile.

He was not used to getting massages while clothed, and removed her bathrobe as well. The room was brightly lit, and Yinghong felt shy and uneasy, even though she knew the masseuse was blind. He, however, lay down stark naked as the masseuse's hands danced on his body, while he reached out to touch Yinghong tenderly with the clear intention of arousing her.

They tried not to make any noise, but the masseuse obviously knew what was going on, and yet she remained focused on her job, a true case of the blind working without seeing. Taking the lead, he touched her first and then asked her to pose in all sorts of ways for him to gaze at or for him to kiss her body while lying down. At first she was hesitant, but the silent movements gave new possibilities to the familiar interactions of their bodies; by guessing what the other was thinking and asking questions, they discovered a harmony that helped them truly know each other.

Little by little, she let herself go and started to respond and lead him on. Sometimes she sat on top of him; at other times she moved away, teasing him with her foot. As he was lying down for the masseuse to work on him, he could not move, forced to let her have her way with him, as he waited for an opportunity to grab her.

Yinghong was free to do what she wanted, for the third person, though present, seemed not to exist, due to her inability to see. For Lin, however, the masseuse's every hand movement on his body appeared to arouse her, making it seem as if they were engaged in a threesome. It was not real sex and they were under some restraints, which helped stoke the fires, creating a different kind of sexual stimulation and carnal pleasure.

Particularly because Yinghong felt she must remain quiet and tried not to bump into the masseuse, no matter how she abandoned herself to the play. The masseuse continued to work, moving down on his neck and shoulder, first one side and then the other, stretching him constantly. In the end, both women moved at the same time, and Yinghong's leg touched the masseuse's calf.

Her first reaction was a shudder caused by the coolness from the masseuse's skin, followed by an unexpected unclean feeling and disgust from the contact with a total stranger. She quickly removed her legs and sat up, while the other woman kept the same posture as she continued to massage Lin's body, seemingly unperturbed.

Owing to the prolonged rigorous work, the masseuse showed signs of fatigue and began to breathe hard, her mouth opened slightly. The forceful movements of her hand caused her body to sway back and forth, matched by the heavy breathing that escaped her mouth at regular intervals—"Uh, uh." The sound did not seem human, more like something totally unrelated to human speech. Truly odd. Yinghong suddenly realized that the masseuse did not work with her eyes closed; instead both eyes were open, showing mostly white eyeballs with tiny incomplete irises, resembling tadpoles sitting at the edge of her eyes, rushing around or rolling up every time she blinked.

With the movements of her hands, she rolled the whites of her eyes and emitted the odd, rhythmical "Uh, uh" sound.

Unnerved by the sight, Yinghong backed away and moved up to Lin, who turned to look at her; obviously mistaken about why she'd stopped teasing him and had come over, he asked the masseuse to leave.

Before the masseuse could slowly grope her way out the door with the help of her cane, Lin turned over and climbed on top of Yinghong to force his way in, clearly highly aroused. At first all she could see were the whites of the blind masseuse's eyes, and amid the premonition of death caused by unexpected apprehension and fear, she let herself go and moved with him.

They spent the night in Beitou. When she woke up the next morning, she could see from where she lay that under a drizzly sky, the bright red flowers continued to bloom on the tips of the old cherry tree. In a room that was totally different from what she recalled from the night before, the man next to her slept on.

What occurred to her at that moment was the thought that she could not afford to lose him again. In order to keep him and, in particular, to retain his normally short-lived passion, she would, she knew, do anything.

It finally became clear to me that his halfhearted performance in bed a while ago was likely caused by his tendency to be bored easily. There might not be other women he sees regularly, but that doesn't necessarily mean he still feels passionate toward or interested in me. The information I managed to extract from the driver I'd personally hired showed that he never takes women back to the suites, but that means nothing.

The dread I'm feeling now is worse than the last time, when he made an abrupt departure. We've been together less than six months, so what sort of future awaits me?

I didn't dare think about it.

It was, ultimately, after our trip to Beitou, that I could, during our intimate moments together, bring myself to ask him about the girls he procured with money.

To my surprise, the girls were not particularly lascivious nor were they all that good in bed. In fact, they liked to pretend that they were not used to it, so their clients would think they were new in the trade and lacked experience.

So after they know the clients better, do they try to keep the men?

Lin smiled. There isn't much chance of that. The men are in it for fun; what's the point in sleeping with them more than a few times?

They ought to have techniques unmatched by the average woman, I persisted. He gave me a tender look and patiently explained things to me. Ten or twenty years ago women from good families were ignorant of such things, and only those girls knew how to please a man. Now there are videos for anyone who's interested in watching.

So I finally learned that I was fighting a battle I could never win. No matter how hard I tried, I could never compete with girls he could change night after night. I was destined to be powerless against a sexual life cultivated in Taipei's business world.

In order to win enough votes for the guild directorship, Lin agreed with Yinghong that presenting prospects of foreign investment in real estate was a workable strategy. He knew there was a lack of stability in Taiwan's politics owing to the long-standing fear of communism and a possible invasion from the other side of the Straits, which made newly rich businessmen eager to move some of their assets off the island to reduce risk. The best investment option was, of course, the "gold country," the target of envy for the Taiwanese.

A real estate investment tour was organized, with help from an American company, to provide investment possibilities for midrange real estate developers who lacked the know-how to do it themselves. This could prove to be effective in getting votes. Lin himself had already checked out the hotels and rental apartments from a distance, and his dream was to buy up landmark buildings in American cities, like the Japanese corporations had done.

Yinghong arranged an exploratory trip for the two of them, with L.A. as their first stop, for it was a city with many Taiwanese immigrants. In her contacts with American businesses, she was able to use her fluent English to her advantage; at a late-spring dinner, she knew to order the new vintage Beaujolais, chilled at the right temperature. Her pretty face and tender concern, which showed her pedigree, added a mystique to Lin Xigeng; there seemed to be something mysterious about a real estate tycoon from the East who could afford to hire such a special assistant. What connections did he have back in his own country, which had recently gotten so wealthy?, they wondered.

Moreover, Yinghong knew the advantage of playing second fiddle; she limited herself to interpreting for him. She'd let him handle even the most insignificant inquiry and never answered for him just because she knew the language. All the time they were dealing with the Americans, she never made him feel uneasy about his lack of English proficiency; instead she made sure he understood that language was merely a tool. Given his financial status, he could have hired thousands of interpreters, but in the end, it was he, Lin Xigeng, who could make decisions without speaking a word of English.

When they were alone after the meetings and dinners, she played out her plan to make erotic moments occur naturally in the car, though she had all the details mapped out beforehand.

Back in Taipei, he'd always preferred to arouse her in the back of his Rolls Royce, reaching under the various types of skirts, not even deterred by a short pencil skirt. With long pencil skirts, he would ask her to shift around for him reach under. She usually tried to fend him off halfheartedly and would say no if he wanted to go further. The driver might be her own hire, but she was never naive enough to think that no one would know. Having been around Taipei's business circles for so long, she had no faith in anyone, for she was not one of those nameless "girls," who could simply disappear into obscurity afterward. No matter whether or not he married her, she knew she must maintain a spotless reputation to gain people's respect.

But she usually consented to his many demands, as long as there was some kind of cover-up. In the daytime, he would pretend to be reading the paper, which provided enough coverage for her to unzip his pants and play with his penis till it was fully erect. He would then, with a proud and confident expression, look at it, at the long, thick, dark instrument that extended beyond the hold of her slender fingers with their fair skin and bright-red nail polish.

At night, when devoid of the excuse of a paper, she would feign fatigue and lie in his arms for comfort, though actually resting on his knees to kiss and suck on his penis. The need to avoid detection and the ruses they had to devise only added to the titillation, making them both excited.

He would often want her to sit atop him, claiming that people could not see through the tinted windows. And as for the driver, he would think she was just being affectionate, but she would not agree to his request, no matter how persistent he was.

Finally in L.A. on the night before they left town, they got into the black stretch limo they'd rented for the trip, after a night of proper interaction and small talk, a champagne toast for future successful cooperation, and the American-style good-bye of hugging and kissing.

She had chosen the limo chauffeur herself. A young white man, he had a sincere smile, earnest enough to promote the American Dream. From a quick inquiry at the car rental agency and casual conversation later, she learned that driving the limo was a part-time job for him, as he had come to L.A. for other prospects, such as Hollywood. Of course. Why not?

On the spring night before they returned to Taiwan, she asked the chauffeur to drive around L.A.'s prime residential areas and main thoroughfares, with the full knowledge that they could drive around for hours in sprawling downtown, even at night, when there was less traffic.

"Let's experience the magic of L.A. at night." She said to the young man with a smile.

Then she began to lead him on, without him asking her to, though she was trembling slightly out of nervousness. Lin immediately knew what he'd be able to do that night.

"Is it safe?" he whispered, biting her ear.

She nodded.

"Then ask the driver to tilt the rearview mirror." He said leisurely, but it sounded like an order.

She slid open the glass partition and, in a dry, unnatural voice, relayed Lin's request. The young driver complied, calm and composed, like his American smile. He didn't look surprised, so obviously this was not the first time for him.

Lin began to take over. As she shrank into the seat, with a practiced hand, he removed Yinghong's clothes until he was able to touch her freely. Blocking her with his broad shoulders, he kissed and played with her breasts but always on the alert to quickly cover up what they were doing.

Fondling and oral sex were what he liked most from her, so his eyes were nearly shut as he enjoyed the pleasure, though he still cast an occasional glance at the world outside the car window.

The streets of L.A., with more than ten lanes of traffic, were just about devoid of pedestrians, and his mind was put at ease, as the car rolled along at a steady pace.

His skill from practice and total control also made her feel safe. Though tall and big with long limbs, he had enough room to maneuver in the spacious limousine, so Yinghong, smaller in size, did not feel crowded, as she had thought.

He guided her in changing positions to increase the pleasure and comfort, which enabled her to once again experience his awe-inspiring style. A sense of submission and dependence turned her body supple and lithe, and, under his instruction, that softened body was able to easily accomplish several difficult positions and unfamiliar moves. Total relaxation and reciprocation led her to forget herself completely, and all she felt was bodily, carnal pleasure.

Feeling disrupted each time the car stopped at a red light, she began to complain about all the stoplights in L.A. While waiting for a light to change, the chauffeur showed visible unease, suddenly not knowing what else to do; moreover, the vehicles that came up to them on both sides gave her the feeling that the windows were useless and that the drivers of the other cars could see what they were doing.

Right after they were done and had tidied up, Lin lowered the window, sending late-spring evening wind onto her sweaty face; caught unprepared, she let out a startled cry.

"Can't you smell it all over the car?" he teased, while reaching out to put his arm around her.

Without the dark windows, L.A.'s night lights leaped into her field of vision in all their glory. As the car drove along, the city seemed to suddenly come alive and became something real; she no longer felt that it was merely a Hollywood set, as viewed earlier through the windows, where the darkened, understated city seemed to be an endless, unconnected background, existing just for cars to drive through.

It was like opening your eyes again to see the real world outside, making the earlier lovemaking scene in the car more like a dream. Tears welled up in her eyes.

"You'll remember me, won't you?" She stammered, "There have to be some moments . . . that will stay with you."

He held her tightly.

"Silly," he said tenderly.

She recalled the conversation in Japanese with Father in the backseat of his newly purchased Mercedes, which was still being driven by the consulate driver, after Father had explained to the driver, who obviously knew no Japanese, that this was their daily language of choice.

"When I was a boy, your grandfather had a black Japanese sedan. He taught a man how to drive so he could have a properly trained chauffeur."

She listened quietly, head lowered, as dictated by their family upbringing; she did not even turn to look at the scenery passing by outside, despite her urge to do so.

"Back then the family driver did not wear a uniform. Your grandpa was so considerate he did not want people to detect the driver's status from the uniform. He often said that ours was a big family in which we were all equals."

Father paused.

"I recall his name—Ah-bing. He wore gloves when he drove. He treasured the car and did not want to soil the steering wheel if he happened to have dirty hands. Ah-bing always sat up straight, his hands resting on the upper curve of the steering wheel with his elbows turned in to maintain a certain angle between arms and body. You would never see him flail his arms to turn the wheel."

Immersed in his recollections, Father began to smile.

"When Ah-bing made a turn, he never turned the wheel all the way; instead, he did it slowly, little by little."

Father looked up to watch the traffic in front of them.

"You'll see how the driver makes the turn when we get to an intersection."

The anticipation made her sit up with excitement during this, her first ride in the family Mercedes. Father and daughter strained to search for an intersection, while the car moved at a leisurely pace, letting trees and farmhouses in the Lucheng outskirts recede one by one. The car seemed to glide over the bumpy, unpaved road.

They encountered no intersections that day until they reached the provincial highway, where the driver needed to make a wide left turn. And indeed, as Father had said, the trained driver did not swing the steering wheel when he turned. Instead, he moved his hands several times to inch the vehicle elegantly to the left. They got onto the asphalt provincial highway without swaying back and forth.

She turned to look at her father and they both smiled.

TWO

Yinghong had heard since childhood that her mother's beauty was widely celebrated.

"Pretty, just like a Japanese lady," they said. "Lady" was used only for pretty women, and since Japanese women were pretty, they were called Japanese ladies. Taiwanese women were not refined enough back then to deserve to be called ladies.

"Have you ever heard of a Taiwanese lady?" Even Mudan felt that way.

Yinghong was too young to know what it meant to be pretty; her understanding of the concept came mostly from mirrors.

In those days, mirrors were mostly oval-shaped, about two feet from top to bottom, with a mercury surface and a support base made of thick coiled wire. As a child, Yinghong did not like to look at herself in a mirror; what attracted her were the colorful photographs of movie stars adhered to the back, popular icons and what the people called beauties such as Asaoka Ruriko, Wakao Fumiko, and Mitsumoto Fujiko.

They were always smiling, revealing slightly crooked front teeth, a common trait among Japanese women. There were usually one or two exposed small canines as well; their uneven teeth added a childlike quality to their faces. Before technology for color printing was perfected, the colors would sometimes be slightly off, shifting the red for the lips to below the mouth, thus adding a second pair of red lips beneath white teeth, while the face remained smiling. Or the eyeliner would be printed to one side, as if the subject had double eyes. In any case, you could still see the double folds of the eyes, the long thin brows, the high nose, and tiny mouth, all in all, the perfect picture of a beauty.

Her mother was a beauty like that, with well-proportioned features, a nose with a straight and high bridge, eyes that were not too big beneath deep and long double-folded lids that slanted slightly upward at the corners. Her brows were long and nicely arched, like crescent moons, with modest shadows. Downy hair grew around the edges of her brows, making them especially graceful and alluring. Her mouth was small, but her lips were fleshy, a perfect match for the preferred solid yet gentle look of the time.

Yinghong had kept an enlarged photo of her mother in middle age. A black-and-white photo, taken by her father, of course, it was a foot high, and hand-colored, a substitute before color photo was invented. Vermillion lips, black eyes and brows; all clearly marked. Her hair, in tiny curls combed back to the sides, gave her a bewitching look. Father had added pink to her cheeks to represent rouge, while the smudges of blue and green were eye shadow, which he had copied from photos of movies stars.

Many years later, when she rushed back from America to Lotus Garden for Father's funeral, Mother's face looked just like that hand-colored, but faded photo; her features remained the same, just suddenly decades older.

After the funeral, Yinghong's two brothers had to leave the country immediately, for their visas to Taiwan, obtained through special channels, would not permit them to stay long. They had to leave before the postfuneral seven-day rites were performed.

On the night before they left Lotus Garden, Mother took an old account book out of a drawer of a craftsman's desk from an upstairs room in Lotus Tower. It had been put away with care, but still looked tattered; the original cobalt blue cover had faded to a dark gray. Her mother's graceful handwriting in ink, recording in Japanese the dates and places of transactions of every piece of family property, graced the red-lined cotton paper.

"Your father was not a spendthrift even in his youth," Mother began slowly in Japanese, obviously prepared for this conversation.

"In high school, young men his age from wealthy families began to frequent the red-light district, on the pretext that they were there to compose poetry, an elegant act of social life. But your father never had any of the bad habits that commonly afflicted the wealthy young, nor did he consider such degenerate behavior the norm."

Mother looked far and deep into the distance.

"When I married into the Zhu family, your father had just returned from travels in Europe after finishing his studies in Japan; he took over the Zhu family business, while devoting himself to perfecting the first modern high school, which the Zhu family had established, with the intention of promoting cultural activities and waking up the Taiwanese to resist foreign rule. Then the incident occurred."

Mother paused briefly, highlighting the sound of the late-autumn gale howling in Lotus Garden. Cold wind seeped in through the latticed windows, gently tousling her gray hair.

She was sitting up straight on a purple sandalwood armchair in the small second-floor parlor. A tall woman, she maintained the usual pose of holding her body away from the back of the chair and placing her feet close together on the octagonal floor tiles. She was wearing a black two-piece dress, a jacket with old-fashioned upturned collars, and a skirt that fell below her knees. Yinghong had never seen her mother in a *qipao* or Taiwanese-style pantsuit. In her memory, that black dress came with a hat in the same color, but Mother was not wearing it that night.

"I thought I'd never see your father again, but he returned. Even though he was more or less a prisoner in Lotus Garden, at least he was back home." Mother took a deep breath. "After the incident, I had to take over everything in the house. When he was in prison, everyone in the clan, convinced that he would never come out, wanted to divide up the family property. At the time, cutting off all ties with us was the best method for self-preservation, and I never begrudged them that."

Her voice sounded neutral, far-reaching, as if narrating someone else's story.

"As the first grandson of the first son, your father was given the most worthless and remote property, land that was only good for a garden, not suitable for farming. The good rice fields and houses in the city were all taken by your uncles. Except that no one could have predicted that a few years later, when the policy of Land to the Tillers was implemented, most of the dozens of *jia* of rice paddies they'd gotten would be appropriated. And us, we were not only able to keep our land, but it turned out to be in the heart of the city, when city planning began, new roads were paved, and new zoning laws were applied."

The flicker of a serene smile flashed across Mother's old, sallow face.

"It's ironic when you think about it. The regime ruined your father's life, but their policies, right or wrong, brought him new wealth."

With a subtle gesture, she stopped her children from objecting to her interpretation of the turn of events.

"I came from a merchant's family. Your maternal grandfather and uncles had foresight, and with their help, I learned to manage the land, property, and houses. I helped keep the family going on your father's behalf so as not to add to his worries. And he could send you to study abroad when you were young. He was free to do what he wanted."

Mother slowly stood up and turned to open a large, partitioned armoire also made of purple sandalwood. Cameras and lenses filled all the spaces, ranging from early German models to recent ones from Japan, and all by renowned manufacturers.

"There are two hundred and thirty-two cameras in here. If you count the lenses alone, including those on cameras, there are two hundred and fifty-four."

Yinghong nearly cried out in surprise at the sight of more than two hundred cameras, stored in an armoire that clearly had been made to Father's specifications. The single piece of furniture took up a whole wall, and every space was crammed full with cameras and lenses. A coat of ash-white dust lay on the black metallic cameras. With so many types and models, they looked less like the cameras she was used to and more like ill-defined contraptions. Gathered in such numbers, they seemed to deconstruct the commonly accepted image of cameras, and had become strange and unrecognizable.

She went up to look for the Linhof she'd used, as well as Father's favorite Leica M3 with its 50mm, 90mm, and 135mm lenses, but it was a fruitless attempt, as she found it impossible to tell one from another.

Closing the doors, Mother next led them to an inner room on the second floor of Lotus Tower, where strewn atop the cupboard, chest, and an old-style carved bed were all sorts of stereo equipment, from early hand-cranked models to models of 78 and 33 $\frac{1}{3}$ revolutions, plus various types of speakers, turntables, and amplifiers.

"There are five turntables, seven sets of speakers, and three sets of amplifiers, plus thirty-seven of the early all-in-one stereo systems."

The speakers were all roughly four to five feet tall, crowding the corners in sets of two, on top of which rested turntables and amplifiers. Some of the all-in-one systems were in boxes piled high; others had extended speakers and had been placed on the floor, lined up from the bed to the door.

Mother took up all the unused space, so the three children had to stay outside and crane their necks to look in.

She pushed open the long, latticed south-facing windows; the walkway lights were still on, dimly illuminating the two cars parked neatly in Lotus Garden.

"There are also the two Mercedes, one from 1953, and the other a later model, with aerodynamic lines."

She then closed the window and turned around, a contented smile on her face to show she was pleased to have accomplished her task.

"I'm pleased that, until the day he died, your father was able to have everything he ever wanted and never had to worry."

Now she turned to face her three children.

"At first I sold off the dowry that my parents had given me, but the money quickly ran out, so little by little I sold every piece of Zhu family property."

Placing her hands together in front of her, she bent deeply and gave her three children a Japanese-style, 90-degree bow.

"I'm very sorry."

Unable to stop her gesture, the three children got down on their knees before her. Yinghong began to sob.

"I know some of our relatives criticize me for letting your father spend money like this, but they didn't see how he suffered each day in Lotus Garden with nothing to do." For the first time that night, Mother choked on her words. "His whole life was gone, so how could I watch him suffer with nothing to keep him occupied?"

She bent forward to help her children up.

"The orchard, the land, and other properties were all sold to outsiders, except for this garden, which is connected to the Zhu ancestral house. It was your father's favorite place, the spot where he spent most of his life, but since I had to sell it, I asked my own brother to buy it."

An unprecedented serious tone crept into her voice.

"I asked them to add a condition that, if in twenty years, anyone in the Zhu family could afford it, you would have first right to buy it back."

Mother died in early autumn the following year, less than twelve months after Father. Yinghong was the only child with her when she passed away.

Within those months, Yinghong witnessed with her eyes how fast a garden can go to seed and how it is intricately connected to the vegetation inside.

After Father's death, the flowers and trees, which had not been trimmed regularly to begin with, quickly overgrew, starting with the weeds spreading from the ground to the paths and quickly covering the flagstone paving. Mudan and Luohan cut the weeds back a few times, but the garden was crisscrossed with winding paths, and another would be overgrown by the time they finished weeding one nearer the house. Mudan had other household chores to tend to, and Luohan was getting too old to care for the plants in such a large garden.

She could almost see the vegetation growing wildly in front of her day and night; it grew any way it wanted, thriving and spreading its tentacles everywhere. And soon fallen leaves began to pile up.

Central Taiwan enjoys year-round greenery, so vegetation grows in profusion in all seasons, including fall and winter. At any given moment, buds sprout on trees, becoming fully formed leaves in a matter of days, only to fall to the ground before long, replaced by new buds that start the cycle over. Leaves fall twelve months a year, spring or summer, rain or shine; they drift softly to the ground in an everlasting cycle.

The fallen leaves were not much to see at first, unlike the deciduous trees in temperate zones, where they fall all at once, denuding the trees in spectacular fashion. Instead, the leaves here fell in small numbers, so no one paid much attention. But they quickly accumulated and, if not swept away soon enough, began to pile up, creating a sight of decay, a blanket of dry yellow leaves. Then they started to rot, lying atop the few remaining flowers, which now looked withered and desolate.

As leaves continued to fall, the trees grew even more vibrantly, with branches spreading and new leaves sprouting. Moss began to form in the shade under the trees; soon the red-brick wall was nothing but a dark-green patch. Even the tiled roof was taken over by weeds with gnarly roots that stuck on anything they came into contact with.

Looking down from the ancient vase-patterned window in Lotus Tower, she saw that the garden was reduced to a patchwork of green in many shades; even in the ponds that had so far escaped the shade of the trees, the lotus and lilies were dying. The water congealed into a deep green, as if frozen over, and if you looked closely, you saw that duckweed had overtaken the surface, so tightly packed that it stopped moving.

It was on an early autumn day when the garden was lost to the greenery that Mother breathed her last, after giving her wish to be buried with Father.

"I've fulfilled my responsibilities. I'm free of all cares."

She said before peacefully closing her eyes.

As expected, Lin Xigeng was elected director of Taipei's Construction Guild, a confirmation to Yinghong that their relationship would continue, except that she had not expected to be carrying his child.

Lin reacted to the news of the baby in his usual manner.

"Great. We'll have a child with the good genes from both families. He'll carry the Lin surname, but would not be a disappointment to your Zhu family," Lin pronounced with customary confidence.

He had five children, three boys and two girls, from two marriages, which to him meant that children were not special gifts from heaven. Too preoccupied with expanding his business, he had no time to think about inheritance, nor did he spend much time with his children. He was simply too busy. But he firmly believed that "they'll come see me on their own when they're old enough to take over some of the business."

"Their mothers may not want them to be too close to you out of resentment, so it may be too late when they're older," Yinghong commented with concern, looking at the matter from a woman's perspective.

"I don't believe so. Children identify with a successful father. As long as I do well, they'll want to be with me, no matter what their mothers say," he replied with self-assurance. "Don't worry. Facts will prove I'm right."

Many years later, after they were married, she had an opportunity to see that he was right. In order to fight for what they believed their children deserved, his former wives not only did not drive a wedge between their children and him out of personal spite, but actually encouraged the kids to fight over favors from him. At the time, along with the continuing economic boom in Taiwan, the real estate business was experiencing another high. Lin Xigeng, known to have large landholdings in the Taipei metropolitan area, saw his total worth increase many times over.

Owing to Lin's views about children, she knew, from the moment the pregnancy was confirmed, that the life growing inside her would bring her only defeat and worry.

I knew it was not yet time for Lin to get a divorce and marry me. He did not want another divorce, not because he had strong feelings for his marriage or any special affection for his wife and children. From his perspective, as long as he was serious, a relationship should proceed in a set formula: first, a woman, then find a place for her to live, deciding on the monthly allowance, followed by children. All these occurred in their designated order, and came to him all too easily. He would tolerate no disruptions in his daily life, particularly if that involved divorce.

No matter how successful and confident he was professionally, he could not bear to hear people gossip behind his back.

"Three marriages is a sign that a man can't handle family affairs, so how could he be expected to devote himself to long-term business deals? He would never be a major player."

People said things like that all the time.

I knew that on an island known to have constantly imported information and customs, a successful man who was acceptable to his peers usually had only one marriage (those who were single could give the impression of inconstancy). The women they had outside of marriage earned them envy and compliments.

I have yet to make him feel that I'm so indispensable that he must get a divorce to marry me. Before that happens, I could ask him to go through with it, but he would never consent, and worst of all, I would lose my current edge. At least, as of now, I haven't moved into the house he set aside for me, and I live on what I earn. To him, I'm still someone he needs to court, not a woman he keeps.

It is imperative that I maintain the current condition. Once I become a kept woman, I'll be doomed, no matter how much he loves me.

Yet, why do I harbor such deep fears? Will the day ever come when he finds me indispensable?

Eight days after she was sure of the pregnancy, Yinghong thought long and hard before telling Lin.

Though there were no signs of the pregnancy at that early stage, she presented herself to be a lethargic mother-to-be by asking for sick leave. When he came to her room, where the fragrance of flowers lingered, she was lying in bed, displaying her soft, alluring chest, framed by the white lace of her nightgown. Didn't articles in women's magazines, newspapers, and books all say that a woman evokes an unusual languid sexuality in early pregnancy?

Her sunken eyes were slightly closed under long lashes as she told him in a listless voice about her apprehension as a first-time mother, while holding his head against her still-flat belly.

He showed all the befitting signs of joy, saying he'd always wanted to have a baby with her. He would take all responsibilities, giving the child the proper surname and, of course, taking the best possible care of mother and child.

"You can ask for anything you want, as long as it's available," he said with confident generosity.

Yinghong smiled weakly and closed her eyes, now truly fatigued. Fear gripped her heart, for, from now on, there was no way out. What would tomorrow bring?

She had another option, which was to abort the baby without telling him, and pretend that nothing had happened. Their relationship would continue as before until the day came when he could not live without her.

That was something she had thought of before, but the intimate connection she felt from carrying his baby convinced her that this might be a turning point.

But he expressed only his willingness to take responsibility, with no mention of marriage. Now she knew that, after she told him, she could not resort to aborting the baby on her own; if she insisted on doing so, that would damage their relationship. All she could do now was continue carrying the baby and get whatever she could out of a disadvantageous position.

She soon returned to work. The newly elected guild director was required to attend many meetings and do something to prove himself, in particular, negotiate with relevant government offices dealing with regulations and policies. Deftly utilizing the Zhu family's old connections as well as the new web of relationships established through Lin's business empire, Yinghong helped him obtain more lenient deadlines for construction companies, in cases involving urban space ratios. The new director thus was able to present his first, outstanding report card.

She worked day and night, in the office during the day, and at banquets at night. In the early stage of pregnancy, the baby in her belly was unusually dormant; she had no symptoms at all, no nausea or other signs of discomfort, and no changes in the appearance of her body. Sometimes she thought it might have been a misdiagnosis. Nothing had happened; she'd just had a mystifying dream that had lasted too long on the streets of Taipei, a city bathed in brilliant sunshine.

It was Lin who tried to get her to work less. He somehow got the idea that the child would be a girl, and promised Yinghong that he would give the little princess what she deserved, more and better than Yinghong's father had ever given her.

His efforts made her wonder if she had been working doubly hard so the unformed fetus might lose its grip on her uterus and leave her body in a natural way. That, of course, would mean she could start over.

But she was not to have that opportunity. Imperceptibly and quietly, the fetus grew inside. It must have drawn nutrients from her, feasting on her life force, and ingesting her energy to grow and develop. And it went on day and night, not stopping. Yet she detected no change in her body; she knew the baby was still inside her only by counting the passing days.

She grew fearful.

Lin was preoccupied with the many tasks related to his new position as guild director, and some of the real estate operations fell to the domain of Masao. Yinghong had always shown respect to the older man, who had started out with Lin Xigeng early on and now owned a substantial share of the company. The only exception was that, privately with Lin, she jokingly referred to the tall, brawny man as a "pile" of Masao.

The real estate boom continued, with daily increases in pricing. Unhinged from all other economic indexes, housing costs, like the continuously rising numbers on the electronic board at the stock market, turned into a nightmare for most residents of the island nation. An average three-bedroom, 1,500-square-foot apartment was now priced above the lifetime earnings of a midrange civil servant.

Just as the real estate market was at its hottest, and real estate agencies were holding back available units, Masao began to sell those sites frozen by Lin earlier. Known to be cautious and given to playing it safe, he obviously sensed the latent danger in soaring real estate prices.

"It's better to make less than to lose money," Masao said resolutely, as he sat, more like "stuffed," in Yinghong's characterization, in the conference room.

Lin was noncommittal.

Yinghong thought she detected fear in Lin's eyes. The timing for a real estate sale naturally involved tremendous, tangible differences in the amounts of money made or lost, but it was also connected to a sense of accomplishment that came from the ability to judge correctly. Everyone in the business was speculating on housing price trends by taking the capital market and government policy into consideration. Everyone was a specialist in analysis, but no one could say for sure. Desire lurked in every pair of eyes, as they waited for the highest price before selling; then, once they sold, they hoped the housing price would plummet, in order to make up for the jealousy stemming from not getting enough money out of the deal and compensate for the frustration of bad judgment.

This time Lin did not say anything, so Masao went ahead with his plan after the meeting.

Within a short time, 90 percent of the sites were sold. The overall sales price didn't go up dramatically, but individual cases continued to bring in high profits; the cost of housing was obviously stuck at a plateau, which meant it would not only not drop, but that another rising trend might be just around the corner.

As real estate prices soared, an island economy that was developed through international trade seemingly began to enjoy the full benefit of the wealth from foreign reserves. Within a year or two, those who owned houses or land saw their wealth increase two or three times, some as much ten. Looking at numbers, some people felt that their sudden wealth was simply too great for them to know what to do with it.

As for those in the real estate business, which helped created the boom, the assessments of their houses and land were so inflated they could hardly believe them. Everyone in the business was studying these numbers and the wealth they represented, hoping to increase the value to an incalculable figure.

Masao was under noticeable pressure, even though Lin had not made a comment. As the days passed, differences between the new and old sales reached several billion, which finally led Masao to get totally drunk at one company party.

It was at a seaside staff club Lin had designed. Amid the sounds of people outdrinking each other, Yinghong walked into the yard alone. The Indian summer was nearing its end, but it suddenly reasserted itself, and the seaside was stifling hot even at night. The Chinese-style garden, with its meandering wall, had eaves capped with small tiles. As moonbeams shone down on the eaves through spaces in the wall's carvings, she thought she saw someone standing by the wall.

"You're drunk, aren't you?" she said in a gentle voice with a hint of reproach.

The man in the shadows looked up; it was Masao. A peachlike carving in the wall shaded his face; even in the dark she sensed that he had nearly drunk himself senseless.

"Masao," Yinghong called out his name in precise Japanese, with a tender edge to her voice. "Go back inside. You've had too much to drink."

The crisp but gentle voice calling out his name seemed to stir memories, for he stared at her woodenly, as tears began to slide down his face.

"It's all right. Seriously, it's all right," she continued in Japanese, made uneasy by tears from a man who, in his fifties, had always maintained the demeanor of a somber Japanese man. She reached into her purse, took out some tissues, and walked up to him.

He reached out, as if to take the tissues, but instead he did something completely unexpected; he pulled her into his arms. As her face came in contact with his flabby chest, foul-smelling from sweat and alcohol, she instinctively tried to fend him off.

"It's me," she cried out, "Zhu Yinghong."

He paused briefly, as if undergoing a confused battle with himself, and then he mumbled:

"Of course it's you. How could I not know it's you? You're Zhu Yinghong and you slept with Lin Xigeng. You let him fuck you. You're his mistress, the concubine, so why can't I, why can't I . . ."

She continued to struggle, but the hulking drunk was surprisingly strong. A rash of ideas flashed through her head. She could scream for someone to come out and rescue her, but with all the employees around, that would cause irreparable damage. Masao was Lin's irreplaceable right-hand man; his steady manner and composure served as a counterpoint to Lin's arrogance and conceit, his willingness to stay behind the scene the sole reason why the two men could work so well together.

With thoughts flashing through her mind, she stopped struggling because she knew she could not fight him off. She did not make a sound, choosing to bide her time, waiting for the right moment for escape. To her surprise, he stopped and, with his arms around her, stammered over and over:

"To be his concubine. Aren't you all the same, the same?"

When he let down his guard, she ducked out of his arms, and as she took off toward the house, she sensed that he was not giving chase, so she changed direction and headed for the parking lot.

She did not go to the office the next day, and she decided to tell Lin about the incident.

She knew that he was the jealous type, just as she'd known about his conceit and arrogance; he wanted to claim sole ownership of whatever belonged to him. To be sure, he would grow tired of something, but relinquishing had to be the result of his loss of interest, not someone else's. By revealing Masao's behavior, she hoped to make him jealous, especially since the violation had come from his preeminent business partner. If nothing else, he had to save face by declaring that Zhu Yinghong belonged to him.

This could be what solidified their relationship.

Of course, she thought about how her action would damage Lin's relationship with Masao, yet she was convinced that, knowing the indispensible role Masao played in his business empire, Lin might not bring it up with the man, but would need to give some sort of signal to her and to Masao. And that would be marriage.

The possibility of driving a wedge between the two men did not concern her. It was too early to feel the existence of the baby inside her, but clearly it was growing day by day, like a persistent nightmare, and it would not take long for it to become a burden by changing her outward appearance. Carrying the child to term without marriage was out of the question for Yinghong, who must consider the reputation of her immediate family and the Zhu clan.

To her surprise, Lin did not fly into a rage; instead, he listened quietly, carefully ferreting out every little detail to determine whether Masao had gotten his way with her. On her part, Yinghong intentionally minimized Masao's insult while stressing his affection for her. She repeatedly assured him that Masao hadn't even touched her lips. Then Lin fell silent.

She stopped going into the office for the time being, and Lin never brought up the incident again; but a few days later rumors began to spread in real estate circles that Masao would soon be leaving Lin's company.

Yinghong heard nothing from Lin. Was he waiting till everything cleared up to tell her? She shook her head. For a major event like this, Lin's personality and style would require that he boast about it beforehand; he was someone who would not stop until he made sure the person receiving his favor knew every detail.

Feeling anxious, she found an excuse to go into the office one afternoon, under the pretense that she needed to turn over some documents right away. She had known, before arriving, that Lin was away at a meeting, but that Masao would be around.

She had her own people in the company, but only those personally involved would understand such delicate and subtle interactions. As expected, she "ran into" Masao in the office, whom she greeted in her usual manner. Masao, in contrast, was so startled by the encounter that his face reddened; the big, brawny man, who paraded his role as the head of the family in his usual Japanese way, gave her a flustered nod before slinking back to his office.

Instinct told her that Masao had been so drunk that night on the beach that he probably did not remember exactly what he had done. Personal consideration for face-saving made it impossible for Lin to lay it all out, which could only lead to speculation that Masao would likely think he had done something much worse.

One thing was clear to Yinghong: with the sense of dignity stemming from a Japanese upbringing that instilled a code of masculinity closely tied to the traditional culture of hara-kiri, Masao would never think of fighting back, and his self-esteem would not allow him to defend himself.

Hence, she knew that in the end Lin Xigeng would have the final say and make all the necessary decisions once she eliminated the possibility of counterattack from Masao, which was what worried her most, and the interference and possible variables that could have resulted from his actions.

She should have been happy now that Masao's sense of shame had prevented him from fighting back, but Yinghong was even more apprehensive; all she could do was wait patiently in her distressed state.

The rumor was confirmed; the explanation offered by consensus was that an error in decision making on Masao's part had cost Lin several billions in revenue.

People in the realty business were critical of Lin. To be sure, it was a large sum of money, but Lin came out looking unforgiving for abandoning a business partner who had been with him for twenty years over money. It simply was not an action suitable for a major player.

Yinghong heard all these comments, including the news of Masao's departure, from various sources, but not from Lin. She knew by then that she'd lost him.

It never occurred to her that Lin would make such a decision because of her. It was entirely possible that he had not been completely happy with Masao and had wanted to fire him, but no matter how she looked at it, she was the cause. Lin could have chosen an easier path by promising marriage, yet he opted for a drastic decision. She was caught by surprise and, moreover, she now realized that she would not get what she had hoped to have after all this time.

Finally Yinghong was thinking about leaving.

Lin continued to call and visit her, but he never asked her to return to work. Furthermore, shortly after Masao's departure, the government initiated a policy to control the overheated real estate market. First, the mortgage interest rate was raised several times, and then reliable sources indicated that more steps, such as limiting construction on empty lots, would be taken, all of which were omens of a declining market to the perceptive real estate business owners.

As soon as housing prices began to drop, the market would be dominated by buyers, highlighting the importance of the flow of capital. The media and experts went into a frenzy predicting inevitable bankruptcy for unsound construction companies with too great an investment in land, because they would face a financial crisis once the banks began to tighten their money flow.

Rumors began to fly; people were talking about which construction company would be the first to fall. They talked glibly with jealous overtones about Lin Xigeng, who they believed would easily ride the storm due to the money he'd made from a large quantity of construction projects that Masao had sold.

Yet, for a few billions that he had thought were lost, Lin had gotten rid of someone with foresight who had made him rich. People in the business criticized Lin with contempt.

Yinghong knew, even before it happened, that the incident with Masao would cause irreparable damage to her relationship with Lin, but she was powerless to do anything about it.

Following the government's measures to rein in the real estate market, housing prices began to drop, even with the immediate worries that the train-engine industry would no longer stimulate and create new prospects, which would result in a general economic downturn. However, the island nation, in the way it has always weathered the assault of typhoons and earthquakes, was equally resilient in terms of its economy, similarly adaptable to the soaring trend *and* the spiral downturn.

Some experts began to argue that no other country could go through such drastic fluctuations in housing prices without suffering major damage to its economy. In other words, the island that had seen overnight wealth from exports not only created an economic miracle but also extended the miracle into its ability to withstand a recession.

While the real estate business alternated between sudden highs and lows, the newly planted roadside golden shower trees steadfastly followed seasonable changes and burst into bloom with clusters of golden flowers. The new heights gained over the previous year sent the flowers higher into the sky, above and around the space below them. When the rains came, the assault of water and wind showered the ground with a blanket of golden flower petals.

True to his expansive nature, Lin suddenly stopped calling or coming to see her.

She waited in despair.

Winter arrived, bringing nonstop rain to Taipei again; gloomy rain clouds hung around northern Taiwan seemingly for an eternity. It rained for nearly three weeks with no sign of letting up. The sky appeared to have a hole in it, as rain continued to fall, never a downpour, but a lingering, unending drizzle that wove into a tight net that enshrouded the city in a basin that tended to retain moisture. The leaden sky pressed down on city streets submerged in grayish rain.

Yinghong was sitting on the second floor, looking through the French door at vivacious wild grass that bowed under the weight of the never-ending rain and collapsed into the water, where it began to rot. The long, thin blades were yellow with mud, emitting a faint, putrid odor. It had been nearly a week since she last left the house, but this time she did not stay inside waiting for the phone to ring. Instead, she spent most of her days sitting there, facing the yard, where the vegetation rotted in the rain.

In a state where everything seemed to have stopped, I waited, day and night, for something that was unknown even to me.

I felt no acute pain or sorrow; gone was the piercing heartache I'd experienced when Lin Xigeng broke up with me after we'd just met. I'd thought I'd have the same nightmare again, that I'd have the strange bodily pain, but that did not happen; I did not feel the unbearable ache from his departure that I'd felt upon wakening back then.

In the daytime I busied myself with minor household chores, emptying out a closet and discovering, to my surprise, many items I didn't recall buying. Then I lost interest; I lacked the will to put them back and merely left them strewn around the room, waiting for a grumbling Mudan to tidy up.

Most of the time I sat alone, with no thought of listening to music. Occasionally, I'd open a book, but I got nothing out of it even though I understood every single line of text. My gaze flitted over page after page, until I realized that I had no idea what I'd been reading. My shock and fear would then prompt me to fling the book down.

I was in a stagnant state of nonaction, feeling no pain but strangely devoid of thought. When night fell, I'd turn on the TV as usual, and it took me several nights to see how TV news programs seemed to leave the least impression on me. There were no connections between the ever-changing, fast-paced segments, making it hard for me to follow, and then I'd be completely lost. I'd look but not really see the images, be they continuing battles in faraway places or pile-ups on local highways; when the sound was muted, what was left before my eyes was a series of flickering shadows rolling over one another, mystifying and unreal.

It turned out that TV drama was easier to follow, particularly the prime-time serials at eight, which tended to drag on forever; I could make the connections in the story line even if I caught only a few minutes of the plot development.

And so I became a couch potato. I'd watch every night till there was nothing on, when I'd be so exhausted I could not only finally get the sleep I so badly needed, but I could sleep through the night. I devoted a lot of time to sleeping. In addition to nine or more hours each night, I took afternoon naps, not because I was tired but because I needed it. I simply longed to sleep, to enter oblivion.

After sleeping away more days than I could count, I began to feel a hint of dizziness and nausea. It could have been a result of too much sleep, but it could also have been a terrifying sign that a life really was growing inside me. I didn't bother to find out. I was constantly reminded, though in a dizzying, delayed fashion, that keeping the life inside meant that I'd naturally have an unbroken connection with Lin. He was not irresponsible; put differently, he would consider taking care of a child a simple enough task that he could not possibly refuse.

So what I needed was to wait, to wait for the child to be born. In fact I didn't even have to wait that long. It would only take a while before the growth of the baby became visible and he'd come forward to claim responsibility. A set amount of child support was without question; he might even lend his last name to the child.

In my hazy state, in which everything seemed to progress with dull slowness, I was actually thinking that I finally understood why women desire or believe that a child can keep a relationship together. Maybe that is the last assurance we women can have. But even when I was most addled and confused, I could sense hidden somewhere in a secret corner a different, clearheaded self declaring unequivocally in a determined voice that:

This is absolutely not what I have in mind.

A week passed before Zhu Yinghong picked up the phone; through the operator and a personal assistant, she reached a clearly apprehensive Teddy Chang and told him succinctly that she wanted to see him.

They met at their usual place around noon, a small coffee shop in an alley, which was not a trendy place for fashionable Taipei residents. Devoid of taste and special character, it was more a community haunt selling simple set meals and sandwiches. She had spotted the place when Teddy took her to a nearby hotel in the past, and had been in the habit of arriving early and sitting down for a cup of coffee. The shop hence became a midway station on her way to a tryst with Teddy, a node between her office and the hotel, like a turning point, where she switched from one need to another.

Teddy was slightly late when he saw her smoking in a corner. She looked visibly thinner and her deep-set eyes seemed gloomier, darker and more shadowy, as if her unease could send her fleeing at any moment. He asked her how she was doing and why she wanted to see him. Her eyes turned misty, but he wasn't sure whether that was caused by the smoke from the infrequent cigarette in her hands or from tears.

He suggested that they go to the hotel, as if to stop her from shedding tears in public. She got to her feet without giving it much thought, following him out the way she had in the past.

They walked into the alley and entered the motel, unlike before, when they had arrived separately and registered under false names. While getting the key and waiting for the elevator, she saw couples leaving after their trysts, but made no effort to avoid them.

Teddy began taking off her clothes the moment they got into the room, and she did not try to stop him; nor did she respond. He touched her with a triumphant air, obviously playing with her body. Not worried that someone might be watching or filming them in secret, he turned on all the lights, examining her naked body with a mocking look.

Then he thrust himself into her, unconcerned whether she was ready, and began to move. Within a minute or two he finished and withdrew.

"I told you you'd come back to me one day."

He got up and looked down at her with a smug sneer.

"A woman like you is insatiable; you open your legs wide and let a man, any man, mount you. See, didn't you come back to ask me to fuck you?" He spoke so forcefully that the corners of his mouth curled. "But who do you take me for? Your sex tool? No way! Let's get this straight. I've been the one screwing you, not you screwing me."

He dressed at lightning speed, as if afraid she'd talk back, though he continued to mock her cruelly.

"Didn't I just screw you?"

He picked up his jacket and walked to the door, where he turned and said:

"Let me tell you this, don't call me again. Go find someone else if you need to be fucked. I won't be back."

A reflexive reaction to the extreme humiliation made her sit up, but before she could get to her feet, she felt a sticky substance oozing down the insides of her thighs, followed by a nauseating odor.

Yinghong thought about how the semen must have squirted deep into her uterus, where it soiled Lin Xigeng's baby. She thought she ought to be tearing up, but no tears came when she raised her hand to dry her eyes.

She stood up, sending the sticky secretion flowing down her legs to her feet; warm at first, it quickly turned cold and clammy like snot. It felt like the first time she realized that a man could leave such a large quantity of semen in her.

While she was trying to find something to wipe herself off, she happened to look up and saw a naked woman before her in a ridiculous posture, standing with her legs wide apart. Her heart raced before she realized that it was a mirror.

A hotel that prided itself on its Mediterranean flair had a large oval bed that took up half of the room and faced a mirrored wall. The other three walls were plastered in paper featuring huge red-and-yellow flowers that seemed to engulf the room in fiery passion. With all the lights on, a white glare was reflected in the mirror, which contrasted with her disheveled black hair and displayed her naked body in an eerie, embarrassing posture. In the mirror, the ridiculously large oval bed behind her, with its full pretension to romantic exoticism, appeared to fill up the room, as if serving as a constant reminder that a carnal encounter had just taken place there.

She turned the water on full and scrubbed herself repeatedly, but she knew she would never wash off the soiled feeling of violation; she was even more keenly aware that, for the rest of her life, she would have to live with the unclean feeling that the baby inside her was contaminated by another man's semen.

She left the bathroom and quickly got dressed. When she reached the ground-floor reception desk, she was, to her surprise, stopped by the staff; it turned out that Teddy hadn't even paid for the room.

After hailing a taxi at the alley entrance, she settled in before calmly giving the name of an ob-gyn on Zhongshan North Road. The young driver glanced at her in the rearview mirror, but she just turned her head to look out the window.

It was already dark outside on a cold, drizzly winter evening. Yet it was only when the driver reached the street and began to search for the sign of a clinic lit up by fluorescent lights that she was startled awake by the sight of neon signs dazzling the streets in the misty evening.

The doctor was a man in his fifties who had studied in Japan. Yinghong had recently accompanied a female friend for a procedure that had gone smoothly. She asked for a general anesthesia, to which the doctor agreed with an understanding nod.

When she woke up to find herself in the recovery room, she placed a call to Lin's office. A familiar male voice answered with a hint of fatigue after a long day's work. She told him in a measured voice, with little elaboration:

"There's no need for you to worry that I will hang on to you. I want to tell you that I just aborted our child."

He raced over. What greeted him was an ashen-faced Yinghong devoid of makeup. She was noticeably thinner but peaceful, with a relaxed, even indifferent composure, as if everything that had supported her in the past was gone. She was no longer the daughter of the Zhu clan, nor was she his most competent assistant. She was, simply put, a woman; she had even lost her intimidating beauty.

Pulling her tightly into his arms, he said:

"I'll make it up to you. I'll do what's right."

At that moment, he obviously had no idea how to react to a self-possessed woman who wanted nothing from him, and all he could do was instinctively mumble a promise.

A few days later, he put all business aside and returned with Yinghong to spend some time at Lotus Garden. In the cassia grove on a hill, in his usual conceited tone, he asked her to marry him.

With an evident decline in the real estate business, construction companies had stopped or delayed work on new projects, which in turn cooled a market that had already been leveling off. While staying at Lotus Garden, Lin continued to run the company in Taipei via telephone, but showed no sign of anxiety over the situation, for he knew he had the edge over the others. The large amount of ready cash meant he could re-launch when the moment was ripe, particularly because, in his estimation, this was just the beginning of the depreciation of the housing market; he had all the time in the world to wait it out.

Because of the certainty of his future success, he held off on new projects and gradually finished the old ones.

"We must wait now so we can maintain our edge over others."

He explained this to Yinghong in a decisive but calculating voice. But he sent secret messages to reliable and viable real estate brokers, who would immediately notify him if they knew of any real estate firm with a shaky financial structure that could no longer hold out and must sell its land units at a low price.

Which was why he had lots of free time while staying at Lotus Garden. The decay in the dying garden bothered him and made him uneasy.

At the time, the tallest structure, Sea-gazing Tower, had suffered damage during an earthquake that destroyed the top floor and reduced the bottom floor to broken walls. Several typhoons over the past few years had blown the roof tiles off most of the pavilions, towers, and terraces, including the second story of Lotus Tower, which leaked every time it rained. Only Flowing Pillow Pavilion, under the aging Luohan's painstaking care, managed to retain its original form and remained habitable.

In the beginning, Lin followed her around the garden and watched as she devoted her time to various tasks: picking up fallen wood carvings from the windows and putting them away after carefully noting the location; reinforcing the finials on posts; and giving additional support to slanting doorframes to hold up a wall.

He lent a hand with some of the physical labor but couldn't help noticing the obvious changes in her. The most inescapable sign was that he was no longer the center of her world and that she had stopped planning her schedule around him. In fact, the decision to return to Lotus Garden was hers alone. Now what he liked or disliked no longer dictated what she said; worse yet, she didn't seem to care what he said either.

In the moonlight on a chilly winter night, when they were looking at shadowy trees and waist-high weeds, he joked, as an attempt to recapture a topic from the time she lived in Taipei:

"There's something funny about you, you know. No matter where you go, there will be a garden choked full of weeds, one that scares you."

She smiled serenely, saying nothing in response.

Her changes extended even to the way she dressed. Shedding the alluring, feminine clothes he'd preferred, she switched back to the black and white she'd worn back when they first met. What remained was only the delicate lace trim adorning the hems of white skirts, the collars of black sweaters, and the sleeves of white blouses.

Mudan came back to Lotus Garden with her, where she cooked the daily meals and helped clean up the garden. With Luohan, the two women shared an intimate relationship and memories about the garden, which often made Lin uncomfortable. Mudan and Luohan were the only two servants left, but everything about their old-fashioned loyalty, manner, and style reminded Lin of Yinghong's highborn pedigree, even though he'd always known that she came from the renowned Zhu family.

He'd planned to return to Taipei after a few days at the garden, but was apprehensive about the distance that had begun to grow between them, as Yinghong slowly regained her self-awareness and superiority. He delayed his departure for fear that all ties would be severed if he left and she would be beyond his reach again.

In order to while away time at a place with no clubs or piano bars, he began to roam the long-deserted garden. At first he didn't think he would have trouble finding his way around, because he had spent years in the construction business and had always prided himself on his sense of direction. But once he began, the garden seemed to transform itself into a maze mired in confusion. He didn't know the various structures to begin with, and now they all seemed to look the same in their dilapidated state. Often he would think that he had traveled quite a distance, only to realize that he had been going in circles around a few pavilions and courtyards.

One afternoon, he took off again, but this time, using the height of Lotus Tower as a landmark, he was able to make it back to Flowing Pillow Pavilion, where Yinghong was going through the cameras stored in large camphor trunks. He took her by the arm.

"I seem to go round and round in the garden, wasting time and energy. But I won't accept defeat. Come, let's go to the hill in the back and look at the design. I refuse to believe there's anything special about it."

She smiled faintly and gracefully got to her feet to lead the way.

When they reached the Jiaping platform by Flowing Pillow Pavilion, she turned right onto a small path; then she led him around the artificial rocks and trees, before moving on by taking a winding verandah by Long Rainbow Lying by the Moon.

Lin stopped by Long Rainbow Lying by the Moon. The hill was now behind Lotus Tower, which was separated from Flowing Pillow Pavilion by a large lotus pond. The location told him that they should be walking in the opposition direction from the verandah. So, ignoring Yinghong, he took off down the path from the verandah, hoping to reach Lotus Tower ahead of her. The path was overgrown with weeds, but stones still showed signs of foot traffic; carefully he followed the flagstones, but the path twisted and turned to the point that he was getting farther and farther away from Lotus Tower and soon ended up in the small yard by Authenticity Studio.

He was flustered, but reluctant to backtrack. Then he noticed another verandah by Authenticity Studio, which, in his estimation, should have been connected to the others in the garden. So he walked across the yard, but when he got to the other side, he saw a low lattice wall blocking his access to the verandah. No matter how hard he searched, he couldn't locate a break in the wall; all he found was a moon gate on the opposite side, by Authenticity Studio, but it was unclear where it would lead.

The crumbling wall, which reached only to his shoulder, had decorated openings with visibly identifiable bat designs. Tall and long limbed, he would have jumped over the wall if not for the imposing air the dilapidated garden still possessed. He looked around before finally deciding to retrace his footsteps.

When he got to Long Rainbow Lying by the Moon, he saw Yinghong leaning against a railing post, her white dress fluttering in the cold winter wind. Obviously, she'd known he'd have to backtrack, which was why she calmly and quietly waited for him.

Seen from the hill, the crumbling Lotus Garden structures, camouflaged by the lush vegetation, showed no sign of decay. The vibrantly green trees and plants spread and wove themselves into a verdant ocean to embrace the fading buildings and cover the disintegrating eaves and rooftops. A sweet, quiet, and serene kingdom was created, where time seemed to stop, and the garden, surrounded by the sea of trees, would awaken from a deep sleep a hundred years later.

Lin could only look down at a garden whose design escaped him, for obviously it was now shrouded in a profusion of trees and vegetation. He was surprised when Yinghong spoke up without much thought:

"Just think, I was born in this garden, so my child—"

She stopped, but unease prompted her to continue incoherently:

"I remember once when I was child, a fairly powerful man, General Chen, came to pay us a visit at Lotus Garden. Father hosted a banquet for him at Lotus Tower and I was allowed to join the adults, probably to create a familial atmosphere."

The recollection brought delight to Yinghong's face, as she smoothed over her earlier incoherent utterance.

"My father had a Western side to him."

Lin nodded in agreement.

"The first dish was a cold appetizer. Carefully following my parents' instructions, I waited until the adults began eating before sampling the food in my bowl. Common with children, I ate the pieces I didn't like first, saving the best for last. Who'd have thought that the adults would lay down their chopsticks so soon?"

He laughed softly.

"So naturally I had to follow suit and lay down my chopsticks. Then the servers came and took away all the plates and bowls, including mine, with my favorite food still in it."

"How old were you?" he asked, his eyes brimming with tenderness.

"I don't really remember, but I know it was before I started school."

"Do you still recall which favorite dish was taken away?"

"I do, actually. It was cashew nuts," she said, with an innocent look that bordered on childishness; the feeling of regret persisted. "With a table laden with fancy food, all I was looking forward to was cashew nuts."

He smiled tenderly, before blurting out in a surprisingly spirited tone:

"Your father saw to it that you were born and raised in the garden, so I, I will help you carry out its renovation. Then our children too will be born and raised in Lotus Garden."

Caught completely off guard, she looked up at him with confusion in her eyes.

"I want you to marry me," he said in a hurried but determined voice.

As she fixed her gaze at the man before her, the first thought that came to her mind was a sense that she did not seem to have ever loved him.

Endless clusters of snowy white silver grass flowers in front of Yinghong blanketed heaven and earth.

It was nearly the heart of winter, and yet the silver grass still raged, with giant bunches of white flowers, like wolf tails, growing everywhere and painting the small hill in white. In dry, cold winters, northern winds carried strands and fibers of the flowers into the garden. Their tiny seeds, covered in gray fuzz, drifted all over the place, and when the wind died down, left a fluffy white film on the greenery in the garden, from the wild weeds, to the moss and ivy on the wall, and to the towering trees that were tall enough to block out the roofs.

Finally I saw my very first snow, but what immediately occurred to me was the "snow" I'd witnessed as a child in Lotus Garden.

I must have been a third-grader. I remember it was a winter afternoon when a gust of wind sent a similar whiteness drifting in the air. I thought, at the time, that it must have been the kind of snow scene Otosan had experienced in Japan and Germany. I ran out into the yard to catch the snow, but all I managed to grab hold of were clusters of silver grass blooms, indeed, gray, fuzzy flowers that were feathery light. They began to float in the wind as soon as I opened my hand, wafting over the place so much so that I could only see a flurry of whiteness.

I never knew that the silver grass flowers could be so abundant and so white they looked like snowflakes. Father couldn't recall such a scene either. Could it be, Ayako, that your homesickness planted a false memory when you saw the snow in New York?

Although I spent so much of my life at Lotus Garden, it was only recently that I was deeply moved by the many wondrous scenes, a result of learning to observe the garden in its minute details. The world is filled with boundless mysteries and wonder; everything is possible and nothing is tenable. I can't be sure if Ayako has been blessed with karmic fortune to see the rare sight of silver grass flowers blanketing the sky; it could be an illusion, just like the world we live in.

After reaching a certain age, I've been thinking recently that everything, including cause and effect, along with retribution, is predetermined, both in this life and in previous incarnations. I still recall when Ayako, as a young child, was nearly bitten by a green bamboo viper, you said that death meant not seeing Father and Mother, and, you added, Lotus Garden. Ayako, you were born and grew up in Lotus Garden, which means you witnessed its various transformations.

You must still recall that year when we set fire to the hill and the wind changed direction suddenly, nearly reducing the garden to ashes. You were the only one who was convinced that the fire would not reach the garden, because you were seeing the flaming hill in the transposed images through the lens of a camera.

And indeed Lotus Garden escaped destruction by fire. Could there be some connection between Ayako and the garden? And what kind of tribulation would the garden, which reached its current state through the efforts of generations of the Zhu family, bring to you? What kind of karmic connection did you have with it?

After spending decades of my life in Lotus Garden, I have yet to see the unusual sight of silver grass flowers covering the sky, as described in your letter. Perhaps this has all been prearranged in some unknown way, for no one can say for sure what happens in life where karmic causes and effects are concerned. Or, it could be that what you saw years ago was, in the end, illusory, like life itself. Even if there were indeed silver grass flowers flying around like drifting snow, the flowers would fall till nothing was left. It would be as if nothing had taken place, nothing appearing and nothing disappearing, for life in the myriad worlds is but a dream.

EPILOGUE

THE LOTUS GARDEN DONATION CEREMONY took place in the morning. At noon, a Taiwanese-style banquet was held in the garden, filling all the structures and empty spots under the trees with round tables covered in red tablecloths, as if giant flame flowers were abloom on the summertime garden grounds.

After lunch, VIPs who had come from afar left, while most of the guests stayed behind for the two o'clock lecture under the coral trees by Lotus Tower, with a tour to follow.

The speaker was the middle-aged architect heading the restoration project; a specialist in traditional architecture, he began his lecture in Taiwanese:

"The Taiwanese term *liaomweigyah* usually refers to a son who squanders his family's wealth. During the three years of restoration, I spent most of my time in Lucheng, and I've often heard the locals speak reverently about the *liaomweigyah* of the Zhu family, the previous owner of Lotus Garden, Mr. Zhu Zuyan."

A man who spent years restoring and maintaining historical sites, the architect continued emotionally, showing his fondness for anything old:

"To me, Mr. Zhu was not only not a *liaomweigyah* but was in fact a protector of ancient structures. Without him, it would be impossible for Lotus Garden to present itself in such a complete state to you all today."

Some people began to whisper among themselves.

"Yes. Without Mr. Zhu, there would be no Lotus Garden today. If he hadn't undertaken a total renovation in the early 1950s, this garden, which is over two centuries old and mostly made of wood, would have suffered major damage that could not be easily repaired and returned to its original state, since no modern carpenter possesses the required skills for restoration."

He continued with self-assurance:

"Most importantly, Mr. Zhu, an avid amateur photographer, photographed every step in the renovation process, thus keeping a record of the old artisans' work and leaving valuable information for future generations. Moreover, thanks to Mr. Zhu's hobby, we have pictures of every detail and bit of scenery of the garden, which have enabled us to repair, with precision, major damage caused by weather and humans over the past three or four decades. Using his photographs as a basis, we are now able to present to you a completely restored garden. Which is why I said there would be no Lotus Garden without Mr. Zhu."

Applause erupted from the audience after a few seconds of silence. Tears began to well up and continued to stream down the face of Zhu Yinghong, who was sitting under a coral tree.

Lin Xigeng, who was next to her, took out a linen handkerchief and handed it to Yinghong, who used it cover her mouth and nose, though she couldn't stop sobbing.

After the brief description of the garden, the guests set out on a tour, led by the relic-restoration expert, who brought everyone back to the entrance with its arch. He gave a detailed explanation of the different parts of the garden, which could be reached by three separate paths—by following the water, by crossing the man-made hill in the middle, or by walking down the winding loggia to the first structure, Square Kiosk. He looked up at the sky before making a choice for the guests:

"It's quite hot outside, so let's take the loggia to Long Rainbow Lying by the Moon. After we finish, we can go boating in Lotus Pond under a setting sun."

As they walked into the loggia, the rocks, hill, and vegetation on the right blocked the view of the lotus pond, limiting their movements to within the posts and pillars of the loggia, but a few exquisite turns and several stone steps later, they were greeted by a lily-scented breeze blowing through an ornamental hexagonal window that framed a corner of Yinghong Pavilion. They could see the pavilion's magnificent eaves with delicate upward curves, contrasting with willow branches that swayed in the wind. The giant lily flowers in the pond seemed to be leaping out of the water to hug stone pillars by the pavilion. Even from a distance they could make out the inked couplets in free-style calligraphy on the pillars:

In a quiet little garden, startled geese soared into the sky with the wind,
On the boundless green leaves, feathered friends frolicked in shadows of red

Some of the guests cried out in admiration.

Continuing on their crisscrossing journey through the garden, they stopped to admire the banana shrubs and firecrackers flowers, with the explosion of tiny clusters of red blossoms. Then they climbed to the second floor to check out the octagonal courtyard, with its skylight, followed by a hike to Sea-gazing Tower to gaze at the distant horizon, where the sky met the ocean. They also got to read the poems left by literati on the loggia and admire the exquisite dragon carved on the doors and partition walls. After watching mandarin ducks splashing in the water, they found themselves trapped between man-made forests and hills. Many stops later they finally arrived at Fascination Scene Stage.

Separated by water and twenty feet from Yinghong Pavilion, Fascination Scene Stage opened on three sides and was encircled by short railings spaced between posts. Behind it was a towering wall with two ornamental doors featuring literary and military themes.

The play that had been put on at lunchtime was long over, so the guests went up onto the stage to examine the double-sided carved screen wall.

The front presented *Chen San and Wuniang*, a drama that had been in circulation for centuries. Regardless of their chronological appearance in the play, all the characters were painted on the six-foot-high wall: beautifully dressed Wuniang and her alluring maid high up in her private residence; Chen San, who had sold himself into bondage to be with her, standing next to a broken mirror; Wuniang's enraged father being soothed by her mother. The only exception was Ma Jun, who would later come to carry Wuniang off in a sedan chair; he was standing to the side, slowly waving his fan, for he wouldn't be on stage for a while yet.

The rousing play was etched on the front side of the screen, while the backside was carved with slender window lattices to hint at the notion of "nothing in and nothing out," which, with light pouring in through the lattices, highlighted the similarity of the play to human life.

After viewing the screens, some among the guests sensed something stir on the other side, but forgot they were on a stage until they turned around to see Yinghong Pavilion across from them, lined up with chairs from the earlier performance.

With the pond before them, they could still see the Cape lilacs by the pavilion, where the late-blooming plants blanketed the trees with tiny white flowers. The Cape lilacs seemed to be all stamens and pistils; with no solid petals, the flowers looked dispersed and illusory. The many white flowers were like layers of misty clouds and fog over Yinghong Pavilion, as if ready to descend and surround the small structure and make everything vanish without a trace.

Under the hazy, melancholic Cape lilac flowers, the guests slowly came to Flowing Pillow Pavilion, recently renamed Zhu Zuyan Memorial Hall, its original furnishing intact and the photos he'd taken hanging on the walls.

Scenes in the black-and-white photographs, which had been carefully stored away, were still clearly visible, though somewhat yellowed. By contrast, the colored photos, which had been sent for development in Japan, surprisingly showed little change in color and quality. Lotus Garden's predominately indigo tone was elegantly reproduced over and over on the woodwork, giving the visitors an illusion that nothing had changed after so many years and that everything would continue the way it was for ages to come.

Locked inside a large, purple sandalwood cabinet that had been fitted with glass doors were two hundred and thirty-two cameras, alongside two hundred and fifty-four lenses; on the wooden shelves of a large new cabinet were forty-seven stereo systems, accompanied by speakers of various size, turntables, and amplifiers.

Naturally, another round of amazed cries erupted, intermingled with whispers among the guests.

They left Flowing Pillow Pavilion and continued on the tour, traversing narrow spaces created by walls, buildings, small bridges, embankments, winding loggias, and ponds. Unable to take in the whole garden in one view, they spent three hours on the tour, one in which each step afforded them a new sight and each turn opened up a new vista.

Some guests hung around; Lin Xigeng, who was taken by members of Lucheng gentry and officials to survey local construction and potential real estate investments, did not return to Lotus Garden until after the sun had set.

Dinner was served in the banquet hall in Lotus Tower, with a nonfunctional kitchen, so the food, simple daily fare, was brought over from the Upper House. The aging Mudan, who remained table side to serve, was no longer capable of doing any household chores, so she supervised two female helpers and continued to be in charge this time when she returned to Lotus Garden with Yinghong. The similarly ancient Luohan, observing the old rules and absenting himself during mealtime, was sent by Mudan to wait outside Lotus Tower, where he would spring into action when needed.

Yinghong and Xigeng sat on opposite sides of a large, round rosewood table in the main hall. Still feeling excitement from the tour that afternoon, he talked animatedly about Lucheng. Yinghong, now tired, was not paying much attention when he abruptly changed the subject:

"The local gentry and elders all think you ought to donate Lotus Garden to the government, which would take over its management. You really needn't go through so much trouble to set up a foundation. It doesn't seem legitimate, and the garden doesn't have what it deserves. That's what they said."

Yinghong laughed softly.

"How could I give my father's garden to a regime that had persecuted him?" She paused and continued in a firm voice:

"I can't."

"That's all in the distant past. What's the point of bringing it up again?" Lin said with a rare tenderness in his voice.

"Yes, it's all in the past. That's why I want this garden to belong to Taiwan, to the twenty million Taiwanese, not to any government that oppresses its people."

Lin went quiet, and they sat in silence as they ate. It was a while before he began again with some hesitation:

"Quite a few people are also against your decision to include Zhu Feng in the clan history, saying that, no matter what, he was a pirate and did not deserve the amount of effort and money that you've spent in research and investigation."

She gazed at him with a look of surprise.

"But the facts show that he was indeed our ancestor. We can't disown him simply because he was a pirate, can we?"

"That's not the reason for their objection. Some families in the Zhu branch openly refuse to accept the family record you created." He continued with his usual willful directness, "I think they're afraid of Zhu Feng's wife, the woman who swore a vicious oath of revenge."

He reminded her:

"Don't you remember the malicious vow that people still talk about?"

She shook her head.

"Didn't the woman swear that whoever dares to include Zhu Feng in the family record will bring ruination to the Zhu clan?"

She looked at him calmly.

"Don't tell me even you're afraid."

He was quiet; a shy look that had long been absent flashed in his eyes briefly. It disappeared almost immediately, but in that instant Yinghong experienced a vague feeling that it hadn't been all that many years since she met him.

She looked at him silently. He hadn't changed much, except that he'd put on a bit of weight; and yet there was something different about his expression. Gone were the poise and expansiveness; he now seemed more grounded, with more gloom showing between his brows. No longer coming across as insecure and fidgety, he seemed somewhat aloof but sure of himself, quite composed; gone also was the momentary apprehension and shyness that occasionally flashed in his eyes.

They finished their dinner in silence. Afterward, she turned on all the lights in the garden, instantaneously flooding the darkness in the open space with a brilliant glow unique to the human world. Bathed in the light, the soaring eaves and winding loggias gained a patina of ancient warmth, like a familiar beacon in the Zhu family bloodline. Time and place seemed to have changed, replaced by a backdrop that framed famous ghost stories, in which a night traveler traversed boundless space in the dark and a splendid, well-lit manor suddenly rose up before him. He was not unsuspecting, but the cozy light was a lure for one's most primitive need for home. It was so nice and welcoming, he couldn't help but walk right into it even if it was a somatic trap, which gave the scene a lasting, dreamy sentiment that would die only with death, the ultimate romantic splendor that one would be willing to die for.

As if mesmerized, they walked around the garden, with Yinghong leading the way most of the time, while Lin walked along at a leisurely pace. Once he insisted on a direction of his choice, only to find himself trapped amid a pile of rocks. Unable to continue, he had to circle back to where he had been and hurried to catch up with Yinghong, who had stopped to wait for him.

"I keep getting lost in this garden when I walk alone," he grumbled.

After a few swift turns along stone paths, she quickly cut across the garden, where she opened the north-facing moon gate and arrived at the hill. Cassia trees grew big and tall, with abundant branches laden with thin, pointed leaves that did not block out the watery moonlight, no matter how densely they grew.

"This was where I let down my guard and fell for you years ago," he joked as he pointed to the grove of cassia trees.

She did not respond, so they continued down the path flanked by cassia trees and walked slowly to the top of the hill, where she finally spoke with some hesitation:

"I don't know what would have happened if you hadn't proposed to me."

Now it was his turn to stay quiet.

After a few moment of silence, he asked gently:

"Do you regret donating the garden? In the future you can't come back to live here, you know."

She nodded and then shook her head.

"It's not that I don't regret it, it's that I can't. Otherwise, what would happen to this garden when I'm no longer Mrs. Lin?"

He obviously knew what she was getting at, but changed the subject anyway:

"Otherwise, I'd raze it to build an apartment complex when the price was right?"

She smiled mirthlessly. Before returning to Lotus Garden, she'd heard he had a new woman, which was only one of many similar incidents in their marriage. A sudden rage rose up, and she said pointedly:

"The garden will at least remain intact when I donate it as a historical site for the public to visit."

He took her into his arms.

"So you're worried, silly girl," he said, holding her tight.

"I thought you wouldn't care no matter what I did, because this garden was all you wanted."

Closing her eyes, she felt herself stiffen. When was the last time he'd held her like that? Too long, so long she couldn't even recall. He bent down to kiss her gently, his overpowering embrace forcing her to lower herself to the ground. Sensing his real desire, she began to respond slowly.

Under the light from newly installed lamps along the path, she saw that the ground was covered in a layer of tiny, fuzzy cassia flowers, each no bigger than a mung bean, but together forming a dark yellow carpet.

He undressed and caressed her, boasting as he readied himself:

"Remember the last time we were here and I said it was as if your great-great-great-grandmother, the pirate's wife, were watching us?"

She looked up at him. Under the light from mercury lamps, the green cassia leaves were dotted with clusters of yellow flowers, as if to fill up the spaces between them; the lush trees with their abundant branches created enough shade to blot out most of the moonlit sky. Suddenly a cold wind blew over, flitting across the tips of the leaves and sending a loud roar over their heads. The leaves fluttered in the wind, and with help from the wind gusts, turned themselves into waves that pushed and crashed into each other; the slender blades offering crevices for the wind to whip through, creating a seemingly unending whiz as they turned in the gust, sprinkling the sky with dots of tiny yellow flowers.

Surprised that a gust of wind could produce such an impressive sight, they stopped what they were doing; he resumed his movements only when the wind had died down. But at that instant, she realized that the man on top of her had gone soft.

Uneasily he tried again and again, but nothing happened. They were both unnerved by the new development, when an idea came to her.

It was the vow, from two hundred years before, that the clan would come to ruin in the hands of whoever dared to include Zhu Feng in the family chronicle. She was the one who donated Lotus Garden, which was a different form of ruination. She sat up, too agitated to worry about Lin, who continued to try in his frustration. Maybe she would never have another child by him, she said to herself. An urgent desire rose inside her; she wanted to see the garden one more time, for otherwise, it might vanish before her eyes, erasing everything that had happened and everything that she had owned.

From where she sat on the hill, she could look down on all of Lotus Garden. In the darkness, the garden was lit up in all its glory, as if it were engulfed in a raging fire.